I0544981

BETRAYAL OF HONOR

Dragon of Eriden Book 3

SAMANTHA JACOBEY

Lavish Publishing LLC

First Edition

Dragon of Eriden Book 3

2018 Lavish Publishing, LLC

All Rights Reserved

Published in the United States by Lavish Publishing, LLC, Midland, TX

Cover Design by: Victor R. Sosa

Cover Images: Canstock

Paperback Edition

ISBN: 9781944985592

www.LavishPublishing.com

Contents

Prologue

"LAMWEN," Pardodan grunted as he landed next to the captain of the king's guard.

"Pardodan," the older dragon replied, holding his tone even.

Looking around anxiously, the newcomer first admired the clearing where his target had been lying. Then turning, he stared down the slope at the cabin below. A girl with unruly blond hair used a tub of water to scrub articles of clothing before hanging them, her line stretched from the cabin to a tree on the edge of the forest.

"I've been sent to summon you," he informed the captain in a surly tone.

"Summoned by whom, might I ask?" Lamwen's voice remained calm, his gaze still fixed on the scene below them.

"The council will convene on the eve. Don't be late." Pardodan did not elaborate. Leaping into the air, he left their spy to decide his next move.

Watching him head east, presumably to return to Adiarwen to inform their king his message had been delivered, Lamwen considered his options. He had been careful since the day the trolls had welcomed the members of New Abolia into their beloved Yilaric. He had only allowed the girl to visit him a handful of times, and none of the others had been permitted to do so, although he knew they desired it.

"Foolish mortals," he growled, turning his gaze to the east field, where three men and an elf were gathered, either planting or tending to their new crops. He had to admit they had tenacity, especially the old man they

1

called the Mate. The troll king had killed him a few months ago, but Amicia had restored his life in the grandest display of power his eyes had ever seen.

And how does he use this second chance? His lids narrowed, he studied Piers as he toiled. *Planting crops, as if the entire Kingdom of Eriden were not poised to rise against them.*

Turning his gaze to the girl, he watched her equally dedicated movements. An unselfish lot, he had to admit. Each had carved out a role within their small society and worked to fill their days with service to the group. The others had accepted his communication with the girl, but if it had changed their perception of her, he could not see it in the way they regarded her, or she them.

"Amicia," he called down to her thoughts.

"Yes?"

"I am summoned before the council," he informed her. *"I shall return when I am able."*

"Be safe," she bade in her typically protective manner.

Taking flight, the gathering below hardly noticed his coming and going these days. Headed east, only a short distance behind Pardodan, he kept his pace slowed in the hope that it would be dark by the time he arrived.

In his solitude, the dragon had come to feel disconnected from his kin. He no longer communed telepathically with any of them, even those strong enough to have reached him in the past. Jarrowan had been his only visitor from their realm, and those had been few and far between. Their numbers still small, the time had not yet come for their group to rise against Gwirwen; at least he hoped it had not.

The fire on the cliff burned brightly when he arrived, as the darkness had covered the land as he had planned. He could hear angry voices floating on the air and surmised a quarrel had taken place. It ended as he grew near, and so the topic of the dispute remained a mystery.

Landing on the edge, he ambled towards the ring. Holding his head high and glancing from face to face, he recognized all who stood close to the flames, but a few others hung in the shadows, outside of his view. "My lord," he spat, announcing his presence as he lumbered to the center of their congregation.

"Lamwen," Gwirwen replied sharply. "Our guest of honor."

I doubt that, their target judged from those who stood near. "You require a report?" he inquired aloud.

"Yes," Ziewen agreed. "What news have you of the mortals? Have the

2

trolls not removed them from their forest or boiled their bones for their supper yet?"

"No, they have been welcomed to Yilaric," he replied evenly, almost as if to brag. Deep anger towards the council had festered within him, and it took every ounce of his resolve to hold his rebellion under control.

He had felt the tension in their midst the night he stood before them after being held by the satyrs. His blood dripping from his torn wing, they had interrogated him, then assigned him to watch over the girl and her companions. He had performed his duties well, and yet his feeling that they distrusted him had grown ten-fold at his current conversation.

"That is quite out of the ordinary," the king observed, turning and walking slowly in front of the council members. "I have warned that this girl is a bad omen. Perhaps now you will confess the veracity of my claim."

A murmur passed between the onlookers, and Lamwen detected the divide in their ranks; those of the council intending a coup were close to unleashing their plan. *"Ami,"* he called into the darkness.

"You're back already?" she asked in surprise.

"No, I have not returned. Gather your friends and pack your things. I fear you may be in danger."

"What? Why?" she whined.

"No time to explain, silly girl. Do as I say," he commanded, his gaze taking in the large forms before him as the argument between them rose again. "May I ask what this is about?" he demanded aloud. "Does the captain of the guard not deserve enlightenment?"

At that moment, one of those from the darkness ambled into the light. *Putwyn*, Lamwen recognized. "My friend," he growled under his breath, certain they had been betrayed.

"I'm sorry, my captain," the smaller dragon stated in a shaky voice. "I had to tell them. The omen was too great to ignore."

"You speak of the prophecy," Lamwen replied. "What foolishness is this? The word of an underling scarcely more than a hatchling? What would he know of the oracle's words?"

"He knows enough to speak of the signs, those which you have hidden," Ziewen hissed. "I asked you about the girl when they arrived, and you insisted she was harmless."

"Nay, my queen, I informed you of her use of magic to the best of my recollection. It was your king who insisted that we proceed with caution and bade I should retire to the role of spy," Lamwen growled.

"Her king?" Gwirwen sneered. "Am I no longer *your* king, my faithful

3

servant?" His long white tail swished in anticipation, confident his former captain's end lay near.

His eyes shifting between them, Lamwen considered their motives. *"Ami, hurry,"* he begged across the miles.

"We're gathering all that we can. Are they coming?"

"Perhaps."

"Why do you stall?" Ziewen asked in turn, toying with him.

"I'm afraid I am at a loss for words," Lamwen said with all the calm he could muster. His heart raced within his chest, and it took all that he could do to refrain from leaping into the air to fly to her side. *My queen is in danger*, his thoughts raced; he knew it in the depths of his being. *But how to protect her?*

"What would you have of me?" he asked aloud, still shifting his gaze between them. "What has this child said of me?" he demanded more forcefully, indicating his former associate.

"You have begun building an army," Freiwen accused, speaking to him for the first time. "This is what you are accused of; is it true?"

Staring with glazed green orbs, Lamwen swallowed. All he could buy was time; *maybe*. If the king's guard had already been dispatched, he couldn't even do that. "I serve my king with the deepest of honor," he all but whispered.

"That does not answer my question," Freiwen spat, on his feet to pace with the others, his side in the argument clear. "Our Supreme Dragon has many traitors, and we suspect his captain to be among them. What say you? Speak the truth, and we will serve your justice swiftly."

Leaping into the air, Lamwen fled. Flying south, he beat his wings as fast and hard as he could, hoping to lead them away from that he wished to protect. Those who followed caught him on the edge of the marshes, one landing on his back and forcing him to the ground.

Rolling, Lamwen flapped and clawed as they dove at him in turns, tearing at his thick hide with their sharp talons. Returning the jabs whenever he was able, he could tell he would not last long against the group who assaulted him. *"Ami, please tell me you have fled."*

"We are away," she replied.

"Thank God," he prayed. *"Be safe, my queen."*

ONE

Crimson Caves

"STAY CLOSE," Piers commanded, leading his comrades up the slope.

Marching into the forest, each member of the group carried a bundle; all accept Oldrilin. She walked, her pouch on Rey's chest in case he needed to scoop her into it quickly. Meena had taught both Ami and Animir to use many of her spells, and so nearly their entire household had been shrunken and packed when the call had come that they must flee. It amazed Amicia how quickly and easily the chore had been accomplished, as little of value remained below.

Their mood tense, none of them spoke of their fears, but each wondered at the dire warning the girl had shared hardly an hour before, and during their dinner no less. They had moved quickly, rolling their blankets and packing food. Meena had brought the water stone in case they needed it. It had not run out yet, so they would have at least one more pot from it if they were able. Supplies would not be the issue this time, but they must hide if they were to escape and ever have a chance to use them.

"Are we going to Lamwen's cave?" Amicia called, doubtful it would be a good place to remain hidden from the other dragons if he had used it.

"I'm not sure where we are going," their leader replied. "At this point, we are just putting some distance between us and the cabin." He hoped the alarm would be for nothing and they would be allowed to return to their lives there by the sea in a day or two.

Reaching the clearing where Lamwen had lain and watched them for

5

almost a year, the group paused to look down at their domain. Their cabin snug in the summer darkness, smoke billowed from the chimney as if they remained inside, preparing their evening meal.

On the beach before it, a half-finished vessel cast a moon-shadow across the sand. They had continued to add to it to keep up appearances, but all knew full well it would never sail. They had all resigned themselves that they would remain in Eriden, as they had each come to discover that the land held a power over them and a grip they had no hope to ever break.

"We should keep moving," Piers ordered gently, his hand resting on Ami's shoulder.

Blinking back tears, she turned to follow with the others falling into line. "I wish we knew where we were going," she sniffed. "His warning sounded dire, and we must therefore not chance being discovered."

"We'll look for another cave. One the dragon has not marked," he clarified, puffing at the steepness of the trail. "Watch your footing!"

Taking it slowly, they had not gone far when a screech startled them an instant before a ball of flame slammed into the side of their cottage. Hunkering down, they formed a small cluster, glaring at the destruction as a trio of Lamwen's kin dismantled the house and boat before they turned on the fields.

"Dear God," Rey whispered, watching as their crops burned. His gaze fixed upon the rows of plants and vines, a tear escaped and ran across his stubble.

Pushing her arm through his, Amicia hugged him. "It's ok, love," she soothed.

"No, it isn't," he croaked. "They destroyed our farms so many times," he recalled. "I never watched them do it, though. We simply awoke to the carnage," he sobbed. His heart aching, he thought he should be angry, but he felt no rage. Fear and sorrow crashed over him in waves, as if he were again a small boy hiding beneath his covers on his family's farm.

"They've taken it all," Bally observed as even their loo burned, along with a good number of trees.

"They are just things," Meena stated quietly. "We have each other, and as long as they don't find us, it will remain so."

"Perhaps they think we are still inside," Animir suggested.

"Doubtful," the Mate grimaced. "There would have been screaming and a try for an escape even if it had only been a few of us."

"I think you're right," Amicia sighed, still gripping Reynard firmly. "They'll be looking for us."

Hearing the sound of bare feet on the trail, Piers stood and pivoted slowly, his eyes narrowed as he peered into the darkness beneath the trees. "Someone is here," he announced. "A troll, perhaps."

"Amicia?" a voice called in a loud whisper, a slender blue body presenting itself from behind a large trunk.

"I'm here," she replied, standing as well and recognizing Traok.

"My father has sent me to assess the damage," the king's oldest son informed her as he drew near. "We feared you destroyed."

"We were not harmed," she grinned, their escape easing their loss. "But we must hide. Do you know of a place?"

Considering his instructions he pointed, "To the east, you will find a shallow cave. Hide within it, and I will let my father know of your location." Not waiting for a reply, he scampered away, the toughened soles of his feet thumping against the earth as he fled.

"Stay beneath the shadows of the branches," the Mate warned. "Their eyesight is keen even in darkness. If they see us moving, they will be on us for sure."

Obediently forming a line, the group snaked along beneath the shelter of the trees. The cave turned out to be almost three miles distant, and it was well after midnight before they reached it. Below them, the dragons had searched the woods all around their former dwelling but could find no sign of their whereabouts.

"I'm surprised they don't smell us," Animir observed of the great hunters. "Surely we leave a scent."

"I have masked our path," Meena chuckled, thumping the ground with the long staff that she carried. "We have been enchanted, at least for the time being."

"Can you make us invisible as well?" Bally gasped, still amazed the old wan had tricks they had not yet seen.

"I'm afraid that would take a bit more doing," she sighed. "The trees will be good enough to hide us. I can see the cave from here," she added, pointing at the dark maw that loomed above a group of rocks on the hill.

"Aye," the Mate agreed, "but it's going to be tricky to approach, as the forest does not provide shelter the entire way. When we make the final climb, we will be easy to spot against those light-colored stones."

"I will try to provide the cover," his wife agreed with more confidence than she felt. She knew of a spell but had never attempted it for herself. Thinking of the hamar gem, she turned to the girl. "Perhaps you can do it instead. I think your talents would lend themselves to this task."

7

"My talents?" Ami gasped. Meena had been working with her for months, training her how to use her special stone. The older woman believed it to be a focus point for the girl's magic but not the source of it, something Amicia herself was yet to be convinced of. "You want me to light it up? Won't that make us easier to see, not hide us?"

"I believe you can cast a shade, as if you are a tree," Meena smiled. "When we reach the edge of the climb, I will explain."

"Yes, explain," her apprentice groaned, often feeling as if her master expected more from her than she could provide.

"Do not fear, Amicia," Animir grinned confidently. "You are far stronger than you know. Casting a little shade should prove a simple task, of this I am certain." He had also been part of the training and had realized the growth of his own strength, but nothing compared to the girl.

Arriving at the edge of the clearing, Piers glared up at the expanse of large stones and smaller rocks. Clearly a point where the snow melt ran, he knew the ground beneath them could be unstable. "Well, I have my own doubts about this," he voiced his concern evenly, "and they have nothing to do with Ami's abilities. This path would be perilous on a good day, much less under darkness and threat of dragon's fire."

"We will be fine," Meena coerced. "A slow climb, be assured, but we are capable."

Glancing at her, he could see her eyes picking out their course. "Fine," he agreed reluctantly. "Show her how to hide us."

"Place the gem in your hand," Meena instructed, observing as Amicia removed it from her pocket and wrapped her fingers around it. The stone naturally glowed when she touched it, and the girl put forth the effort to snuff the extra light. "Good. Now breathe as I have shown you."

Inhaling quickly through her nose, Ami's lungs filled with air, which she then pushed out via her mouth in a slow exhale. The action helped her to focus, and she felt more at ease with each one. On the third, she said quietly, "I am ready."

"Focus on the darkness. Imagine that the moon itself has been extinguished."

Holding up the crystal, Amicia followed the command.

"Good. Now imagine yourself within the shadow of the darkened moon."

Again, Amicia did as she was instructed.

"Holy shit," Bally whispered. "Her arm is gone!"

"Aye," the Mate replied in an equally quiet tone. "You're doing well, love. Can you expand the shadow?"

"How is her arm gone?" Rey asked doubtfully. "It's still there, right?"

"The light no longer shines upon it," Meena explained in a soothing voice. "Ami, increase the shadow."

Using another cleansing breath, Amicia complied, and the entire company disappeared.

"Oh, God," Zae squealed. "How do we climb without bumping into each other?" Hidden from the dragons was good, but unable to see each other as well presented a problem.

"Slowly," Amicia hissed. Reaching out with her free hand, she caressed the smaller girl gently. "Let's hold each other, as we did through the foreboding forest. I will take the front, and each of you stay aware of the one in front of you even if you can't hold on to them all the time," she suggested.

"That's a good plan," the Mate agreed, helping to form the chain and taking up the rear. "At least this time there are no goblins to leap out at us. But be aware of the stones; some of them may be loose, and we can't risk the fall."

Taking a few steps, Amicia could hear the others scuffling along behind her. Pausing to refocus her energy, she smiled at her own abilities. *Meena sees such greatness in me;* even more than she could see for herself. It had been by accident that the older woman had been discovered and joined their group, but the girl had never been more thankful for it than at that moment.

"We go slow," Amicia reminded them, taking a few steps and allowing them to catch up.

"Of course," Piers agreed. "We have all night to get there, if we must."

Continuing until they reached the center of the barren hill, a shadow suddenly crossed their path, then circled for another pass. Pausing, Amicia glared up at the wide wings, noting the darkness of edges and thinner material that almost glowed as the moonlight shone through it. In the pale light, she could not see the color of the beast's belly, but she felt certain it did not belong to her friend. Swallowing, she considered waiting for it to move on before resuming their climb.

Her heart heavy, she only allowed herself a brief moment to contemplate what might have become of Lamwen. "You don't see us," she breathed, confident the dragon did not; if he had, they would already be dead.

Braving another step, the rock shifted beneath her weight, and a few loose stones rolled down the incline. The noise faint, it carried through the still night air, and the hunter made another turn, a large moon-shadow passing near once more.

Undaunted, Amicia used her free fingers to steady herself as she crept another few inches, then paused again as the others slithered up behind her, as if they were a snake coiling its way along. *Why didn't they bring the storm?* Her thoughts scattered, it occurred to her that the dragons had in fact performed a sneak attack, blasting their cabin without warning.

I'm glad they didn't, she realized a moment later, as she felt certain their hiding trick would do little to shield them from rushing water. Recalling how they had weathered the storm at Abolia, she grinned. *Having magic at our disposal has gotten us out of quite a few predicaments for sure.*

Arriving at the top a few minutes later, the cave formed a dark haven as they each crawled inside. Waiting at the mouth to assure each would remain hidden until safely inside, Amicia watched as the three dragons continued to search the forest in a circular pattern. *They've got us trapped here,* she observed to herself. *If they choose not to leave, we will be forced to eat our stores and pray they don't run out.*

When Piers finally cleared the dark orifice, Amicia followed him inside, at last lowering her arm. "The dragons are searching for us," she informed the others in a whisper. "We should be quiet. Maybe not even eat until they are gone."

"Everyone sit," the Mate instructed. "We can't light a fire, so who knows what we'll find in this filthy cave."

"Our cave is not filthy," Yaodus informed him tartly.

"How did you get in here?" Amicia gasped. Using the gem to add a faint glow to the cavern, her hand found his firm, muscled arm in the near darkness to give him a warm squeeze.

"We live within the mountain," the king replied. "Come."

Their eyes adjusted to the dim light, they followed the tall creature through a narrow passage that lay at the back of the cave. Once they had cleared the smaller opening, he turned and spread his fingers, speaking to the earth before it crumbled, closing in behind them.

Her breath shallow, Amicia gasped, "You are a wielder of magic!" She had known the trolls for months now, but she had never guessed this of any of them.

"In Eriden, all possess at least a bit of power," he replied. "Come," he repeated, leading them through the tunnel to their city hidden within the ground.

Holding up her gem, Ami produced a pure white glow to illuminate their path. The walls made of a dark, rich earth, they glowed with a deep rose color that sparkled as small glass stones. Lumbering through the tunnel, the ceiling seemed to open up to allow for his height ahead of them and taper off and close behind. Walking within the bubble felt oddly exciting, and she briefly considered if her friend might teach her how to perform such a trick.

Arriving at a wide cavern, a room spread before them filled with trolls enjoying the night together. "Welcome to the Crimson Caves," the king announced, presenting his palace with a sweeping motion of his arm.

"I can't believe it," Rey breathed, moving to stand beside Amicia. Finding her hand, he grasped it, entwining her fingers between his. "This place is incredible," he gushed, gazing at the sparkle of the walls made of ruby red crystals, which pulsed around them, coating the expanse in a warm glow.

"Thank you for helping us out," Piers offered, remembering his manners. He had never forgotten the king had once taken his life and still found it hard to think of the trolls as friends.

"Is only right," Yaodus replied with a crooked grin. "Come. We will give you a pod along the wall."

After showing them the area that functioned as their toilet, a curiously civilized thing for such wild creatures, they were provided with their accommodations. A pod turned out to be a small alcove, which afforded each family a bit of privacy among their crowded town beneath the crust. The large chamber in the center, long tunnels exited in every direction, even angled up and down so that the mountain itself was actually a honeycomb.

"I can't believe it doesn't collapse," Meena observed. "Or is it magically reinforced?"

"You could say that," the king nodded, indicating the pod that was to be theirs. "You will sleep here. Make a fire in the pit if you require it, and we will have a keg delivered if you desire."

"A keg of the tree root beer?" Bally asked, rubbing his hands together eagerly, as he had developed a particular fondness for the trolls' brew.

"What else would it be?" Yaodus laughed, throwing up his hands in mock surprise.

"Thank you. That would be lovely," Ami agreed, dropping her pack next to one of their walls to stake out the location for her bed. "I'm exhausted, so we'll worry about the food and the fire when we wake up. Or you can, but I'm getting some sleep."

Her mention of rest brought on acute exhaustion within their ranks, as they had fled their home hours ago. "Aye," the Mate agreed, "let's get a bit of sleep, and we'll figure everything out when we are fresh." Helping his wife pull out their blankets, they spread one on the stone floor and curled up together, covered by the second.

Watching, Amicia sighed. She had done her best to get over the fact that he would never be hers, but her worn state made the task difficult. Spreading her own cover, she lay on one half and folded the other over her before she drifted off to sleep.

The girl had no idea how long she had slept. When she realized she no longer did, she raised her hand and rested it on the crystals embedded in the dark soil before her. They glowed gently, producing a red tint on her flesh. Thinking of the night before, she recalled how Yaodus had appeared in the cave from within the earth.

Likewise, he had led them inside and closed the opening behind them. Lying in their pod, she pondered the relationship between the trolls and the mountain in which they burrowed. The caves had obviously not been dug. Instead, it would appear that the soil had a life of its own and had opened itself to prepare the place the trolls referred to as the Crimson Caves.

Running her finger tips over the smoothness of the gems, followed by the sharp edges that threatened to cut her if she were not careful, she sighed. *We're on the run again.*

The reality of the situation had been faint as they fled, but lying in the near darkness with her friends sleeping around her, it came into full focus. Thinking of her winged companion, she reached out, *"Lamwen."*

Only silence echoed in her thoughts.

"Lamwen," she repeated, searching more forcefully.

It troubled her that he did not reply, but then again, she had never tried to contact him while stuck inside a mountain before. *Perhaps the rocks interfere... somehow,* she considered.

Stirring next to her, Rey exhaled loudly. "Anyone awake?"

"Aye," the Mate replied, adjusting the covers over his sleeping bride. "My belly demands it," he chuckled.

"Mine, too," Bally seconded.

"Build the fire, and we'll eat from my pack," Amicia suggested, joining them.

A few minutes later, the flames burned brightly, adding warmth and hope to an otherwise dreary situation. Pulling out dried meat and bread, Ami prepared a small ration for each of them. "I'm not sure if they are going to feed us," she informed the others, eyeing their keg, "or if this will be the extent of their hospitality," she added, pointing at the oversized jug.

"We'll make do," the Mate agreed, accepting his share before sitting on the ground next to Meena, who rolled over to sit up beside him. "I supposed this is all new to you?"

"Yes," she agreed, accepting her own meal when Rey presented it. "The trolls are a secretive lot. We have learned more about them in the months since our arrival in Yilaric than all of Eriden has known for eternity."

"I doubt that," Ami laughed between bites. "Someone has to know them, and I'm sure the dragons do as well."

"Oh, no," the king's son giggled, announcing his presence as he entered their pod. "None have visited the Crimson Caves before or ever will again, I am certain."

"Well, we thank you for the honor," the Mate clipped, cutting his eyes around at his crew and assessing their acceptance of their situation. "We won't be staying long," he tacked on, holding his pause to see if any would object.

Nodding, Amicia frowned. "Agreed. As soon as the dragons give up their search, we should be on our way."

"So soon?" Zae whined, her dark orbs also taking in their surroundings. "This place is amazing. I should want to stay longer if we can manage it."

"I'm afraid we can't," the Mate explained, dusting his hands off as he finished his consumption. "We would only put them in danger by asking them to hide us; even more than we already have."

"Exactly," Rey agreed, pointing a stiff digit at their leader. "Mate's right. We need to be on our way before the dragons realize they helped and it gets them into trouble."

Sulking, her dark lip stuck out in a pout, Zaendra knew better than to argue; but made no effort to hide her displeasure at the verdict.

TWO

Mortals of the Rim

WHEN THEY HAD FINISHED the meal, the group abandoned their pod and ventured down the tunnel, where they returned to the large chamber that served as the center of town. Trolls again filled the space, sitting, lying, and standing around as they conversed in undulating voices.

"Do they stay here all the time?" Amicia asked, as Traok had followed them and appeared to be their guide.

"This is our great hall," the young troll replied with a smile. "We hold ceremonious meetings here, as well as congregations."

"And which is this?" Piers asked, his eyes scanning the room in full.

"This," the boy shrugged, "is an ordinary day."

Nodding as if she understood, Ami agreed, "It seems well suited to many things. When may we see your father?"

"He will arrive shortly, as we have planned a feast for you later today. For now, many are out working," Traok patiently explained.

"Working," Meena repeated, curious what work a troll might engage in.

"Yes," the boy nodded, "gathering the food for the feast, as well as the stores for the winter that must be saved."

"And making the beer," Bally added, still carrying his morning mug in his hand.

"Always making the beer," Traok laughed. "Please, sit and be comfortable until the hour of the feast draws near."

Shaking her head, Amicia sighed. "Well, I guess we might as well do what

15

he says. We can't go out, or shouldn't, until we know the air is clear of demons."

His features twisted, Rey observed, "It sounds odd to hear you call them that, after you've made a friend of one of them and all."

"Lamwen is a dragon," she grimaced. "Those who are outside right now are monsters who want to harm us. There is a world of difference between the two," she observed, taking a seat with the others in a circle around a fire pit; one of many in the great hall.

Warming themselves by the flames, the conversation was sparse after Ami's observation about her missing friend. Watching her openly, Rey longed to continue the conversation and make her see reason; a dragon was a dragon in his book. However, noting the lines crinkling her face, he could see the issue held much deeper meaning for her and decided now was not the time to convince her the mysterious Lamwen was no friend to them.

Instead, he stood and walked casually over to claim part of the rock she sat upon as she glared into empty space. "Does he have information about why we were attacked?" he asked as nonchalantly as he could muster.

Drawn back to reality, Ami blinked a few times before a single tear spilled over onto her cheek. Wiping at it quickly, she shook her blond locks. "He hasn't said anything since he warned us to run."

"That's odd," he observed with a frown, "I thought the two of you had this magic line between you, where you could speak to each other at any time."

"Apparently not," she shrugged, looking away, then down at her hands as she toyed with her fingers. His absence had set her mind to working double as she fought to sort out her emotions for her largest acquaintance. In truth, she had long suspected her feelings for him had grown beyond that of a simple friend but confessing that to the man next to her might prove problematic.

Holding her secret, she sighed, "I'm not sure what it means, love. I only know that he warned us, and that earns him at least some credit; even if you wish to discount his claim to helping us in the desert."

"You miss him," Reynard observed, not fooled by her attempt to make less of her emotional state. Offering her his open right palm, he chose to comfort her rather than add to her suffering by saying any more.

"Aye," she agreed quietly, placing her left over his and clasping her fingers to press them together as they had in Riran. "You are such a dear friend, Rey." Raising her chin to look him in the eye, she managed a weak smile. "I hope one day I deserve all the kindness you have shown me."

"Oh, Ami," he breathed, leaning towards her. The air between them thick, he held his breath, waiting to see how she would respond. He had forced a kiss upon her once, one she had given in to and, as far as he knew, had enjoyed. It had not been proper, nonetheless, and he hoped this time she would meet him.

Ami stared at his closed lids, fully aware of what he intended. She also knew that doing so held great significance in the eyes of those she felt certain were watching them by the lapse in their voices. "Rey," she whispered, not wishing to embarrass him by pulling away. "I'm not ready for this, love."

Raising his lips and free hand at the same time, he caught her by the back of the neck and pressed his pucker against her forehead, holding it there for a half minute, then turning his cheek to lean his beard against her warm flesh. "I love you so much, Amicia," he confessed in a voice he hoped only she could hear.

"I know," she smiled, pulling away and adjusting her grip on his other appendage in case he tried to yank it away. "Someday perhaps I will feel it as you do."

"I will continue my hope," he chuckled, bumping her shoulder to shoulder before glancing around to see that the others were watching as covertly as they could muster.

Making small talk until other trolls arrived, they took turns sharing small stories and laughter, which felt odd after what had transpired the night before. Somehow, knowing they had each other softened the blow of being set back to nothing once again.

As the trolls entered the grand chamber, all carrying cleaned carcasses, one of them brought over a pair of rabbits and skewered them onto a spit. Smiling at the bowl of dried seasonings that he held before her, Ami nodded, "Do you add them, or shall I?"

"I may if you wish." The troll matched her grin, his lavender skin flushed by the fire.

Staring at his large plum-colored eyes, the girl marveled at the manners of the creatures she had heard such terrible things about. "Thank you. It is your meal to prepare, then."

Across the way, the king and his wife set up a large crank with a small elk upon it. The queen and her children took turns winding the handle while Yaodus ambled over to share time with their guests before they were ready to dine. Offering a toast with his wooden cup of beer, he grinned, "Still with us, I see."

"Yes, but we will leave as soon as the dragons have given up their search," the Mate informed him. "Are they still outside tonight?"

"For the time being," Yaodus provided, taking a seat on one of the empty stones. "For now, while the meal roasts, I thought a visit between us would be in order. We have not spent much time in close quarters since the wedding party," he explained, giving the couple a small bow of his head.

"Tell us about your magic," Amicia spoke up. "You said that all in Eriden have a little power; are you certain of this?"

"Quite certain," he replied, slurping from his beverage. "All have a little, while a few have a great deal, of which I'm sure you are aware, princess."

She blushed at the worn term, hating that it had become so popular among the locals to address her as such, but at least he had refrained from calling her queen. She still had not discerned the reason behind it and felt certain asking would be found offensive. "And how much do you have?" she queried.

His large orbs glaring at her, he appeared to consider the question and his response, then confessed, "I am quite powerful," with a laugh. He took no obvious offense, adding, "Our high priest is also quite gifted, and a few of the others almost as much." Signaling to one of the trolls who had been tending the fires and spits, he accepted a small bowl of dried material from him. "Allow me to share with you," the king offered, pinching a miniscule amount of the granular substance and tossing it into the flames.

Burning brightly, with a flurry of sparks and pops, a rainbow of colors washed across the dancing light, and then an image of Abolia appeared before them.

"Wow, are you seeing this?" Bally gasped.

"Aye," the Mate agreed, leaning his head against his hands as his elbows dug into his knees. However, he had been in Eriden long enough, it would take more than a few sparks from a fire to impress him much. Glaring at the scene, he asked, "You know of the ruins?"

"Yes. They are a bit south of our normal territory, but we have ventured that way a few times. And they have stood for many ages; a booming town of several hundred thousand at its peak. But it was destroyed near thirty centuries ago, leaving the ruins you seem to have encountered on your trek to us," he provided.

"Destroyed, as in on purpose?" Rey demanded.

"Quite on purpose," Yaodus agreed.

Glancing at the other native Eridens within their company, Ami could see the mild discomfort upon their features. Whatever history this abandoned city held, they were not eager to discuss it. "How does the fire work?" she asked, hoping to steer the conversation away from the topic that brought her friends distress.

"I'm sure it is similar to my orb," Meena interjected, offering an upturned palm to the fading image. "Can you see anywhere that you like?" she asked, aiding Amicia in her efforts for less hostile discussions.

"I see what needs to be seen," Yaodus explained, seeing through their attempt to dissuade his sharing. Tossing out another pinch of the crystals and causing the scene to change, he grinned crookedly, as if the revelations pleased him in a morbid fashion. Still Abolia, it was no longer a ruin, and instead, people walked among the structures and streets.

"They look like humans," Piers observed, glancing at his bride. "Are they wizards as well?" It seemed unlikely that they would be since she had denied there ever being a wizard community that far north.

"They are mortals," she replied hardly above a whisper. Not meeting his gaze, she glared at the children laughing as they played in the tall grass of a field near their home. "Why do you show us this?" she hissed, cutting their host an angry glare. She had hoped never to divulge her knowledge of Abolia, and here he had forced her hand.

"You knew about this?" Amicia gasped, shifting her eyes to take in her, the elf, and the nymph in turn. "You all knew, didn't you!" she accused more loudly. "There were humans here in Eriden."

"Yes. Long ago," Yaodus answered for them. "Your friends are ashamed, my queen. They have not spoken openly of what became of them for generations, as if to do so were a crime."

"What happened to them?" Piers asked, choosing to ignore their comrades' secretiveness.

"Three millennia ago, there was a rift among the inhabitants of our kingdom. One that nearly tore us apart. The mortals are the least magical of all creatures in this world, and after a great deal of fighting among our races, it was decided that they should be removed from our beloved continent," the old troll explained.

"Exterminated," Meena added, her voice still weak. Glancing at her husband, her lips were pressed together into a thin line. "The magical creatures of our world detested the presence of these inferior beings and sought to destroy them."

"But the dragons would not hear of it," Yaodus added in a gravelly voice, raising a single digit to waggle as if a warning. "It was and is their job to care for all of Eriden and those that call it their home, big and small."

"They attacked us," Amicia observed airily, the breath tight in her chest. "They burned Abolia to the ground."

"Yes and no," Animir took over. "At least that is the version I heard as a small child. The dragons removed all of the non-magical beings from Eriden and scattered them around the rim. Not just humans but all creatures great and small."

"The wolves," Rey agreed with a nod. "Uscan said they are kin to those of the rim."

"Yes," Yaodus nodded. "All that had been born without at least some magic within them were taken to a place where they would be safe and separate from those who were."

"And they put up the barrier so we couldn't come back," Piers growled, less happy with their history at every disclosure. Turning to his wife, he scowled, "You did know about this."

"Only rumor," she sighed. "Legend, if you will. All in Eriden have heard it, but few believe its truth."

"Obviously it's true," he bit angrily, surprising her as well as himself. Reading the hurt in her deep brown orbs, he felt instant regret and gasped, "I'm so sorry, Meena. I did not intend that to be an attack upon you. I –"

"Tis no bother," she sniffed, hiding her tears. "I should have mentioned it," she confessed. "Our ancestors treated such creatures horribly, filling our history with shame. Even if it was centuries ago, it is a dark mark upon our character, one that is visible to this day."

"So, we were taken from here and given the rim as a place to build our own lives, where we forgot all about this place, and you," Amicia concluded. "That's a terrible thing to discover. No wonder you chose to hide it!"

"I wasn't hiding it," Meena defended. "I simply chose not to share it," she explained, glaring at the troll. "Any other dark secrets you wish to expose?"

"Dark secrets," the king laughed, then grew somber. Turning to glare at Amicia, he stated calmly, "I only know of one other that might interest you."

Her heart pounding, Ami met his cold stare. Licking her lips, her voice trembled as she implored, "Go on then; let's have your fun," certain he only toyed with her.

"There is a dragon who lives atop the northern most mountain, a place where the snow never melts," he rasped.

"Yaodus, no," Meena panted.

Not missing a beat, the troll continued. "A giant beast, he is older than any creature who walks or crawls upon these shores; some say he is the first dragon, but of that I am not certain."

His tone clearly intended to put her on edge, Ami shifted her eyes from one to another, taking in the non-mortals in turn. Digging her nails into her palm with her grip, she waited.

"His scales were bright red, and it is legend that he was born from the same magic that created the Crimson Caves we trolls now inhabit," Yaodus continued calmly.

Swallowing, Amicia fought the urge to rush him, ready to get to the part that would be of importance. Her heart pounding, she could hear the blood pulsing inside her ears.

"This dragon is simply called the oracle, and he made his last prediction when the mortals were banished to the rim," the troll grinned, seeing the wide eyes of the humans among them. "The prophecy of Eriden's ruin. They say the power he used to conjure it drained him, and he died from the telling."

"Eriden's ruin," Rey repeated in a hushed tone. "Who's going to destroy it?"

"A great war," their host explained. "A mortal who holds the hearts of dragons and men shall lead the forces of destruction."

Laughing loudly, Bally interjected, "He thinks it's you!"

Turning to glare at him, Amicia could see their cabin boy pointing at her with a stiff finger. "Me? How can it be me?" They had already discerned that she was not a mortal, as a wielder of magic, so it couldn't possibly be her. "What rubbish!" she laughed, standing abruptly. "I need to take a piss," she informed them bluntly, as if to dismiss the entire story out of hand by declaring what she thought of it in a crude manner.

Marching down the tunnel to the facilities, Amicia relieved herself. Her heart pumping, she mused, *How simple my life once was.* In Nalen, she had not been special to anyone, save perhaps Rupert. Even Gus and Arely had not made such a fuss over her. *Now I can't go anywhere without someone making a scene.*

Deciding not to rejoin the others until their meal was ready, she continued to their pod and made her way inside. In the center of their chamber, their fire smoldered. Crossing her arms, she glared at the dark coating of dust that covered the embers, focusing on the coals beneath, their hidden fire matching her rage.

Her thoughts churning, she hated being the focus of so much attention. As she focused on the pit of ashes, the coals glowed beneath their cover; a deep red that caught her by surprise when they flared to open flame. In the same instant, she thought of the great red oracle. *I know how to test his truth!*

The vision had given her an idea, and she located Meena's bag to rummage through the contents. Finding the orb, she dropped the pouch and held the glittering sphere in front of her. Calming her breathing, she searched the mountains of the north. *If there was a great old dragon that lived there, I might find his lair.* The idea of solid proof of his existence gave her comfort.

If I can't find it, it's likely his story is a hoax, she rationalized. Her heart leapt into her throat when she easily came across a large cave, a skeleton lying in the center of it. "Oh, no!"

But how can this be? After three thousand years, his bones would be dust by now. Clutching the ball tightly, she dropped her hand and swung it back and forth in an angry strut as she rejoined the others. "Nice trick," she announced, opening her palm to show Yaodus what she had found.

Glaring at her, almost eye to eye as she stood before him, the troll snickered. "You think I have somehow set a trap for you? Your power is exceptional, my queen," he complimented.

"You can stop with the queen talk," she sneered, folding her hand to darken the orb. "There is no way those bones are your magical ruby-colored oracle dragon. They couldn't possibly still be there after three thousand years."

"I never said he died that long ago," Yaodus quipped, amused at her angry flush.

"You said it took all his magic and it killed him!" she accused, her voice growing louder and drawing stares from those around them.

"Drained him, yes, but it did not kill him until the great war, which was not so long ago."

Her features twisted, Amicia considered this latest bit of news. "The great war where some rose up against the dragons," she surmised more calmly.

"Correct," he nodded. "There was a human, a mortal from the rim, who claimed to be the object of the final prophecy. Another dragon caught wind of this assertion and joined his cause. They visited the oracle, and it is said that it was then that his life was finally exhausted. The pair celebrated his passing as proof that legitimized their claim to the crown of Eriden."

"Oh." Ami's lips pursed as a few details they had gathered since their arrival seemed to make more sense. "They killed him."

"Probably not," Meena intervened. "The oracle was said to be the only true immortal in all of Eriden, and his death signified the fulfillment of the final prophecy."

"Besides," Animir added, "the prophecy speaks of a lover of dragons and men, not a mortal who holds the hearts of dragons and men. He said it backwards," her elf friend informed her, raising his chin in the direction of their host.

His features stoic, the troll made no effort to shore up his claim and said instead, "It means the same."

Cutting her eyes back and forth between them, Ami wondered how they could not see the flaw in their convictions. "But Eriden was not destroyed. So, this guy, whoever he was, obviously was not this harbinger of death he purported himself to be, no matter which side loved what."

"No, but that does not mean the end was not begun," Yaodus sighed. "You see time through the eyes of a mortal, but recall that it flows differently in the land of magic. Centuries old are many who reside here, and a few can boast a full millennium. There are those who believe the great war never ended and it simply fell into the darkness, hidden from sight, while those who plot against our Supreme Dragon remain."

A cold chill crept up Amicia's spine. His dark eyes holding hers, she could not deny that logic, as Lady Cilithrand seeped into her thoughts. "Many died in the great war," she whispered.

"Yes, and I fear that many more will as well before it is truly ended," the king somberly agreed.

THREE

Hiding the Past

"WHAT RUBBISH," Piers muttered upon their return to their chambers much later that night. Not looking at Meena, he kept his voice low, but the air about him spoke volumes.

"You no longer respect our customs," she observed, her tone strained.

Exchanging a glance with Rey, Amicia considered returning to the great room so the couple could argue in private. They had never done so before; not a single time that she had observed. Deciding to stay, she scowled at the pair. "What's gotten into you two?" she snapped, clomping her feet against the rock as she moved to stand between them. "You have never fought, and yet it seems since we arrived here that is all you do."

Glaring at his bride, Piers swallowed, then held out an upturned palm. "I'm sorry, love. I hate feeling as if I have been lied to."

Grinding her teeth, Meena sneered, "No, it is usually you twisting the truth."

"Stop it, both of you!" Rey moved to intercede as well. "Or shall we leave the room so the two of you can really have it out?" he mocked, holding up his fists as if to throw actual punches.

Laughing a short spastic grunt, the Mate grinned. "We sound that absurd?"

"Absolutely," Ami agreed. "We can go out if you prefer, but I can't bear to stand here and listen to you trade insults."

"We will go out," Meena said more quietly, offering him her hand as they exited the pod.

25

"Ridiculous," Reynard observed, shaking his head after they had gone.

Bally and Lin both already lay on their blankets, snoring as they slept. Zaendra stared up at him with wide eyes. "Will they be ok?" she asked in a timid voice.

"They will come to terms," he assured her. "Most couples have a spat from time to time. They love each other, so they will figure it out."

Her face drawn, Amicia felt less confident; it was she who had arranged their wedding after all. If she had not, the Mate would have been free to simply declare their relationship over, and that would be that. As it stood, things were a bit more complicated.

"I do wish to make my apologies," Animir spoke up in a weak voice. "I feel as if I should have part of the blame Piers is bestowing upon his wife."

"And why is that?" Rey asked, preparing his blanket to lie down.

"I have not shared what I knew of the ancient prophecy," he admitted, his eyes fixed on the girl, "but you do seem a likely candidate."

"I don't see how. We have already established that my magical ability indicates that I am not really a mortal; even Meena said so," she countered, removing her boots.

"That is true. But if you are a mortal of the rim and have been blessed with the gift, I feel it makes you more likely, not less," he agreed in a backhanded manner.

Smoothing her bed and lying upon it, the girl said nothing else, unable to argue with that logic. Instead, she closed her eyes and searched her mind, calling into the darkness for Lamwen until she had fallen asleep.

Out in the common room, Piers held Meena's hand tentatively as they selected a couple of stones next to each other and sat down. Deciding to be respectful, he muttered, "I'm sorry if my words have hurt you."

Meeting his gaze, it did not escape her that he apologized for the pain but not exactly for the speaking of the words. "And I," she agreed with a sniffle. Blinking rapidly, she hid her tears the best she could. "I told you, I am an old woman and I know how to take care of myself."

"Aye," he laughed, "as do I. Therein lies the problem, I think. We are both so used to protecting ourselves from others that we have forgotten that we are as one."

Looking up at him, her deep brown orbs glistened with their flecks of green in the fire light. Her jaw dropping, she felt another tart reply forming on her tongue. Clamping it shut, she stood, releasing his hand and smoothing her skirt as she sauntered around their fire. "One of us has to give in here," she whispered to herself, and she considered if that was as close as he would get to groveling.

Turning to reclaim her seat, she smiled genuinely. "Piers, I have always admired your strength. Your caring is not a sign of weakness, and I accept equal responsibility for this rift between us."

"Aye," he grunted, drawing back slightly as he studied her.

"And therefore, I should say the same. I am sorry if my choice to shade the truth has hurt you."

"Aye," he repeated, feeling as if she were still maneuvering to manipulate him somehow, like a snake preparing to strike.

"I wish you to understand my reasons for doing so," she insisted.

Catching on, he grinned. "There comes a time we have to get past all that, love. If you can't trust me with this, then I am the one who must accept it because I trust you."

"Precisely," she nodded, her breath a sigh of relief. "And if we have that faith in one another, then I can share with you what I know, but under the strictest of confidences," she added, her voice lower and filled with foreboding. "If you do not feel you can hear my words, you must accept my knowing and not judge me upon the secrecy. You can, however, be assured I do not fear it will come to harm you."

"This sounds serious." The Mate swallowed, not liking her choice of words.

"It is," she agreed, leaning closer to him. "I will tell you, but you must promise not to divulge a word of what I share with the girl. It will be hard enough for her to accept when she learns of this, and I certainly want no part in the telling."

His heart skipping a beat, the Mate leaned in as well. "Tell me then," he breathed, clenching his knees with a firm grip as if she might knock him from his seat with what she divulged. "I promise to keep your thoughts as secret as my own," he added in a solemn oath.

"Yaodus is fair in his description of our inhabitants," she began. "We all possess a degree of magic, even the wans who do not use, or even are too weak to use, their power. Mortals do not, but that is not to say that it would be impossible. Just as I have manifest greater power than a wan is expected to have, so is it possible that a human could have the gift of magical talents. This could explain her ability to wield magic."

"So, you believe that she is the human in the prophecy," he surmised, stroking his beard.

"She could be," Meena confessed, lowering her eyes. Staring at her hands, she rubbed them against one another firmly. "But I fear she may be something else. I think she could be a dragon."

"A dragon!" he spat, leaping to his feet.

"Shh," she warned, indicating for him to sit. "Please, Piers. Do not involve the trolls any further," she begged, glancing around at the few that shared the massive room.

Retaking his seat, he growled, "Then explain this. She is a girl. Blonde hair, green eyes – "

"I've seen her," Meena chuckled, amused by his confusion. "But the more she uses her magic, the more I feel it from her. I don't know how or why, maybe as a punishment for something she did, but I am hard convinced that she is only imprisoned in her mortal form. You spoke of transfiguration as a difficult spell to cast, and I agree; I alone could never perform such a ritual. But that is not to say there aren't others who could complete such a dark act." Staring at him, she said no more, the rest too much for even her to stand should it come true.

Blinking at her, Piers felt as if he had been punched. "You're serious," he whispered hoarsely. "You think she could be a cursed dragon, and you expect me not to tell her?"

"You can't tell anyone," she begged, laying her hands over his. "Promise me this. Until she is ready to know the truth, none in our company must know, and you must speak of it with no one."

"You told me," he grinned.

"Yes, but we have agreed upon our trust of each other, and you are talented at keeping secrets," she smiled back. "You always do whatever you must to protect those in your charge, and this is something you must. Knowing would only make things worse for any of them. All of them."

Raising his shoulders as he inhaled deeply, he released a loud sigh, "Very well." Cutting his eyes over at her, he accused, "But we still have not discussed your lying to me."

Laughing at him, she shook her head, "I have shared all that I can, my love. You must have faith, as I have in you, that I will share when and what I can. Besides, I am embarrassed at the way the mortals were treated, and I wasn't even alive then. This lie you perceive was merely my way of protecting myself of guilt by association."

"What did they do exactly?"

"They were rounded up, throughout the realm. Animals as well, so that the rim could be populated. The oracle had a great deal to do with all of this, and legend says that he hid away from all, including the other dragons, after they were removed."

"So, he really only died during the great war, killed by those two who found him."

"Oh, he may have died in their presence, but I doubt that they killed him, as great and powerful as he was purported to be," she replied, sorrow in her voice. "Hell, he may not even really be dead for all we know. It's all speculation and myth as far as I'm concerned," she sniffed, pushing the oracle from her thoughts and returning to the mortals. "As far as the humans, it's such a dark history and not one I am eager to share. The mortals did nothing to deserve their treatment, forced from their homes and ripped from their lives. Of course, it was better than what many wanted for them."

"What do you mean?" he frowned.

"Many called for their blood. If they had all been destroyed, there would be no way for the prophecy to come true," she revealed somberly.

"That's horrible," he groaned, his jaw tight with subdued rage.

"Yes, but the Supreme Dragon wouldn't hear of it. He arranged for their transfer and for the stocking of their lands with lessor creatures to provide for their lives and future," she explained, sniffing again. "The dragons are the protectors of the world, not just of Eriden. At least, I believe that they are, even if it has not seemed so in the years since you were moved to the rim."

Stirred by her tears, Piers sighed, "I think I have heard enough, and I understand why this is one story you never wished to tell. Anyone with such a mark in their history would be tempted to hide it. Or certainly never openly share it," he stated confidently, his forgiveness of her whole-hearted.

Leaning against him, she sighed, "Yes. Deplorable. And it has only been since the fall of Ziradon that mortals who have stumbled upon our shores have even been allowed to live."

Frozen, he asked tentatively, "What do you mean? Like the men in Whitefair?"

"Yes. Before Gwirwen came to power, any mortal who managed to navigate the barrier between Eriden and the rim was destroyed, which is why I was so surprised to find you there the day we met. I'm still not accustomed to the presence of mortals within the realm, and so it is with most of our inhabitants."

"Dare I ask how the humans were destroyed?"

"By the mermaids," she whispered, hating to speak ill of Oldrilin or her kind. "That is the duty of the sirens; to lure the men and see to their end."

"So, the legend is true," he breathed, rubbing her arm anxiously. But then again, he had never trusted the mermaids despite how the others felt. "What changed, then? What did this Gwirwen do that made them stop doing their job, if you will?"

"I don't know that he did anything. To be honest, I think those in Whitefair simply came to shore somewhere else and never met them, and as far as you lot…" Her voice trailed away as she searched for the right words. "I think that is the greatest evidence yet as to my suspicions about the girl. The sirens took her in because they recognized the dragon within her, and you were allowed to live by association."

Stunned, he pushed at her. "So, you are saying that they are killing people now, any who wash up on Eriden's shores. Those tiny, innocent-looking creatures really are murderers."

"Well, it's not like this is an easy place to find. You've seen how inhospitable the waters are," she spat. "But yes, if any should, they are our first line of defense. As are the elves the second. The fact that they took you in rather than kill you on the spot of your discovery speaks volumes."

"Then how did Humphray and the others get into Whitefair?" he demanded loudly.

"I don't know," she shrugged. "We have seen the number of wizard communities along the western shores. Perhaps they simply landed at another location and the wizards allowed it. It is the job of the dragons to protect our shores by destroying them as well, which leads us back to the original problem; they have not. Not since Gwirwen became king, almost as if he is hoping to see the prophecy fulfilled."

Looking away, as if searching for something he had lost, the Mate blinked rapidly. "This is horrible news. It sounds as if we have arrived just in time to watch the fall of the kingdom, whether Ami will be the cause or not."

"And thus the reason we should keep it to ourselves," she pointed out.

"Aye," he nodded, finally able to agree wholeheartedly. "I won't say a word; not to any of them. But we can't stay here, and we can't go back the way we came. We have to move on, and get to the bottom of this even if we don't tell the others."

"It will be dangerous," she warned. "The land only becomes more unfriendly the closer we get to the eastern shores."

"Then so be it," he agreed, placing his arm over her shoulder and drawing her near. "I love you, Meena Gavaan Massheby. Please forgive me."

"Nothing to forgive," she smiled. "We all have our rough times, and I am only thankful I am able to face mine with you."

Standing, Piers offered her his hand, and they strolled calmly back to their quarters. When they arrived, all had fallen asleep save Rey, who sat up on his blanket as they entered.

"Who landed the most punches?" the younger man teased.

"None of your business," Piers shot back with a short laugh, holding his voice down so as not to disturb the others. "Good night!"

"Good night, Mate," Rey grinned, lying back and staring at the ceiling.

Removing their shoes, the couple stretched out as well, and within a few minutes, the woman had drifted off to sleep. Piers on the other hand lay in the near darkness, his eyes roaming between the members of his group. Removing his shirt, he tried to get comfortable but to no avail. His bride had pointed out that he always did what he could to protect them, which was true. But how would he stop their destruction if Eriden was really headed to the end?

FOUR

By the Numbers

THE GROUP AWOKE EARLY, their lack of sunlight playing havoc with their internal systems. Hearing the others tossing and turning, Amicia groaned, "Is it time to get up?"

"I have no idea," Bally replied, pushing himself up to sit.

The cave walls reflected the embers of their fire, illuminating their pod with red light. Staring up at the crack in the ceiling, where the smoke disappeared, he sighed, "The trolls are crazy to live inside a mountain."

"Shh," Ami rebuked, also sitting and pulling on her boots. "They have taken us in and protected us. The last thing we should do is speak ill of them."

Across from her, Piers lay with his arm draped across his wife. His eyes closed, he breathed evenly, listening to the younger members of his group trade banter. "You should rest while we can," he growled.

"Why? Is something going to happen?" Zaendra joined in with a shaky voice.

"We are only staying until the dragons are gone," he reminded her, giving up on his slumber and sitting up as well. His chest bare, the dark hairs sprinkled across it stood out against the crimson glow on his skin. Pulling on his white shirt, he added, "If our past travels are any indication, we are headed for one disaster after another."

Hearing his words, Rey laughed out loud, still on his back. "Oh, come on. It hasn't been that bad. We've made it through every one of our misadventures."

33

"Aye," the Mate agreed, rubbing the scar on his chest through the thin material as Meena stood to face the day. He knew some had been very close calls, and by the numbers they would eventually lose a few of them. "Let's get breakfast and plan the day," he said instead. "But we might as well pack and be ready for the opportunity to depart should it arise."

"I'll go prepare the meal," his bride suggested. "Will you prepare my gear for me?"

"Of course, love," he smiled up at her, glad they had repaired the rift in their relationship before it had become too large.

Washing her face and brushing out her hair, Amicia braided it first and then twisted it into a bun that sat neatly near the top of her head. Rolling up her blanket, she placed all of her things together, ready to leave. From the outside, she appeared calm, even collected, with her thoughts and preparations.

On the inside, she was a mess. Her head ran in circles with worry, and she called for Lamwen every few minutes. *I can't believe he doesn't reply*, she sobbed inwardly. *"Lamwen, please speak with me!"*

It was no use. Only silence echoed in her mind.

Deciding to test the distance and the rock, she tried for another. *"Uscan."*

"My lady," he replied promptly, as if he had been waiting for her call.

"Oh," she gasped aloud, shocked at the ease of reaching him. Thinking quickly, she smiled to lighten her thoughts before she shared them. *"How have you been?"*

"I am well, princess. But I had not expected to hear from you. Has something happened?"

She stood still, toying with the merdoe between her breasts. What could she say? So much had happened since they last spoke. *"We are in the north,"* she managed.

"Ah, have you reached out to our kin, the great wolves of the northern pack?"

"No, we have not encountered them as of yet. Do you speak with them, Uscan?"

"I can make the introduction if you prefer. Where would you like for them to meet you?"

"Oh God," she breathed, realizing she would have to explain more than she wanted. *"We're in trouble,"* she confessed. *"The trolls have hidden us within their mountain."*

"The trolls!" he gasped, obviously disturbed. *"Amicia, what in Eriden have you done?"*

"Nothing," she denied. *"We built a cabin and were working on a boat. We've been looked after by a dragon named Lamwen for months, but now he has disappeared, and three others have destroyed all that we have,"* she gushed; the floodgates opened, she felt certain she sounded delusional.

On the contrary, what she said made perfect sense. *"You need help getting out of there,"* her old friend surmised.

"Yes. Please. If your northern kin do not mind, we could use quick transportation away from here."

"I will send Edeill to you; he heads the pack and will know which route to take. Watch yourself, my princess."

"As always," she agreed, relief escaping her lips in a loud sigh.

"Have you reached Lamwen?" Rey asked, observing her trance-like state.

"No, but I have arranged for our transport," she confessed, not revealing it had completely been by mistake.

"What kind of transport?" the Mate asked, joining them while the others prepared their gear.

"I contacted Uscan. He is going to send the northern pack to fetch us." Her wide green eyes met his dolefully as she explained.

"Then they will be taking us to the east," their leader explained.

"East?" Reynard clipped in surprise. "Surely we should go back the way we came and hide among Meena's people."

"No, we push on," Piers replied, raising his chin. "Things are likely to get worse before they get better, so prepare yourselves." Turning his back, he left their pod in search of that breakfast they had spoken of.

Catching up to him, Ami whined, "Why are we going east? It can't possibly be safe there," she pointed out, knowing the dragons resided somewhere on the eastern coast.

"We must face our demons," he stated calmly, not missing a step. Entering the great room, his wife had already secured a fire for them, and their meal was being prepared. "Don't make this harder than it is, love," he said more quietly, turning to face her.

"You decided this last night, while the two of you were having your fight," she accused, glaring at him through narrow slits.

"Aye, you could say that," he confirmed. "It is what we believe is best for us even though our journey will be hard."

Coming up behind, Bally agreed cheerfully, "We're with you, Mate. Where you say we go, we will follow," he added with a laugh.

Cutting her eyes over to glare at the younger man, Amicia wasn't so sure of that logic, but at the moment she knew it would be pointless to argue. Their path would be hard no matter which way they took, as it always had been. "All right," she approved with a pout. "Let us eat and discover if the dragons are still lurking about."

In the midst of their meal, Yaodus joined them to give his report. "There have been no dragons sighted this morning," he said with a rumbling laugh. "Perhaps you will wait another day to see if it holds?"

"We have friends who will see us through the woods," Piers explained. "When they arrive, we will depart."

"Friends?" the old king asked doubtfully, no longer smiling. "We are the main inhabitants of the Yilaric forest," he pointed out, searching for a clue as to who else might come to their aid.

"The northern pack will see us through," Amicia stated bluntly.

"Wolves?" the troll growled, baring his teeth.

"Aye," the Mate nodded. "They are acquaintances of ours through Uscan and the southern –"

"You have given them permission to approach our mountain," Yaodus interrupted, his eyes fixed on the girl.

"They won't stay long, and they will not cause any harm while they are here," Amicia assured, sitting up with a stiff back as she addressed their benefactor. "You have my word on that."

Glaring at her, the rage radiated from the king's pale blue skin, the red tint more than the gems of the walls. "You will leave today," he stated gruffly.

"Yes," she agreed with a nod. "If they do not arrive, we will head out and meet them within the forest." His anger troubled her, and she suddenly felt as if they might be in danger, as the dragons clearly no longer supported her. "After we eat, in fact."

"Very well," he hissed, rising and leaving the group abruptly.

"What the hell was that all about?" Rey demanded after he had gone.

"We've worn out our welcome," Piers clarified in a hushed voice, his eyes following the sovereign, "again. Finish your meals. We have already packed. We simply go to our pod and gather our things."

"We can't leave the way we came in," Amicia pointed out. "Yaodus closed the tunnel behind us, remember?"

"There has to be another entrance. Perhaps Traok will show us the way," Bally suggested, confident they were still on good terms with the king's eldest son.

Meena could feel the eyes of those around them drawn to the group. "Something's wrong," she whispered. "I think we should leave the meal and get the hell out of here." Her staff still leaning against the wall in their quarters, she suddenly felt as if she were naked in the room full of strangers.

"Aye," the Mate quietly agreed, also picking up on the vibe. "Go gather the gear, now!"

Leaving their food, the party stood and made their way down the tunnel to their room with haste. Inside, they pulled their packs onto their backs and carried everything else, including their weapons. Openly brandishing them, in case the trolls were to get any ideas, they made their way back to the great hall.

"And so you run," Yaodus called from across the open space, his voice loud as the rest of his people grew eerily quiet.

"We appreciate your hospitality," the Mate hollered back. "But yes, the time has come for us to go. If you would be so kind as to point us to the exit, we will be on our way." He smiled his best fake grin, his hand gripping the handle of his weapon firmly as he prepared to use it.

Not taking his eyes off the Mate, Bally lifted the siren, placing her in the pouch he had strapped onto his chest. Animir added the string to his bow so he could rain fire upon their hosts for all the good it would do. If the trolls attacked them, the group was as good as dead.

"Amicia," Uscan interrupted her thoughts.

"Not now," she replied. *"The trolls are upset you are sending your friends."*

"You must flee then."

"Yeah, we're working on it," she snapped, her features tense as she studied the posturing of those around her.

"Edeill and the northern pack are to the east of the trolls' mountain. Leave and move towards them; they will take you where you wish to go."

Stepping forward, she pulled every ounce of bravado she could muster. "Great king Yaodus, do not let our friendship end like this," she commanded. "We wish to exit the mountain on the east side if you will allow it."

Studying her, he lumbered forward, skirting one smoldering pit after another as he closed the distance. "Your flame is bright, my queen. Even within the darkness of the mountain, the light of your soul cannot be hidden."

Clenching her teeth, the girl held her stance. "And you are a worthy leader of your people," she agreed with a single nod. "Let us part as friends, that we may once again help one another should the need ever arise."

Halting only twenty feet from the group, a single fire burned between them. His large eyes glazed, her target appeared lost for a moment as he

37

considered the time he had known her. "Why would you bring the wolves to us?" he asked more quietly.

"I seek no enemies in Eriden," she stated confidently. "All who have stood against us have chosen of their own accord. And so it is with you and with the wolves. I would call upon you all and protect you all to the best of my ability."

"The true and noble words of a queen," he nodded his approval. "Your greatness shall spare us our own destruction." Turning to his son, he wafted at him, calling him to his side. "Take them to the eastern passage and let them out into the cavern. Do not look upon the wolves, my son."

Turning to the girl, he glared at her, "You will vouch for my child's safety?"

"Of course," she breathed, blinking back tears. "I vouch for all upon my own life. No harm will come to you as long as I am able to prevent it."

"Then fair well to thee, my queen," Yaodus agreed, kneeling to bow before her, a ripple of whispers sweeping across the room.

Picking her way through the stones, Amicia walked calmly forward until she stood before him, where she also took a knee. "I never did ask you why you call me queen," she pointed out, sniffing with tears in her red-rimmed eyes. "But I will miss you, my friend. And your people."

"Then leave us, and be safe," he replied, lifting his chin to meet her gaze.

Offering her hand, he accepted the small appendage, touching it to his lips before he stood and commanded, "Traok. Lead them to the east, quickly. Let them be gone before any trouble can come from their presence."

"Yes, father," the younger version of him agreed. "Come come," he beckoned with a quick wave of his hand.

With no will to argue, the group formed a single line as they weaved through the crowded room. The trolls stood stiff as stone as they made their way across and followed their leader's offspring into a dark tunnel.

"Are they really letting us go?" Rey asked anxiously when they were all out of the massive chamber.

"It would appear so," the Mate agreed, bringing up the rear.

"Don't talk," Ami warned from the front of the group, next to the troll that matched her height. Giving him a quick grin, she trusted that he would see them out as his father had required.

Coming to a rock-filled wall, they watched as he used his spear, tapping it against the crystals and dirt. Bubbling, as if it were made of boiling water, the dark surface parted, and light entered the tunnel, giving the crimson gems a faint glow.

"My lady," Traok stated calmly, using a hand to indicate she should exit the trolls' tunnel.

"Thank you, son," she replied with a slight bow of her head. "Have a wonderful life," she added as she stepped into the dim light of the cave that served as their hidden entrance.

Following close behind, they remained in the darkness until the wall had been closed behind them, then ventured out into the light. The day bright, Ami squinted against it, using her hand to shield her eyes. "It's been a few days," she said with a laugh, overjoyed that they had made it out of the mountain alive.

"My lady," a voice called from the line of trees before them. Out of the shadow cast by the branches, a massive wolf stepped forwards. A magnificent creature, it matched Uscan in size and stature, but its pure white fur bore a sharp contrast to his smoky black and grey.

"Edeill," she replied loudly, crossing the distance between them and placing her hand against his beautiful hair. "I am so glad to make your acquaintance," she added with a formal air.

"I hear you are telepathic," he dared whisper into her thoughts. *"Will you share with me?"*

Holding her curled lips in place, she nodded as she replied, *"But of course!"* in kind.

Bowing slightly as he stepped back, near a dozen others came forward to stand behind him, presenting themselves to the assumed leader of the band of misfits. "These are my best," the alpha informed her, indicating his crew.

"They will do nicely," she agreed. Hesitating only a moment, she smiled. "We must go east. Can you get us there?"

"I'm afraid that due east would not be possible," he replied with a doubtful glance at the others. "The cliffs on the back side of Adiarwen would be impossible to climb. However, we can take you south and east. If you can navigate the land of the dwarves, you will eventually find that which you seek," he assured, assuming they searched for the eastern shores.

Nodding, she agreed, "Deliver us to the dwarves then, and we will take our chances with them."

Lying upon the ground, the pack of wolves accepted their passengers, each of them taking a single member of the party except for Baldwin. Still carrying the siren, he helped her out of the pack and then placed her onto the back of a wolf before he climbed on behind her. "I hardly recall the last time we rode in such a fashion," he chuckled.

"Ha," Amicia laughed, taking her place behind the head of Edeill. "You were so close to death, it's a miracle you made it," she added. "Hang on," she commanded of her friends as the line formed and the stiff strong legs of the northern pack spirited them away from the dark mountain of the trolls.

FIVE

A Fireside Chat

A FIRE BURNED BRIGHTLY in the center of the haphazard group, with the wolves lying in a larger ring around them. The clearing that they occupied barely large enough to hold them, the trees pressed in and hung over the relaxed forms of Edeill's pack.

Leaning back against the giant wolf's side, Ami waited patiently for their stew to boil so they could enjoy their evening meal. The sun low in the sky, the warm air of summer would soon be spent, as the nights were still cool in the north.

"Can I sit here?" Rey asked, plopping down to join her before she could reply.

Noting the mortal's affinity for the girl, the pack leader probed covertly, *"Is this man your intended?"*

"He courts me," she confessed, staring fondly at Reynard Daye; she had not agreed to marry him, but she could not deny that it was a possibility. Feeling it rude that they should speak where the others could not hear, her cheeks flushed, and she said aloud, "I don't feel right using the telepathy in front of the others."

"Then we will converse openly," Edeill agreed in his low, grating tones. "We could have carried you into the darkness," he boasted, looking around at the group of weary travelers. "You seem awfully tired considering you did little more than ride this day."

"It's been a long week," Piers interjected with a laugh. "We'll be better after a good night of rest, and tomorrow we can push further if you like. How long will it take to reach the lands of the dwarves?"

"Three days," Edeill informed him with a slow nod, curious that the Mate behaved as if he were in charge rather than the girl. "You are the leader of these people?"

"I am. I was the first mate on our vessel before we arrived and have continued to see to the group and all its additions," he replied, raising his cup of water as a toast to Animir, who sat across from him in the dark dirt.

"Interesting," the old wolf replied softly.

"Can you tell us what you know about the oracle?" Amicia asked, changing the topic of discussion abruptly. "We usually have story time with our evening meal, to keep us sharp," she added, grinning at the Mate.

"The oracle?" he growled in reply. "I am surprised you know of him or that you dare speak of him so casually."

"We're only curious," she shrugged. "Yaodus told us about him last night, but I have learned getting more than one point of view on any story helps hone in on the truth."

"The truth," the giant wolf laughed, glaring at her with a single eye as she still rested against him as if they were old friends. "You are a peculiar creature, Amicia Spicer. Perhaps you should share first; what have you heard about Eriden's oldest resident?"

The air caught in her chest, something in his reply gave her pause. "You speak as if he still lives," she observed hesitantly. "The troll king said he had been killed at the start of the great war."

"Some say it is so," the wolf agreed. "But the oracle was as old as the earth, the great provider. To think he could be removed from it so easily is folly."

"The plot thickens," Piers mused, cutting his gaze over at Meena. Rubbing his hands together briskly, he leaned in so he could hear better. "Tell us what you know, then. Allow us to judge your words against those of your kinsmen."

"We are no kin to the trolls," the wolf snapped.

"Magical kinsman," the Mate corrected with a twisted grin.

"You are a scoundrel, sir," Edeill hissed.

"At your service." Piers gave him a mock bow. "Now, shall you tell us or not?"

"The oracle has been known by many names," Edeill agreed to the sharing. "For as long as the earth has turned, he has walked upon it, swam within her oceans, and flown across her skies. He is the earth's mate, as her equal and caretaker." Turning his head slowly, he noted that all of their group as well as his own were hanging on his every word. "It is said he lived as a giant dragon, but that is a lie. The creator is an omnimorph, able to hold whatever shape he chooses. The only one of his kind since the dawn of time."

"So, he chooses to appear as a dragon," Ami clarified.

"Yes, it is his favored form. A giant crimson dragon; but a red wolf is another form he has taken," Edeill explained. "In a time of great sorrow, he appeared to our kind and provided us with a means of escape."

"He is an elf with hair the color of flame," Animir countered. "A thousand years ago, he aided Lady Cilithrand's father in a magnificent quest."

"Oh," the girl giggled, "I get it. Each sees him as one of his own. Curious then that Yaodus wouldn't tell us he was a giant red troll."

"A troll," one of the wolves scoffed, earning laughter from the outer ring.

"He is a shape shifter, able to change his form at will," their story teller insisted. "For centuries upon thousands of centuries has the great globe turned beneath the burning sun. At first, the oracle was alone, but soon he brought forth trees to shade him and plants to cushion his steps when he walked. But in time, he grew lonely, and he called for other creatures to join him; and so the dragons flew across the skies. He spawned the fish of the waters, and the wolves to watch over the woods. Because of this, he was called the creator of all that was good."

"The centuries passed, and in the ages that followed, he added the birds to share the heavens and other creatures to share our lands, and we were given rule over them that they might be strong and flourish," he explained, a few of those around him mumbling their agreement of his assessment.

"He gave the mountains in the center of Eriden to the Dwarves to share with the Elves. He placed the sirens and the nymphs on the southern corners, while the trolls were tasked with the northwest. The northern and southern packs have watched over the forests in between, while the dragons kept the northeast for themselves, and all of our land was blessed," he added quietly.

"So, what happened?" Bally interrupted. "If everything was so wonderful, why did it all fall apart?"

"Because each new creation believed they were superior to all that came before them. The dwarves despised the elves, and the elves plotted how to steal the mountains for themselves. The trolls refused to share with anyone, and the wizards forced any who dared to cross their desert to pay a heavy toll," he replied, glaring at the wan, who hung her head.

"We deserve to be destroyed," she mumbled.

"What of the men? The mortals. We've been told they were banished from Eriden because of some supposed 'final prophecy' that he made."

"Yes," the wolf hissed, "they were the lowest of all the creatures. No magic were they given and easy prey to those who were ranked above them."

"But that's not fair," Ami spat. "If we are the lowest, how are we supposed to be the end of Eriden?"

"That is the error in the interpretation of the oracle's final prediction," the old wolf laughed. "Everyone assumes that it will be a mortal."

"No, it says that it is a mortal," Animir corrected.

"A lover of mortal and dragon," Edeill professed. "Those are the words spoken by my ancestors."

"You didn't hear them?" Rey asked. "Was anyone alive today there to do so?"

"Of course not," the wolf snorted. "I am only a century old, and although I can expect to live many more, no creature lives for thousands of years."

"Except the oracle, who can take any form that he wishes but prefers to be a dragon," Ami pointed out, the connection clicking.

"Yes, the oracle is as old as time," Edeill agreed.

"And he loved the dragons and made them to be the greatest in all of Eriden," Ami continued, "which is why they rule over all the others as their protectors. You think that the oracle himself will be the destroyer because he also loved the humans and refused to kill them, which is why he moved them to the rim."

"Ah, very good," Edeill's deep laugh rumbled. "Uscan said you were a brilliant young woman. The creator is the destroyer. I am certain, yes."

"Rubbish," the Mate muttered under his breath. "He's as good a story teller as you," he nodded at Baldwin. "Much to say and not a word of it believable."

"Piers," Meena gasped, "you should be so bold to speak to our hosts in such a manner?"

"Such ceremony," her husband laughed. "He has insulted you as well."

"There is no insult in the truth," she confessed. "All of Eriden bears their flaws. My people are no different. Apologize," she commanded, glaring at him.

Studying her for a long moment, Piers rocked his jaw side to side, considering his words more carefully than he had a moment before. "My deepest regrets," he said to the alpha, pressing his hand to his chest and bowing his head. "I have spoken out of turn, it would seem."

Loud laughter rolled from the wolf, as it did from those who surrounded them. "And now we see the true leader of your group."

"Certainly not," Meena gasped.

"But it would appear so," Edeill assured in a softer tone. "Sensible ladies, both," he nodded at the girl next to him as well. "Hear my words, sweet Amicia. The creator and the destroyer are the same, as nature intends. The prophecy is but a story, and you should not trouble yourself. You are in Eriden now, as will you remain all the rest of your days."

"Yes," she agreed, her expression somber. "I was drawn to this land since I was a child, and I will be pleased when we find the place where we may finally build our home."

"Well, it won't be tonight," Piers laughed, undaunted by his wife's rebuke. Standing, he claimed the ladle and served the bowls, passing them out to his charges.

Watching him, the old wolf wondered at how the members of his party cared for one another. Elf and siren, nymph and wan, no rank could be discerned between them, even as he professed to see it. *She is truly special,* he mused, observing the girl who held his deepest concerns.

The sun set, the group ate their meal in near silence. Amicia had hoped for clarity, but she had discovered none in the wolf's words. To the contrary, his telling had seemed to only add to the displeased air that hung over the group. Pulling out her blanket to rest once the dishes had been washed and put away until the morn, she lay on her back and stared at the stars above.

"Will you speak with me now?" Edeill asked.

"I suppose," she sighed. *"What is it that you require?"* Sleep would not find her for hours she felt certain if her scattered thoughts were any indication.

"Tell me about the trolls," he proffered. *"How might one gain access to their home within the mountain?"*

Her heart leapt at the question, her pulse doubled in an instant. Clenching her fists, she searched for the right words, as making him angry would only leave them to walk the rest of the way to the dwarf mountains, if not worse. *"Why would you need access to their city?"* The troll king had been most disturbed by the wolves even coming near their home; could this be why?

"I am only curious," he replied smoothly.

"I cannot tell you anything of their sacred dwelling."

"Cannot or will not?" he pushed.

"Neither," she snapped, unable to hold the anger from her reply. *"I consider you a friend, Edeill, as I have Uscan and every other creature we have met along our journey. I would never betray my honor or duty to one for another. Leave my thoughts and do not speak of this again."* Turning onto her side, with her back to him, she pulled her blanket up beneath her chin to punctuate the end to their conversation.

45

Leaving her to her slumber, the wolf stood and ambled into the darkness of the trees around them. *"Uscan,"* he reached to the south.

"Edeill," the grey wolf replied.

"I have spoken to the girl. She is as you have said."

"Indeed, my brother," Uscan agreed.

"Yes, a more noble creature I have yet to meet. But you have underestimated the radiance of her power. No creature of Eriden will encounter her without knowing who and what she is, save herself."

"No, she has not yet realized what blood flows within her veins. But she will in time; we must be patient in her awakening. Being forced to see her true self might damage her ability to fulfill her destiny."

"Then we will wait," Edeill agreed, turning to make his way back to the group. Stretching out next to Amicia, he watched her as she slumbered, waiting for the dawn.

SIX

The Wandering Gnome

A LIGHT FOG coated the ground, masking the morning sun with its haze. Preparing their meal, Amicia tried to control her anger towards their guide, but his attempt to use her knowledge against the trolls disturbed her. Around her, the others chattered harmoniously, but she could not quite reach their level of enthusiasm.

"We will depart as soon as you have eaten?" Edeill inquired, hoping to speed the process.

"Yes, we will pack and be ready in no time," Ami assured, avoiding looking at him as she tended to the food.

Sensing her foul mood, Rey joined her. "Can I help?"

"You can," the girl forced a smile, glancing up into his hazel orbs. "I'll fill the bowls with porridge while you hand them out."

"Agreed," he said with a chuckle, calling to the others. "Everyone sit and I'll give you a share."

A short time later, they ate hungrily at their morning rations, Bally joking, "Will we have better food once we find the dwarf kingdom?"

"Unlikely," Aelalle, the pack's beta, grunted. Turning to clean himself after having devoured a fresh kill, he added, "They are more likely to eat you instead."

Frozen with her serving ladle in hand, Ami cut her eyes over at him, demanding, "I'd rather you didn't tease us in this manner."

"Who's teasing?" came his retort. "Edeill said we would get you there, but

47

we never said they would accept you. If you want my advice, you should avoid them altogether if you are able."

"And you have suggestions on how we can accomplish that?" the Mate asked, also feeling cross with their latest wolf encounter. In his eyes, Edeill did not measure up to Uscan in so many ways, and his followers behaved more like thugs than guardians of the forest.

"We will deliver you to a part of the mountain that may be climbed. If you can pass over the top and not be noticed, you will be better off," Edeill intervened, the conversation growing tense. Telepathically, he instructed his beta, *"Do not provoke them; we have not yet gained the knowledge they can provide."*

"We'll have to turn east at some point," Animir added as the group considered the suggestion. "The other end of the range is occupied by more of my kin, and we wouldn't want to run into them, either."

"We'll manage," Amicia declared, taking her own bowl and having a seat to partake of it. Glaring around at the group covertly, she regretted their situation, but at the moment, a way out seemed unlikely. Instead, they would have to continue on and hope for it to work out once they were at the mountain.

When they were finished with their meal, the group gathered and stowed their gear, then the wolves allowed their passengers to board. The fog slowly lifted as they continued on their journey, and they caught glimpses of the peaks they intended to cross in the distance, the very tips still touched by patches of snow that had not melted.

Ahead of them, a small hunched creature hid among the shadows while roosting inside one of the gigantic trees. Craning his neck while moving to peer over, under, and around the branches, the small gnome observed their procession, grinning to himself at their folly, as few of the northern inhabitants actually trusted the great white wolves.

Remaining still and quiet, he waited until they had passed, as they walked almost directly under him. His eyes glued on the girl perched upon the back of the leading wolf, he gasped, "What a beauty to behold."

Lumbering along behind, the rest of the pack presented each of the group's members for his inspection, which only added to his curiosity; a more diversified group of travelers he had never imagined, or seen for that matter.

When Rey passed, the siren snuggled in front of him, the gnome laughed out loud, bringing the procession to a halt, all poised and still as they listened for a second shout or any other disruption to the quiet of the trees.

"Who's out there?" Amicia yelled, holding firmly to Edeill's fur as she pivoted to have a look around.

"I see nothing," the wolf growled. "We should keep moving."

"I swear I heard someone laugh," she replied, annoyed that he didn't take her seriously.

"I heard it, too," the Mate called forward. "I think we should have a stop and investigate."

Making the decision for them, Amicia threw her leg over and slid off the side, landing on the ground with a loud thud. Pain shot through her body, and she instantly regretted the move. "Ow!"

"What the hell did you do that for?" Rey demanded, his wolf lying to allow him to climb off. Reaching the girl, he ran his hands over her in a much too familiar manner, earning him a slap on back of them.

"Stop that," she shouted. "I'm not hurt. It was just farther to the ground than I realized."

Laughter sounded again, a small boisterous peal, both above their heads and a bit to the left from the direction of their travel. Swinging around and scouring the canopy, Piers pointed as he gasped, "I see it. It looks like a miniature man!" They had seen so many creatures in Eriden a precise identification would require closer scrutiny.

Aware that he had been discovered, the gnome scurried down the trunk, using a rope, which had been wrapped around and held by one end in each hand. Leaning back, he used a bit of leverage to speed the movement as the rope held him in place for short bursts of descent. On the ground, he spun around to face the group members, who had closed in around him.

"I mean no harm!" he offered, holding up his hands as if to surrender to those who had encircled him.

Pushing through the others, Amicia stood before him. A short creature, all of three feet, the only one of less height in their party was Oldrilin, and it wasn't by much. "Who are you?" the girl demanded, noting the tiny robe that covered him, including his head and most of his face.

Looking up at her with wide brown eyes, the tiny man confessed, "I am called Sevoassi. I am a gnome from the Falconmarsh."

"Gnome," Edeill growled, "you are a long way from home. How did you come to hide within our forest?"

"Well, firstly, I would argue the forest doesn't belong to you," the miniature creature snapped. "Secondly, how and why I have come is of no concern to you."

"Please, don't argue," the blonde sighed, deeming the gnome peaceful. Stepping closer, she held out her hand. "I am Amicia Spicer, traveler from Nalen and mortal of the rim."

Blinking up at her, the gnome doubted she were any of those things, but disagreeing would certainly only lead to more trouble. Instead, he accepted the appendage, inspecting her fingers, then releasing them. "Why are you here?"

Surprised by the question, Ami considered how she should reply. On the surface, they were merely passing through, but deeper, she knew there was a great deal more to it than that. "We wish to visit the dwarves," she replied evenly.

"Visit them," the gnome cackled. "Unlikely." Looking around at the others, he pushed his hood back so he could have a better look, exposing his deep red hair and beady eyes, almost black. A long auburn beard and mustache sprang from his crinkled face and wiggled as he spoke. "Come. I will see you have dinner before the dwarfs remove your limbs from your torso."

Taken aback, Amicia gasped in short, "Oh my."

"What an odd thing to say," Reynard observed, placing the siren on the ground.

"Tis true," Sevoassi replied, pointing at him with a short digit. "Nasty creatures are the dwarves, so filled with their own importance."

"We'll judge them for ourselves, thanks," Amicia snapped, regaining her voice after the previous shocking statement.

"My burrow is this way," the gnome continued, indicating the direction he intended to take. His feet pattering as he moved, he didn't bother to look back.

"I advise against this," Edeill growled.

"You know this guy?" the Mate intervened. "I mean, this is your forest. Surely you would know if a gnome had moved in."

"I have never laid eyes on him before," the alpha replied tartly. "We have a large area of land, so we don't watch every inch of it, but I dare say he has not been here long. We would have seen or heard of his arrival in time, I assure you."

"Anyway," Amicia sighed, "should we take him up on the offer of a meal or not?"

Glancing around at one another, no one in her party seemed to have a clear opinion on the idea despite the wolf's objection. Craning to see in the direction he had taken, the girl grinned deviously, "Well, in that case, I'm going to see what a gnome home looks like. Follow me," she commanded, taking up the lead as she hoisted her pack and bow into position.

"I do not recommend this course of action," Edeill growled. "In fact, we still have a few hours of light left. We should keep moving."

"Go if you don't want to wait," she yelled over her shoulder, eager to be rid of the wolves.

"Ami," Piers called after her, hurrying to catch up. In front of her, he turned to announce, "Let's not be too hasty. If we lose our rides, it might take us days to reach the dwarf mountain, and it could become a more dangerous journey as well. They say we should keep moving, and I think we should heed that advice."

"Are you pulling rank?" she snorted, closing the distance between them before she said more quietly, "I have a feeling, Piers. Something tells me we need to visit with the old gnome, and to be honest I don't really like these wolves. They may be kin of the southern pack, but these are not Uscan and his clan. If they leave us, I don't see it as a loss."

Staring at her then flicking his gaze beyond her head, he could see the alpha glaring at them. He hated to admit he had felt the same about the northern pack almost from the moment they met them. His gaze back on her, he announced, "We're breaking here for the night." Pushing past her to speak to the large white figure bearing down on them, he added, "We appreciate your help –"

"What good is it to have the advice of a local if we don't take it?" Meena complained, almost certain the displaced gnome would be nothing but trouble.

"Please, love," he addressed his bride more softly. "Amicia and I have discussed it, and we would rather leave the company of the northern pack."

"Tired of us already?" Edeill growled, his blue eyes burning as he glared at the man in charge.

"We'll get along," the Mate replied evenly, hiding his racing heart behind a calm facade; if the wolves turned against them, it would be one hell of a fight, one they would probably lose. "Again, thank you for getting us this far."

Obviously upset, the wolves formed a ring around the group for as much as the trees allowed. Her pulse quickened, Amicia stared at the path the gnome had taken, noting that he had paused and turned to watch the spectacle. *"Help us,"* she directed at him, breathing deeply as she focused on their latest acquaintance.

Growling, the pack appeared to be conversing using the telepathy as well, as several of them snarled and pawed the ground, but their final decision was reached quickly. "We will leave you," Edeill announced gruffly. "Good luck with the dwarves."

Howls echoed through the trees as the group disappeared, leaving in the direction they had come. Panting, Amicia chortled, "Oh my God. For a second, I thought they would turn on us."

51

"As did I," the Mate agreed, pulling Meena into his arms and rocking her gently.

"Your supper awaits," the gnome called, drawing them back to the present and their altered company.

"We're coming," Bally yelled back, rearranging their gear now that they would be forced to walk the rest of the way.

SEVEN

Gnome Home

"DO you think they have really gone?" Rey asked doubtfully.

"I fear they may return," Ami agreed.

"Good riddance," the Mate muttered. "Everyone grab what you can carry. It does not appear to be far if we must make two trips."

"We'll have to repack everything now that we are reduced to foot travel," Meena observed, glancing in the direction of their new host.

"We'll manage," Piers countered. "This forest would not lend itself well to the litters with these massive roots cluttering the trails, but by reducing the size of our gear, we should be able to carry it upon our backs easily enough."

"Well, there is a limit to the shrinkage," Meena grunted, hoisting her load onto her shoulders and reminding him of the first time he saw her, carrying a large jar of water back in Whitefair.

"We'll make do, love," he said more softly, a smile curling his lips.

Noticing the grin, she scowled, "You appear awfully pleased with yourself."

"Not really," he chuckled, watching as the others limped along, leaving the pair of them behind. "Remember our discussion about trust?"

"Of course," she agreed, keeping her balance as she passed him.

Catching her arm, he held her, turning her to look at him. "I need you to trust me," he informed her before their lips met in a fiery kiss.

Resisting for a moment, Meena felt stiff, surprised by the open display of affection. Relaxing into the passion of their connection, she breathed heavily

53

when he released her. Licking her lip, she slurred, "That would be one way to convince me." Opening her eyes, she stared into his. "You are not typically so forward, sir."

"And I am usually unaffected at the thought of losing a woman. But you are not just any woman, love. I know we have spoken our vows, but there is more than words to a happy marriage. We have said our apologies, but I fear there is still some bitterness between us."

"You want my support," she cut to the chase.

"Yes. I don't think we needed them, and what's more, Ami thought as much. Please do not undermine our leadership, love," he practically begged, glancing to see that the others had disappeared. "I need you to be united with me, especially as things get harder."

"And here I didn't think you had it in you to grovel," she smiled more fully, leaning forward and pressing her lips to his for a shorter kiss before she agreed, "I will restrain my negative commentary despite my misgivings in this matter. I understand you not caring for my opinion."

"I didn't say I didn't care for it," he laughed. "I would just prefer you gave it to me in private from now on," he replied, lifting his own burden and following her down the narrow path. "Can we agree on that?"

"I'm sure that we can," she called over her shoulder, ahead of him on the trail.

Arriving at a giant tree, he could see that a large hollow had formed at the base of it. Dropping their packs with the others next to what appeared to be the door, he indicated the entrance. "After you."

Sitting and sliding her feet in first, Meena turned and wriggled her way in, her toes finding the small indentions carved into the dirt wall below the doorway that served as the stairs. Using them and the roots that gave her something to grip, she made it to the earth floor inside Sevoassi's home.

Before her, the small chamber appeared cramped. Giant roots acted as chairs along the walls of the dugout basin in the earth below the massive tree, and each of their group had located a place to sit to maximize the space. Ami sat next to the fire with Rey, and Zae on the right. Facing them on the opposite side, Bally and Animir left room for her and the Mate to join them.

"What a quaint home you have," she observed, taking her seat as her husband joined her.

"I do not entertain many guests," the gnome replied politely. "Be comfortable, and I will serve you," he proffered.

Before the fire, two small stools sat, Oldrilin occupying one of them.

54

"Thank you. Quite cozy is your home," she praised with her typical grin as she did so.

"Why thank you," the gnome smiled, handing each of them a cup of cool water to sip while they waited, served from a large bucket and ladle next to his hearth.

Once they were comfortable, he used the group's larger pot and placed his smaller one on a hook next to the hearth. Adding water and small chunks of meat, followed by vegetables, the gnome hummed to himself, then spoke to the girl he assumed to lead them. "Far from the rim you have come. How is it you have gathered so many from the magical realm?"

"Well, we're friends," Amicia explained, looking around at the others with sad eyes. "It is quite a long story, truth be told."

"The truth should always be told," Sevoassi observed, his hands busy as he added spices and then gave the boiling liquid a taste. "Please, tell me of your adventures," he beseeched, sitting upon the second small seat next to the siren.

Taken with the diminutive creature, Ami admired the sharpness of his gaze as he looked at each member, as if he could peer beyond the surface and see what each held within. "Well, I guess I could begin, but mine is by far not the most exciting of our tales."

"Pfft," Rey countered. "You only think that because you lived it. To those of us looking in, it is a grand adventure indeed."

"No more exciting than yours," she laughed. Turning her attention to their host, she started with her mother's funeral. "I lost my mum. That's really where the story originates for my part. Well, that and my childhood dream of crossing the sea. After she had gone, I had no reason to stay, as Nalen no longer felt like home." It saddened her that her quest may have been folly, and the simple act of running away from her loss rather than facing it.

"Nalen," Sevoassi parroted.

"Yes, a port town along the rim," Ami explained. "I caught passage on a ship –"

"Our ship," Bally cut her off. "She stowed away and had to be rescued by the Mate here before the crew could –"

"I'm sure he can picture what the crew wanted to do," Piers took over smoothly. "Suffice it to say we've been together a long time. Two years, or near enough," he grinned.

Noticing the rapport the group seemed to share, the gnome agreed, "Yes, but that doesn't explain how you came to Eriden, not in the least."

"A dragon," Rey spoke up, then took a large gulp from the cup of water

55

he'd been served. Wiping the excess from his lips with his arm, he elaborated, "A giant dragon scuttled the ship; burned the masts down around our ears. The Mate got us out of there though, and we floated along on a raft until we crashed upon the shores."

"Most sad," Lin agreed, blinking her wide blue eyes and sporting a full pout.

"You saw Riran?" Sevoassi asked in awe.

"Aye, the sirens put us right," the Mate admitted half-heartedly, "but the dragons did not allow us to rest there long."

"They attacked the mermaids, and we were forced to flee," Amicia chimed in. "Oldrilin was injured and we took her with us… Then we were taken in by the elves."

"It sounds like you have had a grand adventure indeed!" the gnome exclaimed, checking their stew.

"I'm not sure the word adventure quite covers it," Meena laughed, hoping she sufficed as civil. "We have had little rest in our travels, and the dragons still hunt us."

The group mumbled agreements, nodding their heads and adjusting themselves in their seats anxiously. Seeing their discomfort, Sevoassi shook his head. "Have no fear, my friends. There would be no cause for them to discover you here. You will be safe within my walls."

The group seemed pleased with their new companion, and so the story continued, each adding commentary that seemed appropriate. Leaning against Rey as the evening wore on, he laid his arm across Ami's shoulders and pulled her snugly against his chest. She took comfort in his presence, distracting her from the loss of her dragon. She had made few attempts to contact him that day, as it only made her more forlorn as each failed to make the connection.

By the time they were explaining Jerranyth, Bally had taken over, and quite a few embellishments were added, which left the remainder of them in fits of giggles. Noticing the aroma of their dinner, Amicia politely interrupted as they were building the cabin in Esterbrook. "Pardon everyone, but I think we may be ready to dine soon."

Leaping up from his stool, the gnome stirred the pot, then agreed, "Yes, a delectable dinner awaits." Considering the consumption, he added, "I'm not sure how we will serve everyone, though; I only have a few dishes."

"We each have a bowl," Bally boasted as he climbed the tiny steps to fetch them from his bag, "I made certain that they were packed along with our cauldron when we fled before the dragon attacked us a few nights ago."

"Ah, right then," Sevoassi agreed. Using a large scoop, he filled the bowls, which were passed down the line on each side until everyone had been served. Once they all had begun to eat, the gnome turned to Amicia to observe, "So, you have met many of our natives, and you have many more to come."

"Yes," she agreed between bites. "After we left the glen, we picked up Meena in the desert. Then in the north, we met the trolls, who helped us escape when the dragons returned for us," she explained with a sigh.

"The trolls," Sevoassi gasped, his eyes wide with disbelief. "Surely not. The trolls are friends to no one," he corrected.

"They are friends to us," the girl insisted somberly. "We built a cabin there in the forest. Their high priest performed the wedding for Meena and Piers as well," she added, tears forming in her eyes as she recalled the celebration that followed. "They are dear creatures." The idea the wolves would try to harm them disturbed her, stealing her appetite as she stirred what remained of her stew.

"Dear creatures... trolls," the gnome whispered, blinking at the young woman before him. Few had he met who possessed such an accepting heart and none who would refer to the ground-dwellers as anything but savages. "You are indeed unique, Amicia Spicer. Speak of what you need."

Cutting her eyes up at him, the girl blinked back her drops of sorrow. "I wish them to be safe. Edeill asked me about their home within the mountain, as if I would reveal to him how they could be reached. I fear for their safety even now, as the wolves have left us and returned in their direction."

"The trolls will be protected," the gnome assured, his voice stronger than it had been since they met. "Many eons have they guarded the northern corner of our beloved Eriden, and the wolves will not bring their fortification to an end."

Smiling, the girl agreed, "Thank you, Sevoassi. I hope that you are correct," she added, fairly certain he only said so to make her feel better.

"You seem to know a great deal about this land," the Mate spoke up, setting his empty bowl on the root-bench next to him. "Share with us, as we have learned far more since we have entered the north. The southern peoples were very secretive," he teased, glancing between the siren, elf and nymph in turn.

"Indeed," the gnome chuckled. "The tension of the south has been brewing since Eriden was a young continent, even before the mortals were cast to the rim."

"You know of Abolia and our fate," Amicia sighed, still toying with her food.

"Your fate," Sevoassi whispered, his eyes glazed as he considered her choice of words. "Your fate is so uncertain, princess."

Her face snapping up to glare at him, she spat, "So many have referred to me as such I grow weary of the term. I am no princess, or queen for that matter, and I wish them to cease in using it."

A slow smile creeping across his crinkled features, the gnome agreed with a small nod. "I will refrain from the term, but I assure you no insult is intended by its use. You honor us, the inhabitants of Eriden, with your presence. The depth of your caring is a testament to your nobility. I will speak of it no more, but when you are ready, there will be much for you to discover. For now, let us prepare a place for you to sleep by my fire."

Standing, he moved around the room, directing them where to spread their blankets so they could rest. Doing as he instructed, the fit was cozy, and reminded Rey of the days they had languished beneath their shade as they crossed the desert. Watching as Amicia brushed out her hair and braided it again before she lay down to sleep, he wondered what the old gnome had meant by *"much for you to discover,"* as they seemed to learn something new every day, in fact.

Eventually, they would have to run out, as there would be no more secrets left to uncover. "Goodnight, love," Rey said quietly. Stretched out beside her, he rested his hand on her shoulder so he could feel her respirations as he drifted off to sleep.

Listening to him breathe, Amicia wiped at her tears, not able to stop herself from reaching out into the darkness. *"Lamwen."* No reply came, but she had not really expected one. She searched out of habit or longing for something she should accept; her dragon was no more, she felt sure.

Hearing the snores of the others, Ami gently lifted Reynard's digits so she could extricate herself from his grasp. Picking her way between the bodies, she used the shallow steps at the entrance to climb her way out. Carved to fit gnome feet, only her toes were firm against the earth, and she gripped the sides to prevent falling as she made the ascent.

Outside, the dark earth lay in moon-shade from the large trees that made up the thick forest. In a few patches, the bright white light pierced the branches and shown upon the ground. Walking aimlessly forward, she stuck her hand into one of the beams and admired the sparkle of her flesh beneath the glow.

"You are troubled," Sevoassi observed.

Startled, a small squeak escaped her lips, and she panted, "I did not see you there. Why do you not sleep?"

"Why do you not sleep, pri –" he replied, cutting himself off before he used the term he had sworn off over dinner. "My lady?" he offered instead, closing the distance between them on padded feet.

"I have much to contemplate," she confessed, the sorrow leaking into her words. "I have lost a dear friend, and I fear he may never return."

"Walk with me then. I have words to share only meant for your ears, so it is fortunate that we have these moments to do so," he said with a smile. Offering his hand, he held the small appendage up and waited for her to take it.

Staring down at his dark robe, the red hair atop his head and in his beard glistened in the pale light. "You are an old gnome," she observed, accepting his fingers and giving them a squeeze, something familiar about him she could not quite place.

"Very old," he agreed, leading her down the path. "I have seen many moons in Eriden, watched as numerous kings and queens have risen and fallen over the ages."

"This is a sad time for all the land, or so I hear," she sighed.

"You know of Gwirwen?" he asked, stopping so they could peer through a thin patch in the canopy.

The dwarf mountains before them, the sight of their looming majesty caused her heart to skip a beat. "They appear so close," she breathed, then blinked a few times. "Yes. We have been told by many how things have become unbearable under his reign as the supreme dragon. Alas, I fear there is little that can be done to change what lies ahead."

"Ah, you have learned of the prophecy as well," he mused, squinting up at her as if to study her more closely.

"Yes, Yaodus explained the magical creator, who is also the destroyer. At least that is what he believes, or the wolves believe; someone believes," she stammered with a shrug. "I myself am not certain what to make of it, yet." Dragging her eyes away from the sharp peaks, she smiled down at him. "Would you have any advice to add?"

"Only that you are on the path," he nodded.

"So, I am the lover of dragons and men," she sniffed. "I feared as much. I wish someone would just tell me what I'm supposed to do."

"No one can do such a thing," he advised while digging inside his robe with his free hand. "However, I can offer you this, on one condition." Holding up a small round orb, it sparkled a bright blood red in the moonlight.

"An orb of truth," Amicia gasped, then remembered the previous versions had all been gold. "Why is yours crimson?"

"There are many of the gold, but there is only one like this," he informed her. "Unique, as are you. I offer it to you," he stated calmly, holding the sphere out to her.

Accepting it, the color shifted to a lighter burgundy, almost pink, when her fingers touched it. "It's beautiful," she breathed. "What's the condition?"

"You must not show it to anyone else. I fear your possession of it would bring out the worst in those around you if they knew."

"A secret," she chuckled, thinking of her lost friend. "I had a dragon friend; he was my secret for many months, and the others have yet to meet him," she confessed. "I fear they never will."

Shifting her gaze to stare into the gnome's dark eyes, she agreed, "I will hide it among my things, but how will I know when to use it? I mean, if it's so rare and precious, why would you give it to me?" she asked doubtfully.

"Soon, you will meet my kind, and you will understand. To reach them, you must face many perils, more dangerous than any you have so far."

"Oh, great." She swore under her breath, studying the globe once more. The pink glow against her flesh calmed her. "We must go forward. There is nothing for us behind, and I fear all of Eriden will be lost if I do not complete the task that lies before me."

"You do not believe you are the destroyer, then?" he mused. "The prophecy speaks directly of one who will be the end of Eriden."

"I am not," she bit curtly. "I would never destroy such a beautiful place, filled with people no less."

"Then you are not yet ready to see what lies within the orb. Hide it, and you will know the time that you must look."

Closing her fingers around it, she shrugged, "I'll add it to my collection."

"Collection?"

"Of magical tokens," she snorted. "I have a merdoe, a hamar gem, and now a red orb. I've done well for a mortal of the rim."

Shaking his head, the gnome held his tongue, keeping anything else he knew locked away. Instead, he raised a hand towards his home. "We should rest. You have a long day ahead of you on the morrow."

"Aye," she agreed, walking slowly towards the old tree. "Thank you, Sevoassi, I will cherish your gift and use it when the time comes to the best of my ability."

EIGHT

Veil of Secrets

"WHAT THE BLOODY hell is going on?" Piers shouted, waking Amicia from a deep slumber.

Turning on her back, she looked around at the others, who all sat upon their blankets. Staring about them in disbelief, the group mumbled inaudibly as the reality of their host's quarters sank in.

The light low beneath the tree, Amicia could see no sign of the diminutive creature's presence or any indication that he ever had been there, in fact. His pot no longer hung on the wall, the small seats were gone, and even the fire no longer burned.

Fighting to get to her feet, she grabbed her bag and shoved her hand inside. Rummaging around, she located the small sphere in the bottom, where she had hidden it the night before upon their return to his home. "It wasn't a dream," she assured, rubbing it fondly but refraining from producing her evidence. "Obviously, he is a magical creature and has decided to take his leave of us."

"Obviously," Meena agreed, withholding her retort for Piers's sake. She had feared the gnome would be trouble, and his hasty departure only confirmed her suspicions. "We should have our porridge and be gone from here."

"Agreed," Amicia replied; breathing heavily, her gut roiled between anger and fear. Turning to the entrance, she glared at the hole above them. Placing her pack on her back, she used the roots that hung down the walls to hoist herself up. The small set of steps that had been carved into the rock the night before was gone, along with everything else, and it was far more difficult to fight her way to the top without them.

Arriving at ground level, she found that Baldwin had scampered up before her. "Here, let me help you," he offered. Grasping the pack, he pulled to aid her in gaining her balance as she worked her way out of the pit beneath the trunk.

"Hand me my bow and whatever else you can," she commanded, dropping her pack and leaning through the opening to take what she could. Passing it to Bally, they piled everything to the side, then helped the others make the climb.

Her tiny feet on the ground, Oldrilin rung her hands as she wandered around, peering up at the mossy trees around them. "The gnome is gone," she moaned, her fear of his deception evident.

"Aye," Rey agreed, climbing out of the narrow space. "Don't worry. He didn't hurt us. In fact, he might have helped us get away from the wolves." Gazing into the sunlight canopy, he continued, "We'll have to set a fire for the breakfast."

"Aye," the Mate seconded. "Let's get to it and get the hell out of here as quickly as we are able. Bally, you and Animir gather a bit of wood for us. Rey, there was a stream that we were following before the northern pack left us. Can you locate it and fill the pot?"

"I'd rather use the water stone," Meena informed him.

"It could be our last," Piers countered, doubtfully.

Seizing her bow, Amicia clipped, "I'll go with him. We should save the stone for when we have no other choice in case it truly is the last."

"Very well," Meena groaned, sad that they ignored her advice often and wishing she had not promised to hold her tongue. Watching the young couple disappear, she shivered violently. "I do not like this, my husband." Glancing around, she kept her voice low so that Zae and Lin could not hear. "The gnome knew her, I am certain of it. Whether his removal of our guides was a blessing we may never know."

The look on her drawn features tugging at his heartstrings, he pulled her to him, wrapping his bride in his arms and holding her against his muscled chest. "Are you sorry you have left your home in the desert to join us?"

Pulling back, as if his words stung her, she gasped, "Of course not! My old heart is filled with love again, and I shall never regret you nor our young friends," she supplied, indicating the others with an arching sweep of her hand. "But I certainly wish you heeded my advice more often," she added with a sniff.

"Aw, love," he whispered, his eyes swimming with regret. "Let's prepare to make the meal," he suggested to keep her busy.

A short time later, the pot simmered, and the group took seats on the ground around their fire. Finding a spot on the roots of the aged tree, Ami opened her bag, her breath coming in shallow pants as she confessed, "I have something I must show you. Sevoassi bade I should keep it hidden from you, but in light of his disappearance, I would feel better if you had seen it," she explained, cutting her eyes up at the older woman.

Her fingers finding the smooth surface of the orb, she grasped it firmly, closing her eyes and whispering to herself, *They are your friends; you can trust them with this.* Pulling the object out, it glowed slightly between her digits as she turned her hand over to open them, presenting the sphere to the group.

"What is that?" Bally demanded, leaning closer to get a better look.

"It's an orb of truth, like the gold ones," Ami grunted. "The gnome said when I was ready, I would be able to see what lies within it."

"It's red," Meena observed, her voice faint. "I have never seen a red orb."

"He said it was unique," the girl explained, beckoning her closer. "Would you like to hold it?" she offered, shoving it towards her.

"I dare not!"

Withdrawing the extended hand at the sharp reply, Amicia frowned, "Was I wrong to show you this?" He had said to keep it a secret. Taking in the circle of concerned faces, she said more quietly, "I was warned to hide it. Have I erred in sharing it with you?"

"No, but you may have been mistaken to accept it," Meena clarified. Tearing her gaze away from the warm crimson glow, she stared into the pale green eyes of the girl.

"You are afraid," Amicia whispered.

"Petrified. I do not wish any harm to come to you or any of us. This magic is beyond me," the wan confessed.

"Should we go back?" Rey asked, equally concerned for the girl's safety. "Perhaps this is a warning that we should give up."

"We cannot go back," Piers reminded him firmly. "We must go forward until we have resolved our conflict with the dragons. There is no place behind us that is any safer than what lies ahead. Either way, our future is that way," he said, pointing at the home of the dwarves.

"We have no idea what lies ahead," Reynard quarreled. "We might all die before we make it over the next set of mountains, much less get to the land of the dragons."

"Aye," Piers nodded, "or we might make it through. We must push to defeat one obstacle at a time. If we clear the mountains, we will make it to Falconmarsh, city of the gnomes; then to the north of that we will find the dragons. There, we will discover what became of Lamwen and if we will be able to put an end to their pursuit of us. It is the only way we will have a home, whether it is here, to be returned to the rim of mortals, or somewhere we have yet to imagine."

Their breakfast ready, Amicia shushed them, "I'm sorry I have upset you. I only wished to share what I had discovered. Keeping my dragon friend from you was wrong, or at least I have come to believe that it was; it might have cost us dearly. I do not want to be the cause of our demise by hiding something important from the rest of you."

Serving the porridge, Meena agreed, "Then thank you for the sharing. You have accepted the gift, and that cannot be undone. Hide it away in your bag, and do not show it to any that we meet. I do not know what the significance of the object is, but I know that it would attract undue attention if anyone else were to know of its existence."

Glancing around at the others, the first mate amended, "None of you will speak of it, either. Not to anyone, including among ourselves. Understood?"

Nodding and mumbling various affirmations, they each accepted their morning ration. Eating in near silence, the depths of their thoughts swallowed them, as each knew the risks that they would face, and all felt powerless to escape them.

Once they had eaten, everything was laid out and another round of shrinking took place. Taking up their loads when all had been repacked, Amicia wished she could repair the damage their party had seemed to suffer. "I'm sorry I have brought everyone down," she apologized quietly.

"Rubbish," Piers countered, clamping her on the shoulder to give her a squeeze. "You cannot help who you are, and we are your friends. We will stick together and make our way forward – together."

"But I have lost our rides," she whined, falling into step behind him, with the others following along in single file.

Walking between Ami and Rey, Oldrilin did her best to keep up, calling after the girl, "Sweet Amicia. You are a true princess even as you despise to hear your praise. We are blessed with your company and thank Eriden for your presence."

Not convinced, the girl lifted her chin but said no more. They marched toward the mountain, making several miles through the forest before they came upon another clearing that would make a good camp as the sun sank into the west.

"I think we've gone the distance for this day," Piers observed, drawing everyone in and making the assignments. "Bally, you and Animir see if we can have some fresh meat for our dinner. Zae, you and Rey use the water skins to bring us plenty of water from that stream that continues to flow to the west of us."

"Are you sure it's still there?" Reynard queried, dropping his gear next to a fallen log that would serve as a seat for them once they were able to rest.

"Fairly so. I believe it flows down from the mountain, and I have caught glimpses of it throughout the day," the Mate assured.

"Amicia and I will tend to the vegetables if you are going to set the fire," Meena suggested, glancing at the girl in a hurried manner.

Her gut tightened, Amicia did not miss the furtive gaze. "You wish to speak with me?" she suggested as they began a slow circle through the trees in search of tasty edibles.

"I wish to make an apology of my own," Meena sniffed, her emotions raw after the events of the last few days. "I have been ungracious since the dragons attacked our home."

"Our home," Ami parroted, noting a group of tubers and kneeling to dig them up. "It is my fault that they came, and you have nothing to be sorry for."

Joining her, the older woman disagreed, "Fault is of no consequence. We are on this journey together, and it has only been made more difficult by my words. Piers is right; we cannot go back, and I have not been as accepting of my place within our group as I should be."

"How so?" Amicia asked, pausing her hands to study the features of the older female. Seeing the deep lines in her brow, she reached to catch her hands. "Meena, what has happened?" Thinking of the gnome's gift, she dared not speak of it, but she knew the object weighed heavily in all their thoughts.

Lifting her chin, the wan prayed for the strength to keep her secret veiled, as informing the girl of what she had come to accept as the truth would only add to their burden. "Nothing yet, my child," she breathed, "but I fear what is to come."

"You are afraid for yourself?"

"No, for you; for all of us," she whispered. "I have come to love you all so dearly. For so many years, I was alone in my life. In the midst of your camaraderie, I have discovered what it means to have that which can be taken." Flicking her gaze between her soft green eyes and her hands, which the girl still held, she sobbed, "It would be horrible to lose you; any of you."

"You will not lose us," Amicia soothed, using her grip on her to pull the woman forward. Wrapping her in a strong embrace, she exhaled loudly, as if peace had enveloped them as they held one another. Feeling the shudders as Meena sobbed, the girl shed tears of her own. "You are dear to me, as well. We shall not fear any of the things that may happen and will focus on that which makes us strong. We decided this long ago, when we floated on a barren sea, and I beseech you to take heart as well."

"I will try," Meena sniveled, hugging her tighter. "When my words are sharp, I pray you will see the love behind them."

"Always," Amicia agreed, a smile creeping onto her lips. It had been many years, if ever, that she had felt so loved by another woman, and she would do all that she could to protect the one who held her.

"What's going on?" Rey demanded, coming upon them as he and Zae returned with the water.

"Nothing," the wan replied, forcing her sorrow away as she released the smaller girl. "We were discussing –"

"I was telling her about our positive attitude motto," Amicia interrupted, hoping to prevent further tears. Dropping their find onto a piece of cloth she had spread upon the soil, she folded it over to carry the tubers back to the camp. "We will have a delicious dinner and a story before we rest this night, and we will all do our best to remember our pledge," she insisted as she stood.

Eyeing her doubtfully as they returned to the clearing, where a ring of stones now held the center, Reynard agreed reluctantly under his breath, "We will indeed, my princess."

The days warm, the group followed the stream, always keeping it within reach for their water as they crossed the forest. Above them, the blue sky remained clear, both of clouds and wings, as they constantly searched out of fear at being discovered.

However, if the dragons knew of their whereabouts, they kept their distance, and six days after their encounter with the gnome, they arrived at a rock wall that extended both to the east and west. Following it to the point where the stream cascaded down, they found the only place it appeared to be accessible.

"Climbing this thing is going to be more difficult than the wolves led us to believe," Piers observed, his dark eyes scanning the face of the rock for hand and foot holds.

"We could walk along it for a day or two and see if there is a better place," Rey suggested, kneeling to help himself to a drink while they paused to plan their next move.

"No, I think this path that has been eroded by the water will be our best bet. However, I'm leery of the climb, as we will be exposed against the light-colored stone," their leader insisted.

"As when we entered the troll cave," Amicia observed. "Perhaps I should shield us, as I did before."

"I don't think you can climb and maintain the shadow," Meena warned, stroking the girl's hair fondly.

"We brought the robes," Zaendra added. "They are earth tones, as the stone. Perhaps wearing them will help us from standing out."

"Or in the least help hide our identities," the Mate agreed. "Good idea, nymph," he chuckled. "Break out the packs, and let's dress for the occasion."

Dropping their gear, each member of the group donned a wizard's robe, and Bally pointed out with a chortle, "At least that wild blond frizz won't be as visible."

"Thanks," Amicia grimaced as Rey gave him a dark glare.

Searching up the face of the rock, Piers pointed, "I see an indention a few hundred yards above us. We have plenty of daylight, and I think we can make it before dark. Do we want to take some wood for a fire?" he asked, directing the question to his wife.

"I'm afraid it would only draw attention to us. No, we will eat dried meat and some of the fruit this eve, but the alcove will offer us some protection from the elements while we slumber," she pointed out.

"What about the dwarves? How do they get in and out of the mountain do you think?" Amicia asked in a quiet voice.

"They will have a grand entrance," Animir advised. "They are arrogant creatures, as are the elves, and will want all to know when you have approached their gates."

"Another good reason not to wander too far in either direction," Piers added with a nod. "I'll go first, and the rest of you can follow. Take your time and make sure you maintain three points of contact with the rock."

"Why's that?" Bally bit tartly. "I've been climbing my whole life; a few rocks don't scare me."

"They will if someone slides down into you," Rey replied with a scowl. "Everyone move slow and only move one limb at a time, like he said."

Looking up doubtfully, Amicia swallowed hard. She had never climbed much of anything, other than a few trees back on the farm. The path before them appeared daunting, and she feared she would let the others down if she weren't careful. Adjusting her robe that hid her and her pack beneath it, she drew in a deep breath and pushed it out slowly through her nose.

"We'll be ok," Zae assured, taking her hand and giving her a squeeze as the older couple started the climb ahead of them.

Returning the gesture, Amicia agreed, "Yes, we'll be fine." Her turn, she grasped the rocks and hoisted herself up, only then realizing that the face of the cliff was not a sheer drop as it appeared, and it angled slightly towards the peak. The climbing easier because of it, she was able to keep up despite her lack of past experience.

Arriving at the flat surface as the sun set, as the Mate had predicted, the group fell upon the floor of the shallow cave and panted loudly. A fit of laughter rippled through them as they realized they had passed their first hurdle, and each felt more relaxed as they pulled off their robes and gear, preparing to settle in for the night.

NINE

King's Ransom

THE SUN SHOWN off Onothwyn's dark brown scales as he turned in a wide slow circle, watching the face of the cliffs with his flame red eyes. He had been left in charge of the hunting party, and it would be his call how to deal with the group if this was indeed their prey. He hoped that it was; he had been looking for a chance to prove himself and thereby move up in the ranks.

Flying next to him, Putwyn observed, "That is them."

"Are you certain?"

"Positive. Her flaxen mane gives her away now that her robe is removed," the smaller beast explained. "Do we go in and finish them?"

"The cave would not be a suitable place to attack. We will allow them to climb to the top and take them there. If they survive the ascent," his superior suggested. "We will make a kill for our meal and bed down for the night. They will still be there when the sun rises."

Following his lead, Putwyn flew low over the tops of the trees, searching for an animal to serve as his dinner. Spying a small elk, he slayed the creature cleanly and carried it across the forest to an open area next to the stream the group had been following, where he and his partner would rest for the evening.

Onothwyn joined him shortly after, sporting a larger elk for his sustenance. The two devoured the fresh meat and then drank from the brook as Pardodan landed near them and ambled up to the stream.

"We have found them," Onothwyn informed him, then returned to his slurping at the cool liquid.

Pardodan lifted his large blue and green head, his green accents glinting in the fresh moonglow. "Why have you not destroyed them?" he growled.

"They hide within the caves of the cliffs where we cannot be certain they have been slain. Who knows how deep the tunnels go. We will set against them when they reach the top," the junior dragon informed their leader of their plan.

"Negative. We will set against them at first light, when they move from the shadows. They will be vulnerable on the face of the cliffs."

Glaring at his superior with a glassy eye, Onothwyn instantly regretted giving up his quandary; not only would Pardodan take all the fun out of the kill, he would take all the credit for it as well. Turning his back on him, he realized he should have denied their location and pretended to continue the search, knowing he could have picked them up at the top as planned and the other dragon would be none the wiser.

But it was too late for second guesses. Sharing a glance with Putwyn, the two younger members of the team had no cause to argue. Pardodan had served with Lamwen in the king's guard and held rank over them. They would do as he commanded or they would stand before the council under the charge of mutiny.

Discerning that they would obey, the older dragon turned to their clearing and selected a boulder to lie against. When he was comfortable, he announced, "The war has begun."

"War," Putwyn gasped. He had hoped that turning on Lamwen would prevent the altercation that seemed to be brewing all around them. "Have there been casualties?"

"A few," Pardodan explained, shifting his gaze to fixate on Onothwyn. "We still have not located the body of Lamwen, and a few of the others have fled Adiarwen. They hide across the lands, but we have hunting parties searching for them and will attack them when we can. When we have dealt with the mortals, we will return to our king and be given a new target. Perhaps the sirens."

"The sirens," Onothwyn growled, "surely not. They have been allies to the dragons for many eons. Perhaps you mean the nymphs. They are more likely to stand against us."

"Gwirwen suspects all of treachery, even those within his ranks," the leader barked. "If he orders the mermaids destroyed, we will obey."

Exchanging another glance, the reasoning behind such a cause could not be determined. "The sirens are our first line of defense against the mortals,"

70

Putwyn observed meekly, knowing they had already suffered great losses the first time Riran was attacked.

"We do not need protecting from the mortals," Pardodan snapped, raising his head to glare at him angrily. "You have no right to doubt the plan of the supreme dragon or the council. Get some sleep, and we will complete our task on the morrow."

Staring back at him, Putwyn's heart raced. He had betrayed his friend in the hope that peace would win out, but to the contrary, it would appear that his actions had not prevented the slaughter. Instead, he would be asked to aid in the destruction of many innocent creatures.

Rolling onto his side, he breathed deeply as he watched the waters rippling past. *Surely I will find a way to prevent their demise*, he thought with great pain. He knew that he would have to at least try. The sirens were defenseless against most of the creatures of Eriden; good and faithful servants of the dragons, they did not deserve to be struck down.

Shifting his gaze, he could see the outline of the dark cave where an unlikely group of travelers hid. Amicia, a mortal of the rim, or so it would appear, lay among them. Putwyn had watched her raise one of the men in her company from the dead, or she had from what he had witnessed at a distance.

It could have been a trick. Lamwen was the one who had declared the act a miracle. *Lamwen, who is now lost and presumed a rotting corpse somewhere on or around the lands of Eriden.*

Closing his eyes, the smaller dragon breathed deeply. All he had ever wanted was to fit in; to be accepted by the king's guard, but he had never been deemed good enough. Lamwen and Jarrowan had accepted him, and he had brought them down with a loose tongue. The pain rumbling in his gut, he squinted at the cave once more. *Decide.*

He had chosen the king's side because he thought the benefits would outweigh his disloyalty. *They will never trust you again*, he mourned. Besides, there would be no way to help them, as he would be no match for the two dragons who slumbered beside him.

Listening to them breathe, he considered ways he could stop the slaughter that would come with the light. *I could go and carry them away... or warn them.* Running through each scenario, he quickly realized the flaws in either plan. *I'm not telepathic, so I have no way to reach them, and to go physically could cost me everything.*

I cannot help them directly, he concluded. Staring at the cave, but not focusing on it, it grew hazy, and the mountain behind it stood out against the star-filled sky. *The dwarves.*

71

But why would they offer aid? *They are greedy creatures, perhaps on promise of payment they could be persuaded,* he mused. Getting to his feet, Putwyn stood still, listening to the rumbling snores of his companions. Certain that they slept, he leapt silently into the air, gently leaving the earth so that no stone would be disturbed by his departure and alert them to his flight.

Arriving at the front of the mountain, he landed before the great maw that served as the entrance to the dwarf kingdom. A massive expanse four times his height, it held a rock path that layered the opening so that troops could defend against attackers with a rain of spears, arrows, and stones should the need arise.

In front of the opening, a bridge crossed a deep chasm, one that held jaggedly sharp rocks that would impale or dismember any who fell from above. On his side of the bridge, two large statues flanked the platform, each of them a likeness of a previous king.

On the far end, closest to the mountain, stood the current ruler's version, only larger and grander, with gold and leather armor to protect him. On either side stood a guard, presumably to ensure no one touched the sculpture.

Looking up at the few guards who stood watch higher up, he pondered the conversation he would have with the king. He had never been more frightened, for being caught would mean certain death and, worse, the loss of all he hoped to protect.

"What say you, dragon!" one of the short, round creatures called into the darkness, the moon illuminating the silver and grey scales of their visitor.

"I must share words with Baeweth," Putwyn slurred, delirious with trepidation at his course of action.

"Nay," the guard replied, "our king is in his chamber and requires his slumber."

"You must bring him to me!" the young dragon snarled, bolting towards the dwarf. "The future of the entire Kingdom of Eriden may rest upon his action."

Seeing that the gate's protector was unmoved, he growled more quietly, "Bring him, and I will see to it you are rewarded."

"Rewarded," the gateman laughed. "Have you pockets, my lord? Carry you gold or jewels with which to buy my service?" The others joined him, and the night air vibrated with their taunts and mirth.

His blood boiling with indignation, the fire in Putwyn's chest grew hot as he contemplated scorching them. Although the course of action would ease his wounded pride, he realized it would be foolish to bring the dwarves in against them. An idea springing to mind, he realized the dragons were a divided race, and he currently served the king as far as any other knew.

"Gwirwen commands it!" he bluffed, hoping the use of their supreme dragon's name would get him results.

Their laughter subsiding, the guard demanded, "Why did you not speak of this before?"

"Because, you insolent fool, I did not expect your stupidity to stand in the way of my cause. Now, present Baeweth with my request for an audience, and be quick about it!" Fire dancing between his teeth, the young dragon hoped he offered a fierce image for them to reflect upon as they scurried to do his bidding.

The minutes ticked by, but within half an hour, the king himself appeared at the gate, standing at the top row of the rocks as he called, "What business have you with me, dragon?"

"I am Putwyn, here by order of the king's council," the creature lied, boldly hiding the fear that ate at his gut. "I would speak with you in private."

"Bah," Baeweth spat, pulling his robes around him as he worked his way to the exit below. Coming out through the bottom and stomping across the bridge that spanned their gaping moat, he groaned, "This should be of great importance."

"I assure you that it is," Putwyn replied, lying so that he faced the north with his back to the guards. Glaring at the dwarf king with a massive eye, he hissed, "I'm sure you have heard of the war that has begun among the dragons."

"War is such a broad term," the king growled. "From what we have observed, a simple uprising by a few misfits would be more like. Gwirwen will deal with them in short order, to be certain," he added, his confidence in their supreme dragon evident.

"Would you not like a bit of assurance on that cause?" the dragon growled. "Perhaps to turn a profit from the squabble?"

Rubbing his belly, Baeweth groaned, "I'm listening."

"In the caves on the side of your mountain, which lie next to the western stream," he explained, indicating the location with a lift of his chin, "there hides a group hunted by the king's dragons. A group he would pay a handsome salary to recover if they were to become prisoners of the dwarf kingdom."

Turning to glare at the location through the darkness, Baeweth stroked his beard. "And why would you share this news with me? It does not sound as if you serve our good king."

73

"I serve justice," the dragon replied quietly. "Other dragons will attack the travelers at first light, ones I do not believe deserve the fame of killing these enemies of the realm."

"You wish the glory for yourself," the dwarf laughed loudly, seeing through his plan. Narrowing his gaze, he suggested, "You would provide an equivalent reward for your prestige?"

"Yes," Putwyn hissed. "Take them into your kingdom and hide them. I will come later and barter for their release, and I will receive the credit for their capture," he chortled, excited to see how his plan might succeed.

"This will cost you dearly," the king nodded, still caressing the dark hairs on his face. "We will have to retrieve them before the sun comes."

"Yes. If you do not, it will be too late and the opportunity will be lost. Is there a way to reach them unseen?"

"I may be able to achieve it," the king muttered, considering what he knew about the narrow opening. "The cave behind it is quite large, and one of my dwarves has fancied a project there for some time."

"I suggest you allow him to begin this very night," the dragon pushed in a hoarse whisper.

"Yes, we will make our best attempt to bring them into Rhong. You will come in seven days with payment for their return," the dwarf stipulated. "I have not named my price, so suffice it to say you will impress me with riches should you wish me to comply."

"Of course, my lord," the dragon bowed, "I will see you in seven days, and I will deliver riches beyond your dreams," he repeated the terms, then leapt into the air.

Watching him fly, the king muttered, "I can dream of quite a lot." Shuffling over the access, he called to the guard who had awakened him, "Quickly, locate Hayt and send him to my quarters. Tell him to bring the plans for that vista he is always on about, and hurry."

"Yes, my lord," the gateman replied, turning into the dark halls and making his way to the living quarters above the great chambers.

Meanwhile, the dragon returned to the clearing by the stream, where his two companions slept soundly. They were not disturbed when Putwyn retook his place among them, and he coiled back into his spot, his heart beating loudly within his pointed ears.

Lying in the darkness, his pulse slowed as he considered his success. The plan rested in the hands of the dwarves; he had done all he could for the moment, and it would be up to Lord Baeweth to secret the princess and her friends away.

TEN

Rhong

ARRIVING at the king's quarters, Hayt smoothed his unruly blond locks. Clearing his throat, he called as he entered the door, "You have sent for me, uncle?" Crossing to the table, he lay the rolls of paper that held his plans upon it, catching one as it escaped and fell to the floor.

Being in the king's personal chamber always gave him an odd feeling in the pit of his gut. His grandmother's brother, and therefore his great uncle, he had been an unwilling member of the royal family, as he preferred the work of an architect and structural engineer. He enjoyed getting his hands dirty as he helped to complete the plans he made for their growing community within the mountain, something that did not earn him much respect within his kin.

"Yes, yes," Baeweth replied, securing his favorite gown across his shoulders. "I have given consideration to your plan for a lookout in the northeastern caves. How long would it take to open up the vista?" Stepping up to the younger man, he gazed up at him, as his great nephew towered above all of the other dwarves at over five and a half feet in height. The average was closer to four.

"How long?" his nephew blinked at him, confused by the question. "Weeks at most, as the cave is already there –"

"No, I mean how long would it take to access the cave tonight. Could you open the wall or expand our closest tunnel?" the king clarified. "Show me your charts, son."

Searching through the scrolls, Hayt located the one he wanted and

75

unrolled the yellowed piece of parchment, then frowned, "What do you mean tonight? All of my crews are asleep, and we are currently working on the new tunnels on the eastern boundary."

"Yes, the new tunnel," Baeweth muttered, running his fingers over the drawings for the proposed addition. "But if I were to need the opening tonight, could it be done?"

"I suppose that it could," Hayt sighed, stroking his full beard. His blue eyes studying the shorter man, he added, "You want it built at night?"

"We live inside a mountain. What do you care if the sun shines outside or not?" the king growled at being questioned.

Blinking a few times, the younger dwarf agreed with a shrug, "I don't suppose it matters." Pointing at the location the connection would be made, he speculated, "A few hours is all we would need to tunnel between the cave and our corridor. We did the testing last year, before you decided against the addition…" He hesitated, then asked, "Why are we building it now?"

"No reason." The king brushed him off with a wave of his hand. Cutting his eyes over, he could see his great nephew would not be so easily persuaded. "All right," he whispered. "I've been told there are enemies of the Supreme Dragon hiding in the cavern. If we can bring them within our walls, a reward might be offered for their captors."

"Oh, uncle," Hayt grunted, raising his hands in disgust. "You've dragged me from my slumber to add a bit of coin to your coffers?"

"Well, yes," the old man laughed. "But you get to build your guard tower."

"Yes, in the middle of the night," Hayt spat, rubbing at his red face. "My crew will be angry enough. What are we to say when a group of vagabonds are discovered?"

"Say nothing," the king offered, waving his hands about in the air as if he were hiding the truth from plain sight. "Bring them to my throne room and present them to me, and I will deal with them. And do not tell them anything, either."

"Oh, uncle," Hayt repeated with a shake of his head. "One day, will you be satisfied with the wealth you have hidden away? Our vaults are full, and we add new ones every year, but it is never enough."

"Do as I say," the king replied curtly, thumping the pages before them as he spoke. "The access must be dug before first light. Now go!"

Shaking his head as he rolled the page, Hayt marched out of the room and through the corridors. "Awaken Firen and have him rouse his crew," he instructed the guard who followed him, "and be quick about it. Have them meet me at the second level up, where we measured for the emergency vista."

"Where?" the guard asked doubtfully.

"Just tell him that; Firen will know what I'm talking about even if you don't. I'll get the equipment gathered so we can begin as soon as they get there," he grumbled, stomping through the doorway into the great hall at the center of the city. At the other end, he worked his way through a few more tunnels to arrive at the storage caves.

Selecting picks and shovels, he loaded them into a deep wheel barrel, then set up a second. "We'll get complaints for sure," he ranted under his breath, certain the rest of the mountain would not be happy about the late hour and the racket that would echo through their halls.

Pushing the first cart up the slope of the path, he arrived at the section of wall he had marked back when he first realized the fissure had opened up on the great rock face of the cliffs outside. "This is preposterous," he grumbled, sliding his hand over the faded symbols. "Years I have thought of this, but it only matters to him when there is a coin to be made from the venture."

Leaving the wagon, he marched to the storage to retrieve the second, noting a few of his crew had arrived when he drew near the second time. "Ah, glad you could make it," he teased, setting the back feet of the device on the path and indicating the wall. "The king wants us to open up the passage for the vista tonight."

"Tonight," Firen grumbled. "Have you both lost your minds?"

"The king would be happy to hear your protests," Hayt agreed. "I'm sure there is room in the cells for you to return to your rest."

His features drawn into a heavy frown, the chief of Hayt's crew growled, "That does not amuse me."

"Ah, well, then perhaps you will cease with the unpleasantries, and let's make a hole, shall we?"

"Why tonight?" Firen pushed, seizing his tool and using it on the rock. His swing a perfect arch, the tip of his pick landed against the jagged line of a crack and sent bits of the stone flying, widening the crack with every blow.

"I believe he is concerned about our safety. He wants to get the vista opened as soon as possible, now that the dragons have begun fighting among themselves," the king's nephew lied expertly.

The fib convincing, the other man took over the spreading of it, informing each of their arriving crewmen the reason for their haste so that the new entrance into their intended cave would be ready to begin the next phase well before the day had dawned outside their dark mountain.

Hours later, Amicia lay within their cave. The night before, they had sat within its darkness, praising how well it would hide them if the dragons had been watching or scouring the mountain.

The stream that flowed beside the shelf that had formed in the rock babbled and gurgled as it rushed by, its cascade almost a dull roar as it poured onto the layers of stone. At some time in the past, it had pooled there on the shelf, and the cave had been eaten away by the swirling water, as the soil inside had been less dense and easily removed.

The mouth of the cave heavier and made of firmer sediments, it had remained, so they could sit out on the narrow space, which spanned a mere six feet deep and ten feet wide, while the cave itself had turned out to be more than thirty feet long and nearly as much in width.

Lighting the room with her hamar gem, they had found it to be dry and almost completely free of bugs or other infestations, so they had placed their beds inside, feeling safer than the open air of the cliff on the front of their cave, as if it were a porch and they were still inside their cabin at New Abolia.

Lying still, the girl could hear the scrape of shovels against the rock and the thump of picks as they landed against the wall above her. Sitting up, the breath in her chest grew hot with fear. The others slept, and her mouth felt dry at the thought of having to wake them and flee before the sun rose.

Climbing out of her cover, she tiptoed among them, carrying her boots so that she could sit on their entrance stones and contemplate the path they would take when they left the cave. Up, she presumed, but would they get far if the dwarves made it out and realized their presence?

"Good morning," Piers whispered gruffly when she arrived at the mouth of their cave.

"Good morning," she echoed, her lungs still burning with dread. "Have you been awake long?"

"Since I realized what I was hearing," he sighed, "assuming you have noticed the sound as well."

"The dwarves digging against the wall," she confessed, closing the distance and sitting beside him so that her feet hung over the side next to him. Putting on her boots, they clicked as she kicked her heels gently against the rock below.

"Aye," he agreed, "almost as if they are digging into our very cave. I wonder if they know that we are here."

"If you suspect this, why do we not flee?" she gasped.

Raising a hand, he pointed straight out over the top of the trees. The moon in the west close to setting, the light shone across the tops of them with brilliant, glittering light. Dancing along the top of the canopy, dark shapes flapped their massive wings as they circled, seemingly so close they could spew their fire and reach them.

"Dear God," she breathed. "Do they know we are here?"

"I suspect that they do. If we had lain out on the shelf, or if there had been no actual cave, they could have killed us easily. With us hidden inside, they needed to wait for us to come out and continue our climb; only then could they be sure we were all destroyed," he explained somberly.

"We're trapped," she whimpered, angry tears spilling onto her cheeks. "Do we face the dragons or hope the dwarves get to us first?"

Shrugging, he growled, "I fear the dwarves less, but I believe they will not open the gap in time. As soon as the sun is up and we do not come out, the dragons will probably attack the mouth of our cave out of desperation. They will in the least fill our hiding place with heat and flame, and we will be cooked if not burnt into blackened lumps of flesh."

"A lovely image to look forward to," the girl bit in reply. "So, what is your plan for getting us out of here? Can we hide in the water and make our way back down?"

"Doubtful," he shrugged, grasping a few loose stones and tossing them over the side one at a time. "I was going to let you sleep until the first light and hope the dwarf diggers win the race," he admitted in a quiet tone.

"Can we not dig towards them?"

"Have you brought a pick or shovel in your pack?" he barked with a spastic laugh. Shaking his head, he commanded, "Sit quietly, and enjoy what could be your last morning, love." Offering his hand, he waited for her to place her fingers between his.

Her lip forming a small pout, Amicia accepted the digits. He might have woken his wife and spent the minutes with her, but he had chosen to keep her suffering short, as each second that passed would be pure agony, knowing either fate that awaited them would be painful and most assuredly the end.

Behind them, the noises grew louder and yet remained faint enough not to awaken the others. Before them, the moon disappeared, and only a few minutes later, the sky to the east began the slow shift of sunrise.

"It's beautiful," Amicia observed more calmly. The deep purple of the sky snuffed the stars, with pink and orange slowly creeping into it before the bright red edge of the sun topped the barren side of the mountain to the east.

Leaning towards her, his lips puckered, Piers gently pressed a kiss against her forehead. "I have enjoyed our time together," he whispered, but only an instant before chaos erupted within the cave.

Shouting echoed across the tops of the trees as both Lin and Zae screamed. The men shouted at the dwarves, reaching for their weapons.

"Piers, the dragons come!" Amicia cried, pointing at the three shadows flying towards them at top speed.

Pulling her by the hand, they joined the others inside the cave, where he called loudly, "Everyone calm down! Stop with the squealing. We have attracted the dragons for Eriden's sake!"

"Dragons?" Meena breathed as the others fell silent. "They have found us."

"Aye," her husband nodded. "They've been circling outside."

"Well, the dwarves are digging through this wall," Reynard informed him angrily, indicating the place where loose rocks had begun collecting on their side.

"Aye," the Mate said again, "let us pray they make it before the dragons –"

At that moment, the wall gave way and crashed in upon them, sending their smaller members sprawling. On the other side, eight tiny man shapes could be none other than the dwarves. Holding up a lantern, one of them gasped, "Why are there mortals in our new vista?"

Grabbing his pack, the Mate stepped towards them. "We don't have time to explain. Dragons will fill this hall with fire at any moment."

"Dragons," a second clipped, laying his pick over his shoulder as he inspected the lot.

Taking charge, Hayt helped Amicia to her feet, then paused when Zaendra placed her small dark hand into his, which sharply contrasted with his pasty white flesh. Rubbing at his filthy hair, he mumbled, "I'm Hayt, the king's nephew and head of this work detail."

"That's great. May we come inside?" Piers insisted, already shoving Bally towards the narrow hole that had been made.

"Yes, of course," the tallest of the dwarves replied, still holding the girl's appendage firmly. "Here, let me help you," he offered as he grasped her elbow and guided her over the rubble.

Within minutes, they had gathered their things and carried them through the new opening while Hayt dared a closer look at their cave's mouth and the flat shelf in front of it. Seeing nothing, he ventured closer, where he could see the three forms turning in a rapid circle and watching the mouth of the party's hiding space, seemingly eager to greet them should they go out.

"Well?" Piers demanded when he returned to them. The group had been brought inside and were cowering along the rock wall of the path.

"They are waiting for your exit. Soon, I daresay they will resort to fire-blasting the cave." Looking anxiously at the passage they had formed between the two, his mind raced. "I wonder if we should try to wave them off from that endeavor or try to reseal this so our cave isn't possibly burned in the process."

"Hayt," his uncle called as he scampered up the ramp, his favorite robe lined with fur flowing around him. "I hear we have guests," he announced loudly.

"Aye, Piers Massheby, at your service," the Mate replied thickly with a mock bow. "Unfortunately, the dragons outside won't be too happy about it."

"Dragons," the king laughed, pushing through the opening. "Allow me to handle them," he boasted as he disappeared into the darkness of the cave. "Uh, hand me a light," he instructed, his hand poking back through the hole.

Taking a lantern that was offered, Baeweth hurried over to the exit of the cave and stepped out onto their new vista, laughing loudly at the sight of it. Moving around so that he could clearly be seen and recognized, he discerned the three brightly colored creatures against the morning sky.

Seeing they kept their distance, he simply offered them a wave, then wrapped his cloak around him and strutted back inside, confident the plan he and Putwyn had hatched earlier in front of his stone gates was well in hand. Marching calmly back through the new opening, he announced, "The beasts seem content to fly at a distance. I dare say you will be able to finish our new addition unharmed," he practically sang with joy, clamping his great nephew on the arm.

"For now," he continued, turning to the refugees, "let us give our guests a place to rest and collect themselves, and we will speak later this morning over our breakfast," he instructed as he floated past and made his way back down the maze of tunnels, the way he had come.

ELEVEN

Halls of Stone

WALKING through the tunnels of the dwarf kingdom, Rey glanced around them anxiously. Few moved, but behind arches and doorways, he could see the members of their vast society waking and preparing to face the day.

Ahead of them, a dark-haired dwarf, shorter than most, led the way. Stopping outside one of the arched entrances, he held up his hand to present the suite that would be theirs.

"Fantastic," the young man grumbled, finding it far below their accommodations in Jerranyth. Along the far wall stood a set of beds of sorts, with three levels more like racks. The dwarves would have to climb to reach the top, and perhaps even the center, and a wide set of slats had been attached for that purpose. A plain table with four chairs occupied the center of the room, and a large pit on the right-hand wall held a fire. The space open above the flames, he could see clearly into the next room, where a dwarf family was dressing and preparing their morning meal. "We share a community fire," he observed, pointing into the next chamber.

"Leave them," the Mate commanded, dropping his gear on the table and admiring the large mural stitched in the cloth that covered the left-hand wall.

Still with them, Hayt held Zae's hand firmly, smiling at the girl that nearly matched his height. "I wish to make you comfortable," he decreed.

"Well, you can start by letting go of her," Piers clipped, cutting his glare over at the king's nephew.

Dropping the appendage, Hayt rubbed his palms together, glancing from one newcomer to another. Reaching Animir, he froze, a deep frown etching his features. "You've got an elf."

"Aye," Bally stepped forward to defend his friend, "but don't say it like he's a dog or something."

Glancing at the girl he had been leading, the dwarf cleared his throat. "Sorry. We don't get his kind in here."

"His kind," Meena groaned, also inspecting the décor. "The king wished to see us, did he not?"

"Yes, once you have prepared to enter his chamber," their smaller care-taker explained while stepping aside to allow two more dwarves to enter, each of them carrying a basin filled with water.

"I was not aware that dwarves took baths," Animir sneered, observing as the receptacles were placed on the table, with a dish of soap and a stack of small towels placed between them.

"Only those of rank," Hayt replied, lifting his chin as he glared at the elf.

Instantly aware of the tension between them, Piers intervened, "We are guests here, Animir. I ask that you respect the dwarves as you have any other creature we have encountered on our quest."

"Yes, sir," his target agreed, folding his arms across his chest.

Hayt chuckled to himself, silently observing, *The elf takes orders from the mortal. Interesting.* Glancing around at them once more, he pondered how his uncle had discovered their presence in the outer cave. "Why do the dragons hunt you?" he asked coolly.

"Why do they hunt anyone?" Piers replied with a full grin, as evenly as their host, not bothering with an honest reply.

"Well, I'll go first," Amicia snapped at their posturing, glancing between them. Using the water, she quickly washed her grime-covered face and hands. Drying them on one of the cloths, she grinned, "God if feels good to be clean." Handing their servant the rag, she then retrieved her brush and mirror from her pack and set about making herself more presentable.

"Are you going to remain with us?" Zaendra grinned timidly at the king's nephew as the others stepped forward to follow Ami's example. She had felt instant friendship with their rescuer and hoped to learn more about the dwarf of such unusual stature.

"I would be honored," Hayt observed, giving her a small bow, which brought a wider smile to her lips.

Nodding at his attempt to be a gracious host, the nymph took her turn at rinsing her dusty flesh, then dried it on a towel as well. Returning it to the servant when she had finished, she looked around them with wide eyes. "Your home is quite lovely," she praised.

Glancing at one another, the mortals of the group appeared surprised by her observation. But then again, she had not been a guest of the spire, so her frame of reference lacked any points of comparison.

"I believe we are ready," Piers announced, irritation still clear in his voice.

"Very well," Hayt agreed, offering his arm to Zae. "Please, come this way."

Accepting the appendage, the couple strolled ahead of the group, where they passed many more dwarves along the way, none of whom could match the height of the one who had taken a fancy to their dark-skinned companion.

"I think they are as tall as they are around," Amicia giggled, walking next to Rey. "Quite jolly, as well," she added, noting their pleasant dispositions.

"I thought from the way everyone in Eriden described them, they would be more hostile, like the trolls," he agreed, offering her his arm as Hayt had done.

Accepting the appendage, Ami smiled up at him as she surmised in a quieter tone, "Perhaps we should reserve judgement until we know them better. We thought the elves were nice, too, and look how they turned out."

"Aye," Rey agreed, calling ahead to their guide. "Do you eat with the king often?"

"Typically, when I'm not busy with the construction crews." Hayt chuckled, leaning closer to Zae to whisper, "The king is my great uncle," so only she could hear.

"Wouldn't they make an odd couple," Bally chortled at the cozy behavior of the pair in the lead, speaking to Meena as they moved through the corridors.

"Shh," she warned. "Nymphs who leave the glen are often married to outsiders. Please do not offend the king or his kin with such ignorance."

"How about do not speak at all," Piers countered, frowning at the boy. "Not until we are certain where we stand with these people."

"Aye, sir," Baldwin agreed, hanging his head slightly at the rebuke.

Arriving at a grand hall, one that would rival even the elves and their magnificent chamber beneath the stars, Amicia gasped in awe, "It is beautiful." The rustic simplicity of their décor pleased her, helping her tense nerves to relax. Dropping Reynard's grasp, she turned in a slow circle, taking it all in.

A long room, each of the walls held a row of murals similar to the one in their chamber. Candles hung from elaborate chandeliers so that the room was well lit by a hundred small, dancing flames. A single table sat in the center, with chairs lining both sides. A fire burned in a large hearth on the far end, but the depth of the room allowed a few feet between it and the head of the table. Occupying a large chair with a tall back that matched the others, the king sat facing the door, awaiting their arrival. On the closest end sat a smaller seat, where a dwarf woman also waited for them.

"Grandmother," Hayt greeted her with a bow before he took the chair to her right.

Unsure what to do next, the procession stalled and gathered into a small clump just inside the door. Seeing their confusion, the king called, "No ceremony here. Please enter; sit."

Five chairs on each side, there would be plenty of room for them all, and a box was produced for the siren so that she could reach her plate. Seeing they intended to feed her from the roasted meats and breads that lined the center on large platters, Amicia intervened, "Would we be able to have some of the broth for Oldrilin?"

"A siren," Asyng, the king's sister, observed. "Yes, of course. She will be tended."

"Oldrilin has been with us almost since we arrived in Eriden," Reynard boasted, claiming the seat next to his small friend, with the king to his right. Bally sat between Lin and Zae, facing the empty chair of the group.

On the opposite side of the table, Amicia took the seat next to the mistress, with Animir to her left, while Meena and then Piers filled the two on the other side of the emptyseat, next to the king. Glancing around at the group, Amicia emitted a small sigh as she recalled the last time they had shared an actual table, before the dragons burned their cabin to the ground.

A bowl of broth was promptly delivered, and the group only hesitated for a moment before serving themselves from the grand feast. Smiling at the assembly, the king folded his hands and rested them on the table, already counting the reward he would receive.

"Do you always eat like this?" Bally asked, forgetting he wasn't supposed to speak.

"On occasion," Baeweth replied, still smiling, at least until he noticed Animir. "Bugger me, he didn't say anything about one of you being an elf!"

Seated to the king's right, Piers paused in his consumption, "So, you did dig into our chamber on purpose. Who sent you to retrieve us?" he demanded.

"Well, a dragon, naturally," the king confessed, studying the collection of misfits more closely. His smile gone, he counted them several times, then inspected their features more closely. "Four humans, a wan, a nymph, a siren, and an elf," he mused under his breath. Chuckling, he wondered at how such a group had ever formed, much less remained intact.

"A dragon!" Amicia looked up with a smile softening her features, certain she knew the one. "It was Lamwen, wasn't it!" she claimed, then mumbled, "He's alive."

"Lamwen?" the royal stammered. "You mean the former captain of the king's guard?"

"Former captain," Rey clarified. "Has something happened to him?"

"He was replaced a few years ago," Asyng informed him stiffly. Scowling at her elder sibling, she felt unsure about their guests or their intentions.

"Yes, quite right," the king agreed. "Lamwen was a fierce dragon in his day, but he fell out of favor with Gwirwen and the king's council twenty or thirty moons ago. He was banished, if not killed, as I have not seen or heard of him in all that time. These days, Vaudien holds the rank of captain of the guard, and he comes and goes across the northern wood whenever he likes," he rattled, shaking his head to clear it, "but he didn't make the demand, either. It was a dragon by the name of Putwyn who requested your retrieval," he professed with a smile, hoping to calm the group.

"Putwyn," Amicia breathed, unable to hide her sorrow. "Not Lamwen. Why did this other dragon make such an appeal?" she asked aloud, holding the greater question of why the king had agreed under her breath.

"I am not certain why," Baeweth laughed with a boisterous rolling echo, his jovial mood returning, "but he did promise a handsome reward for your recovery; one I intend to collect."

Bringing the entire group up short, everyone turned their heads in unison to stare at their benefactor. Pausing in mid bite, the king's sister glared at him across the length of the table but said nothing. Noticing the stare, Piers mentally tallied at least one possible friend among them; two if Zae's charms over the tall blond held.

"Well, we are certainly happy you were motivated to agree," the Mate stated evenly, lifting his mug of grog. "Now we simply hope that this Putwyn has honorable intentions where we are concerned. To the dragons," he made a toast by wafting his beverage towards the boy across from him.

"Hear, hear," Rey seconded, lifting his as well and smiling down at his small companion.

Seated across from Hayt, Amicia glanced down the length of the table at him but could not bring herself to join the salute. *Lamwen was exiled months ago.* That meant the entire time she had known him he had been out of favor.

She had always thought Gwirwen had sent him to spy on her, but that might not have been the case.

"My lord, if you please," Ami began, interrupting the pleasant moment. "Is there anything else you can tell me about Lamwen? He is a dear friend of mine," she admitted, then paused, realizing she mustn't reveal too much and may have already done so, "but I have lost track of him as of late. Any news you might share would be most greatly appreciated."

Staring at the girl, the king blinked rapidly, as if seeing her for the first time. Her blond hair pulled back into a neat braid, she held a regal air about her, one he had failed to recognize. Her insistence on the dragon's whereabouts bore deeper scrutiny, to be certain. "I could make a quiet enquiry if you would like," he offered, his smile strained.

Inside, the king's heart raced. Putwyn had asked that the group be saved, but staring at her, he realized the creature before him was undoubtedly his true target. He would be paid handsomely for her return, and the others would be worthless, he felt certain. Giving her a nod, he felt it wise to hide what he knew, at least for the time being.

"That won't be necessary," Piers intervened, leaning forward and giving the girl a stern, *shut up* glare.

Seeing the look, Amicia sighed, "No, I suppose that it would not be."

The silence that followed strained, the group finished the meal with only Hayt and Zaendra speaking in small spurts. Seated next to the girl, the dwarf appeared smitten and she equally taken with the fair hair and skin that lay in perfect contrast to her own.

As soon as they had finished the meal, the king stood, announcing, "I will let you know when I have news about your benefactor. I'm certain he fully intends to deliver you safely to the dragon council."

"He said that?" Piers frowned, finding such a circumstance hard to believe.

"Indeed," Baeweth affirmed. "He intends to present you to Gwirwen himself from what I was told. Return to your quarters and rest; you are in good hands, my new friends."

His smile broad, Amicia studied him, almost certain she knew the face of a liar when she saw one. However, none of the others gave any indication of distrust, so she held her tongue on the issue as they followed Hayt back to their chamber.

Arriving outside their door, Zae offered the dwarf her hand as she inquired, "Will you return for our dinner?" Faltering, she gasped, "Or have I presumed too much that we will eat again with your family."

"You are my uncle's guests, my lady," he assured, bowing and planting a small kiss on the soft skin covering the back of her hand. "I am going home for some rest, but I will return for you in the eve and escort you there myself."

Smiling up at him, the girl curled her fingers as she reluctantly removed herself from his grasp. She had never met a man who gave her heart such a flutter. "I look forward to it," she breathed, then darted inside with a giggle.

"Did you have a nice breakfast?" Reynard teased, observing the whimsical grin on Zaendra's typically stoic features.

"It was divine," she replied, borrowing Amicia's mirror to toy with her hair.

"Great," Piers muttered, shaking his head as he turned to Meena. "What did you make of all of it?"

"I do not trust we will be delivered safely to anyone," his wife warned. "However, what will be done with us is equally hard to define. I do not recognize the dragon he referred to, so it is safe to say he is of no rank, and probably lacks the power to protect us if we are turned over to him as promised."

"How'd you like the part where the king is getting paid?" Bally sneered.

"Dwarves do little without payment," Animir replied tartly. "They are well known for their greed."

"I'm going to have a positive attitude about this," Reynard countered, stretching out on one of their bunks. "Nothing has really gone the way we think it will, so worrying about it won't do us any good, and the good news is we didn't get burned to a crisp this morning."

"I have to agree," Ami sighed, helping Zae with her primping. Noting the girl's dimpled cheeks and broad smile, her obvious joy lifted Ami's spirits as it took her mind off of Lamwen.

"So, what are you going to say to Gwirwen?" Piers asked, taking a seat in one of their four chairs.

"Who say?" Bally asked, looking at each of them in turn. "Do you think we will all get to meet him?"

"Amicia," the Mate clarified. "I believe that we're on this quest to get her to Adiarwen, where she will meet him. With each step we take it becomes clearer that the dragon cliffs are where we were intended to go from the moment we landed, and I'm simply curious what she will say when we get there."

"I'm not even certain that is what we are doing here, but your judgement has proven sound a majority of the time." She grinned as she recalled his one glaringly fatal error and the scar he carried to remind them of it. "If we make it that far, I have no idea what I'm going to say. I haven't really thought about it," she added, shaking her head side to side.

"Well, you should get started then," Rey teased without moving. "If the king is telling the truth then Adiarwen is exactly where we are headed. We will probably be there in a few days, in fact, and you don't want to stand before the Supreme Dragon and look like a fool, do you?"

"Why me?" Amicia snapped. "You're the one in charge," she accused, glaring at Piers.

"Only because you allow me to be," he pointed out. "In Eriden, nearly everyone we have met has reacted to you and or treated you as if you were our spokesman, and I'm inclined to think the supreme dragon will be the same. Therefore, I suggest you plan ahead exactly what you would like to say."

Staring at the floor, the girl sighed. "Without Lamwen, I really have no idea what good it will do, but I guess I can try."

"That's my girl," the first mate cajoled, standing to wrap her in his arms. Holding her against his chest, he soothed, "And don't worry about Lamwen. Maybe there's a reason he has disappeared. It's only been a few days since we left the cabin, even though it seems like a lot more, and he may turn up yet."

"I hope so," she sighed, listening to the beat of his heart and thankful that she still had her friends to see her through.

TWELVE

In the Shadows

STROLLING THROUGH THE CORRIDORS, Hayt greeted the dwarves he passed while suppressing a wide grin, earning him a few odd glances at his atypical behavior. Most dwarves were not the grumpy cusses they were purported to be, but he himself seldom had a reason to smile, much less whistle as he walked, as he was this particular afternoon.

After leaving the group that morning, he had gone home for some much-needed rest. However, after a short nap, he had found himself awake and unable to stop his mind from turning over the last few hours repeatedly. Arriving at the new cave they had opened, he chuckled, "Firen still here?"

The dwarf there loaded a wheelbarrow with some of the debris they had left when breaking in, or out as the case may be. Turning and looking him up and down, he growled, "He called it an early night; said you got him up too soon this morning and he was done."

Laughing out loud, their head engineer replied cheerily, "We did indeed. We'll have our new vista in a matter of days, though, and that will be well worth it." Thinking of his uncle's cover story, he added, "Especially in these dark times with the dragons fighting among themselves."

"Dragon affairs are no use to us," the shorter dwarf growled, continuing to remove the rubble.

"Yes, well," his superior rung his hands for a moment. It was true they seldom had dealings with those outside the mountain, so a few were certain to see the flaw in their cover story. Stepping over the mess, he made his way into

91

the new tunnel and came out into the cave where their visitors had slumbered before they were awakened by his crew.

Glancing around, they had staked the walls and hung lanterns to work by. "It's perfect," he mumbled to himself, recalling the visit they had made via the outside the year before. "It's a shame this is what it has taken for my uncle to see reason."

Crossing the near flat, smooth floor, he noted the few large rocks that marred the otherwise ideal location. "Our new vista is going to be a great improvement," he informed the other two crewmen who remained, each of them measuring for the support beams that would be added to ensure the mountain did not come down on them unexpectedly.

"That it will," a fair-haired worker clipped.

Sensing there was still a bit of animosity within the ranks at their rough beginning, he soothed, "The rest of you should call it a night. We'll start fresh in the morning and get on a proper schedule with this."

"Yes, sir," the third member of his detail grunted, dropping his tools and making for the exit back to their previously existing caves with his cohort close behind.

Alone in the wide chamber, Hayt swept the room again, thinking of the group that had occupied it; his thoughts resting on the girl of ebony skin. His smile returning, he forgot all about his disgruntled underlings as he fought his way over the loose stones once more and headed for her chamber, where she would be waiting with the others for his arrival.

At the door a few minutes later, he announced, "Would anyone be interested in a tour after our supper?"

"Oh, me!" Zaendra squealed, earning a dark glance from almost all of the others, save Bally who seldom noticed what was deeper than the surface in any of their affairs.

Nodding, he offered her his arm. "Very well. First, I am to present you to the king's chamber for our meal, and then I will give you the grandest of viewings." Glancing around at the others as she accepted his appendage, he tacked on, "The rest of you are welcome to join us, of course."

Leading the way, the girl beside him rubbed his muscled shoulder as she clung to him. Noticing her beautiful white teeth as they contrasted with her exquisite dark features, his smile matched hers and perhaps then some. "You seem quite content here," he said softly, leaning over so that the words remained between the two of them.

"I have enjoyed our visit, yes," she confessed, glancing up at him with large ebony pools of happiness.

Arriving to find the dining room empty, the group spread out and assumed their previous seats, but as the king and mistress entered, Baeweth observed in a boisterous tone, "Ah, I see you have arrived before us. I'm afraid we must reseat, as I have looked forward to sharing a word with Lamwen's grandest admirer."

All eyes shifted as Amicia flushed at the declaration. "I hardly think I am his admirer, grandest or otherwise," she grumbled as she stood to trade seats with Rey so that she sat facing Piers at the king's left hand.

Her move prompted a general shuffling, as Lin moved to the center, next to Zae, and Bally took the vacated spot next to Asyng. Grinning at now sitting beside the girl he longed to court, Reynard took the chair between the Ami and the siren while observing, "Your kingdom is quite large. How many dwarves would you say you have here?"

Looking up at him after adjusting into his seat, Baeweth spat, "Of what concern are our numbers to you?"

"He's simply curious," the Mate smoothed, giving the boy a stern glance to silence any further inquiries. "We've passed through many kingdoms to get here, which I am sure you are aware; learning about them as we travel has been fascinating."

Staring at the wan, the king nodded, "She is your wife, yes?"

"Aye," Piers confirmed, offering her his hand.

Accepting the digits, Meena gave them a brief squeeze before dropping them as she returned to filling her plate. "We met last year when the group came to Whitefair. I was obliged to leave with them, and our love blossomed thereafter." Cutting her eyes over at the couple next to the mistress of the hall, her brown eyes spoke louder than any words she had spoken.

Glancing at his nephew as well, the old dwarf folded his hands in front of his face, blowing into the cup formed by the pudgy palms to calm himself. He knew a romance budded within their ranks if the whispers and giggles were any indication; one that he would take care to squash as soon as the evening meal had ended.

For now, he had more pressing matters to attend to, which is precisely why he had insisted that the blonde in their company sit beside him. Turning to her, he smiled his best, his eyes shining as he scrutinized her. "You have come a long way indeed, Amicia Spicer. Tell me of your quest."

Swallowing her lump of meat, Ami flicked her eyes around at the others. The silence of their end of the table marked, she knew they would not help her, and she alone must decide what would be shared and what would remain hidden. The four of them had spoken of the king while in their chambers, and it had generally been agreed that he could not be trusted even if he had promised they were to be presented to the supreme dragon and his council.

"I am from Nalen," she managed. "My mother and father are gone, and I decided to see more of the world," she simplified, then lied flatly, "I booked passage on the Sea Serpent, where these other men were part of the crew."

Shooting a quick glance at Bally, she hoped he would not contradict her, only then noticing that he had set about his own private conversation with the king's sister and appeared to be yammering non-stop. Smiling at the spectacle, she continued a little more bravely, "We were attacked by a dragon six weeks out, which sank the ship. We barely escaped with our lives and a small bit of rations, which we used to survive until we crashed upon the southern shores here in Eriden."

Giggling on the other side of Rey, Oldrilin added, "Happy day friends come to Riran."

Nodding, Amicia agreed, "Yes, happy indeed. We were there almost four moons before the dragons realized our presence and drove us from our new home."

"You intended to remain with the sirens?" Baeweth asked doubtfully.

"Oh, yes," the girl smiled. "The lands there are unimaginably beautiful, and we had made a home within the trees."

Across from her, Piers gripped his fork tightly, squeezing it to hold back his own thoughts on the matter.

If Baeweth noted the gesture, he said nothing, his attention fixated on the woman to his left. "Unfortunate then that you were driven out," he observed.

"Indeed," she breathed, taking a sip of her grog before she continued. "After we left Riran, we were taken in by the elves but only remained there a few days before we made a hasty departure."

"I should think so," the royal said with a robust laugh. "Our food not good enough for you, elf?" he needled, glaring down the length of the table at the one picking at his meal. It sickened him that the creature dined in his hall, but he only must tolerate him for six more days; that is if there weren't any accidents that removed him before then.

"Your food is divine," Animir replied, not looking up from the plate.

Laughing again, Baeweth let it go and refocused on his target. "So, you got out of Jerranyth intact."

"Yes, we left in the middle of the night," she offered with a half grin. "Animir was good enough to show us the way, and we arrived in Esterbrook a few days later. We wintered there, then headed north through the desert in the spring."

His forehead crinkled, the king listened on without comment, gleaning almost as much from what she didn't say as he did from what she did reveal.

"We arrived in the far north as winter was upon us, so we built a cabin in the Yilaric forest, where we lived until the dragons again set against us only a few days ago," she finished, pronouncing the end by resuming her consumption of the meal.

"A brief tale considering the amount of time you have been here," their host observed suspiciously.

Not pausing in her chewing, the girl's heart raced. The merdoe still hung between her breasts, and the hamar gem dug into her hip within her pocket. Could he know that she possessed them? Her mind leaping to her latest acquisition, her bite became more difficult to swallow.

Thinking of the red orb, she gulped more of her beverage. It still lay hidden at the bottom of her bag... in their room, which could currently be under search. Her eyes fixed on the Mate, she stared at him, unblinking as they spoke, *"What do you suppose that he knows?"*

"Hard to say," he replied, holding the connection.

"I left the new orb in my bag."

"It will be safe," he assured. *"We will draw attention if we keep this up,"* he added, blinking rapidly as he hoisted his mug and offered, "It really hasn't been that exciting. If not for the dragons, it would have been a most pleasant holiday."

"Holiday!" the king snapped, then laughed as he pounded the table. The group hid much, he felt certain, but discerning what held little reward for him. He would be paid for their delivery in under a week, and that was good enough for him. Clapping his hands twice, he seemingly ended the interrogation.

Through the door, a group of short round musicians marched in, each carrying an instrument. Setting up in front of the left-hand mural so that Amicia could see them clearly, the five newcomers played a variety of melodies.

"Oh, they are lovely!" she observed, wiping at a few blond strands that had escaped from her braid as she listened. One carried a small set of drums, which added a solid rhythm as they chanted rather than sang, while the others played stringed instruments that vibrated the air around them.

Clapping softly to the beat, Asyng smiled at the boy next to her. "Do you like our music?"

"It's different, but we have stringed instruments back home as well," Bally replied, joining her with his palms smashing together loudly. "Too bad we're leaving or I might be tempted to learn to play."

Nodding, the matriarch smiled. She had gleaned much from the young man who held no filter and felt certain her brother should have grilled him rather than the girl. At the other end of the table, Baeweth had ordered the musicians as a distraction, and he would soon begin his second round of questions.

"So, when did you meet Lamwen?" he asked smoothly as they enjoyed a thick pudding, seeing that she had relaxed at the entertainment.

"Well," she stammered, thinking where to insert him into her previous narration. "He was shot down by the satyrs the night we arrived in the glen," she offered.

"By the satyrs," Baeweth gasped, his eyes wide. His mouth hanging open, he looked down the group, one face to another until he arrived at the elf. "And?" he cajoled, glaring at the decorations in the pointed ears of his enemy.

"They tied him up, and I met him that night, but they let him go. He came back to us as we crossed the desert and stayed close until a few days ago, when he disappeared," she finished, her voice soft as she realized the time frame aligned perfectly with that of his removal as Gwirwen's captain.

"So that's where he's been," the king breathed quietly, still watching the elf.

"Yes. He's been looking out for us," Amicia agreed, lifting her chin. "I told you he's our friend," she added, almost as if it were a threat. "If he's still alive, I feel sorry for anyone who might harm us."

His gaze snapping to meet hers, the king tapped the table with the tips of his fingers, his palm resting against the wooden surface. "Brazen," he muttered. "You will stand before the council, of that I am certain," he lied boldly, convinced they would be left as piles of ash as soon as Putwyn had claimed them. "For now, I grow weary and ready for my chamber." Pushing his chair back, he stood. "Please, stay and enjoy the music until you are ready to retire."

Rising as well, Asyng bowed to the young man next to her. "Thank you for the company, Baldwin. It was a most enjoyable meal." Her dark eyes sparkling, she followed her sibling out of the dining hall before catching up to him as he entered his private quarters.

"I would speak with you, brother," she informed him curtly.

"I figured as much," he growled, removing his fur-lined robe.

"The boy had much to say," she continued, her nose in the air. "It would seem the girl is indeed of Eriden. He says she possesses a magical gem of the elves, a shell of the sirens, and uses the golden orb of the wan."

"The wan carries an orb?"

"Yes, as she is equally as gifted in the arts."

Glancing at her, Baeweth rolled his tongue, then surmised, "These are no ordinary travelers. No wonder the dragon wants them alive. Perhaps I have been hasty offering them to him. Another bidder might have paid more for their release."

"Oh brother, must you always think of coin?" Asyng growled.

"Well, we are dwarves," he shrugged. "I am concerned, though. It has been many centuries since our people declared ourselves against the use of such tricks. I still have my orb, passed to me by our father, but I daresay I wouldn't know the first thing for using it."

"And rightly so," she gasped. "We must not let these people taint us! You know this was the cause of our uprooting and why we were forced from the southern tunnels."

"Yes, yes, I know about the daemons of the dark and why they fell upon us," he sighed. "But that was centuries ago. We have been safe within these caves since the great war."

"And we wish to keep it that way! You will deliver these outsiders to Putwyn on demand and be rid of them?" she asked, fearing what he might have devised after his learning of their worth.

"Right you are, and so it will be," he agreed with a nod. "I have struck a bargain and have no desire to cross the dragon who holds my word. However, I fear they may try for an escape before the day arrives." Walking to the door, he called as she strode down the corridor, "Guard!"

"Yes, my lord," a short dark-haired servant replied when he stood before him.

"As soon as our guests are back in their room, I want them moved to a proper cell. They may keep their belongings, as that might appease them, but take their weapons. We wouldn't want them attempting to depart before we are ready to see them gone," the king instructed.

"Yes, my lord," the guard replied. "I will see that it is done."

Returning to his sister, Baeweth sighed, "And that takes care of that. Anything else, my dear?"

Eyeing him through narrow slits, Asyng replied tartly, "I have let you sit upon the throne for many years, dear brother, and have tolerated your decisions until now. Perhaps it is my age that loosens my tongue. I believe you should release these people; cast them out of our midst this very night, before they bring any harm to our realm."

"If they were capable of harming us, I would see to their deaths myself," he growled.

Shoving a finger in his face, she snapped, "You see the piles of wealth they will bring you, that is all; gold you do not need. Baldwin shared much this evening, and I fear the girl they call Ami. She is a lover of dragons and men, a mortal of the rim."

"Pfft," he spat, laughing as he taunted her. "You think she is the destroyer. A foolish old woman to believe in such silly myths. Take to your own chambers before you share their cell."

Her jaw dropped, Asyng gasped, "You should not treat your own kin so unkindly."

"Do not presume to tell me of my own choices! I am the king, the heir to our throne, not you. Get out of my sight!"

Her lips puckered into a firm scowl, she spun on her heel and marched out of his chamber, muttering under her breath as she left him to his royal concerns. Deep down, she felt certain she was right and this bit of gold would buy them more trouble than he had bargained for, but in the end, it would work out as it always had; and if it didn't, it would be time for her grandson to assume his seat at the head of the dwarf kingdom.

THIRTEEN

Love's Bliss

AMBLING ALONG BEHIND THE GROUP, Hayt walked with his hands behind his back. Zaendra had her right arm looped through his left, gliding next to him in her beautiful shimmering dress. "You were meant to walk in the sunshine, my lady," he commented sternly.

"I have seen my share of the golden rays," she agreed. Arriving at their quarters, they followed the others inside before she asked, "Is no one going with us to see the rest of the city?"

"I've seen enough of dwarfland, thanks," Rey grumbled, glancing at their host. "No offense."

"None taken. I know my uncle and grandmother are quite the pair," Hayt agreed, gazing down at the girl who held a firm grip on his elbow. "I will return your maid to you, then."

"See that you do, and at a reasonable hour," the Mate replied sharply, giving him a stern frown.

Exiting the cramped quarters, the dwarf released his grip on his own hands and curled her fingers between his. "Is he always so protective of you? I assure you, you are quite safe here."

"Always," the girl giggled. "Piers was in charge of the group when they came into the glen, and we have followed him ever since we left."

"What of Amicia, though. She seems to have quite a bit of say in your affairs," he observed.

Shrugging, her smile diminished, Zae tried to explain without revealing

99

more than she should. "Ami is a very gifted young woman, especially for a mortal of the rim. Many have recognized this in her along our travels, and so we have all come to respect her wishes." Biting her lip, she paused, then added, "I owe Amicia and the others a great deal; a debt I fear I will never repay."

Blinking up at her host, Zaendra breathed deeply as he considered her words. It was true, for the most part, but there was something hidden within Amicia; something most in their kingdom would recognize. If Hayt had seen it, he would know she had not been honest with him, but would he be bold enough to call her on it?

"I see," he nodded, wafting his freed right hand at the path ahead. "This way leads to many of the private rooms our people hold. Most families live in a single, such as the one your group now shares."

"Yes, we can see one through the fireplace on the other side."

"Ah, yes; we share those as well when need be. We are underground, so the temperature here is easy to control but not quite warm enough for most of us to feel comfortable," he observed, taking in her bare shoulders. "Are you not cold?" Grinning at the sight of her beautifully delicate skin, she definitely wore far less than a typical dwarf maid.

"I am well. I do not mind it so much," she agreed, happy he had not pushed her about Amicia and curious if that meant the dwarf had not recognized the girl after all.

"Hmm. I have heard much of the nymphs but had yet to meet one. You are lovely creatures, as promised," he flattered, his heart skipping a beat at the thought of giving her exposed flesh a brush to test its texture.

"And what exactly have you heard?" she asked, radiating confidence as she toyed with him. During the last few hours, she had realized her power over him, and it only bolstered her resolve to get to know him better if she could.

"I know that you live in a land of hills and meadows near the southern coast. That you are a simple and yet magical people and that it is rare that you should leave your homeland," he supplied with a raised brow. "Why did you choose to follow Piers and his group of misfits?"

"Misfits?" she clipped, not liking the sound of the term. "There is nothing unfit about my friends," she defended tartly.

"I mean no disrespect," he soothed, placing his hand over his chest as an oath. "I simply mean they are an odd collection; surely you can agree to that."

"Yes, I supposed that we are," she admitted more calmly as they continued their casual strides. "But I have always known I would leave the glen." Regret panged her heart for an instant, and she added, "Not that there was anything wrong with living among my kind. I simply knew I would not spend all of my days there."

"Ah, some magical premonition?"

"You could say that," she giggled, swinging their hands as they made a turn. Entering a long stretch of open cavern, the roof lifted far above them. "Wow, this place is amazing!" Overhead, the high ceiling revealed numerous levels, with a balcony overlooking the floor below on each one. "Is this your great hall?" she asked, thinking of the trolls and their giant common room beneath the mountain to the north.

"Yes," he agreed absently, not really listening at the moment. Her breathless observation stirring his blood, he paused to face her while she took it all in. "But not so beautiful as the company," he whispered.

Her dark eyes shifting to meet his, her heart beat wildly inside her chest. *He's going to kiss me,* she surmised, not sure how she felt about such a prospect. Lifting her face, he moved closer, and panic stole her nerve. Turning away at the last moment, she prevented his lips from touching hers. "Are dwarf boys always so forward?" she asked, her voice thicker than it had been.

"I'm sorry," he stammered, stepping back to put a few inches between them. "I just thought..." His voice trailed away as shame stained his cheeks.

No longer holding his hand, she continued their stroll, her fingers toying with the fine material of her dress. Calming herself, she confessed, "I am an earth nymph. I love the land; the soil and the rock. Your home is amazing. I am very glad I have made the visit and thank you for the tour."

"You would like it to live here," he dared.

Shaking her head, she grinned, "You are again bold in your desires."

"Should I not be? No prize is ever won without the effort."

"Tell me of you, then, if you wish to win my heart," she challenged, cutting her eyes over to glare at him.

"I am the king's nephew. His sister is my grandmother."

"This I already knew. Where are your parents and the rest of your kin?"

Exhaling loudly, he shook his head. "Zae, we have not lived a charmed life in these caves. At least I haven't. Illness and accidents have stolen all but a few of us. If I live when Baeweth finally passes, I will sit upon our throne," he divulged bluntly. Holding his tongue, he waited for her reply, half afraid that the news would scare her away and the other half terrified it would be the thing that drove her to him.

To his relief, she appeared to have no real opinion on such a faraway prospect. Instead, she declared, "Your king is not so aged and appears to have his health. You may have a long wait if you are counting the days until you wear his crown," offering neither a smile, nor a frown.

Laughing at her observation, he shook his head side to side. "I do not wish to wear it at all, if I could avoid it. I love my life as an engineer. Our projects and plans are more than enough for me, and I wish very much there was another who would succeed him."

"Then you understand why I have left the glen," she agreed, taking his hand once more as she drew near him.

"You wanted something more than what life there had to offer," he speculated.

"Yes. I love my people, but there is far too much of Eriden to be seen to waste my years frolicking in the meadows of Esterbrook."

His heart stopping, he realized she would be in danger if and when his uncle turned them over to Putwyn. "I wish I could help you," he said quietly, alluding to the dark days ahead.

"It's ok," she allowed, seeing that they had made a large circle and were again approaching her temporary quarters. "I will share the time I have here with you if you are of a mind. I enjoy your company, Hayt of Rhong," she confessed quietly.

"And I yours, Zaendra of the glen," he replied, coming to a stop outside her door. "I wish the kingdom were larger, that we might stretch our walk until the dawn." Staring down into her large pools of ebony light, he breathed deeply, not daring to attempt another kiss, yet unwilling to say goodbye.

Seeing his reservations, she smiled broadly and announced, "You may kiss me now, if you wish."

"Oh, I wish!" he coughed, gathering her in his arms and pressing his mouth against hers. Her warm skin smooth beneath his palms, he groaned, the taste of her divine.

Fire shot through them, and her hand snaked up his arm as she slid her palm to the back of his neck. Caressing his nape beneath his blond locks, her fingers trembled. Half-heartedly ending the kiss, he laid his forehead against hers, his eyes still closed as he licked his lips.

"Zae," he whispered.

"Hayt."

"I would love to spend my days with you."

"Then I will see you on the morrow," she agreed, pulling herself free and leaving him in the hall as she entered their quarters.

Turning on his heel, he strutted away, almost at a run. His heart pounding in his chest, he felt light-headed as the rocks of the path crunched beneath his stride. He leapt into the air a few times, kicking his feet with joy as he skipped along the path, then regained his composure and marched firmly to the family quarters.

"She kissed me!" he sang in a low voice to himself, exhilarated at the prospect of courting her. King Baeweth would never allow it, he felt certain, but she would only share his days for a short time, and he would take every moment he could get.

Confident that no harm would come from their folly, he reached his small home and dodged inside. Only then did he unleash his full delight, leaping into the air and pumping his fist above his head a few times. "She kissed me!"

Entering their quarters as Hayt walked away, Zaendra searched the dimly lit room. To her surprise, not everyone had gone to bed without her, and Piers Massheby sat in one of the chairs, glaring at the fire. "Glad to see the dwarf kept his word," he grunted. "Was he a gentleman?"

Detecting his stiffness, she grinned, "What if he wasn't? Do you intend to defend my honor?"

Cutting his eyes up at her, he growled, "If need be. King's nephew or not, he has no right to touch one of us out of turn."

"Oh, Mate, you are such a dear friend," she sighed, hunting for a spot where she might squeeze in on one of the beds. "I'm going to get some sleep, and I advise the same for you."

However, before she could make it onto the mattress, a guard appeared at the door and bellowed, "By the king's order, I am here to see you to new quarters. Please, gather your things and follow me."

"New quarters," Piers snapped, leaping to his feet. Peering past him, he could see the guard had not come alone. "Prepared to make it stick, I see."

"Yes," the dwarf nodded. "You may take all of your belongings save your weapons," he repeated as the others stirred. "We will hold those for you until it is time for you to depart our kingdom."

"What's going on?" Amicia asked, sitting up on the top bunk.

"We're being moved," Piers replied calmly, offering a hand to help her down. Then giving Rey a firm shake, he added, "Gather our things quietly. The family next door slumbers, and we do not wish to disturb them."

"That's considerate under the circumstances," the girl grumbled, unhappy at the turn of events.

"Aye, but what can we do," he soothed, waking his wife and the others in turn.

Retrieving her brush and mirror from the hearth, Ami placed them in her bag. Turning in a slow circle, she ensured there was nothing else that had been pulled out for use. "Don't forget our blankets," she reminded when the beds were empty.

"Aye," Bally agreed, rolling his into a ball, "but why can't we take our swords?" he pushed.

"Silly question," the Mate growled. "Leave them on the table," he added, eying the girl and hoping her dagger remained hidden within her bag.

Meeting his gaze, Amicia placed her bow and arrows across the grain of the wood. Seeing their leader give her a firm nod, she grinned, understanding his intent perfectly even without the telepathy. The small blade would not be much, but it might come in useful if they dared an escape.

When they had packed and stood in a line, the guard led them through the halls to a smaller chamber with a single long bunk along the right-hand wall.

Near fifteen feet in length, the bed stuck out across all but a narrow band for the walk way, and a bucket in the back left corner would suffice for their toilet.

Seeing that there was no place for their things, Amicia sighed, "Now can we complain?"

"What good would it do?" Reynard countered, claiming a section of the bunk and using his pack as a pillow.

A large metal door clanged shut behind them, and Amicia turned, placing her hands on the bars. "Is this how you treat all your guests?"

"We don't get many," the dwarf laughed. "Be glad you weren't dismembered and fed to the wolves or dragons," he replied.

"Not yet," she snapped, "but we might as well have been." Dropping her grip, she took the last place on the bunk, following Rey's suggestion and putting her bag under her head before she drifted off to sleep.

Next to her, Zaendra's heart still burned. The tall dwarf had stirred the magic within her, and she lay awake recalling every moment of their walk. Reliving the kiss time and again, it saddened her that they had been locked away, as it meant she had probably seen the last of Hayt of Rhong. *So much for love's bliss,* she sighed into the darkness as she finally slipped into her dreams.

FOURTEEN

All's Fair

"UNCLE!" Hayt announced his presence as he stomped through the door of the king's private chamber, his face flushed in outrage.

"Yes, my boy," Baeweth replied, adjusting his robe and standing straighter as he turned to greet him.

"I have come to you about our prisoners," the younger man stated angrily, his lips set in a firm grimace.

"Ah, I was afraid you would be displeased, but my decision is final. They shall remain in the cell until the dragon comes to retrieve them." Seeing the disappointment on his heir's features, he added, "What should I do? Tell Putwyn our supreme dragon may not claim them?"

"No, uncle," Hayt groaned, nodding slowly at his reasoning. "I understand you cannot go back on your word. But must we give them all of the group? I mean —"

"I know what you mean," the king snapped, studying his relation with a hard glare. "You have formed an attachment with the nymph. Oh, Hayt, I would be so disappointed if you were to marry outside of your own kind."

"Why? Shouldn't I be the one to decide? Besides, if you send her to the dragons, her sentence will be death. I could not bear to see that happen to her, Uncle, I swear it." Tears in his eyes, the boy blinked rapidly to remove them.

"You feel that strongly about her?" the old man faltered, recalling how he had loved his only wife. His eyes glazed for a moment, he reminisced aloud,

"I do miss my sweet Dorfa even as the years have grown long since her untimely passing."

"Yes, most assuredly; I love her as no other. But of course, there is the matter of the Mate, as they call him. I'm sure I would need his agreement, since she is in his company. I would like your permission to ask for her hand," Hayt sniffed, seeing a glimmer of hope as he wiped his nose on his sleeve.

"You may ask, then; but you will abide by his word," his uncle stipulated while shaking a finger in his face. "If he does not grant you permission to marry her, you may not remove her from the prison."

Gaining the goal, Hayt pushed for more. "I intend to ask for her servant as well," the young man declared.

"Her servant?"

"Yes, Oldrilin the siren. She is in the service of the nymph by some arrangement between them. I will bring her as well if you can agree," he lied, thinking quickly how he could save as many as he could.

Pursing his lips, the king studied him. "I used to know you," he sighed, shaking his head.

"Do you not trust your own kin?" Hayt asked in disbelief.

"In the days we now live, trust is a hard thing to come by. All's fair in love and war, as they say," Baeweth chuckled, still thinking of his own past. "Fine. Ask for the girl, and you may bring the siren as well. They are noble creatures, after all, even if they are a bit simple."

"By simple, you mean stupid," his heir clarified, his mood still hovering on foul.

"Call it what you will," the king replied while wafting his hand at the door, "but you better go before I change my mind."

"Thank you, uncle," Hayt replied with a bow. Turning to leave, he grinned to himself, happy he had gotten his way. *Now, to convince Zae of my love, or of reason if that does not work.*

Marching through the tunnels into the depths where the cells had been dug, he rung his hands anxiously as he rehearsed what he would say. He had hardly slept at all last night, as his head and heart traded turns playing havoc with his emotions.

He had awoken with the clear idea that he would somehow convince the girl to be his bride, no matter what it took to do so, and thereby sparing her departure with the others. He had been sorely disappointed when he arrived at the group's chamber to discover they had been moved to an actual cell. *Thank God Baeweth has seen reason,* he prayed as he made the last turn.

"I must speak with the prisoners," Hayt informed the guard standing outside their iron door.

"You may do so," the shorter elf replied with a bow, indicating their chamber with his palm.

"Open it so I may enter."

Hesitating, the guard stammered, "That would not be wise. Speak to them through the bars."

"I assure you, I have the king's permission," the blond insisted, noting that Ami stood at the gate with the others behind her, observing as he fought for his right to converse with them.

"What news have you?" Amicia called, unable to stand the suspense.

"Open it!" Hayt shouted, towering over the guard.

"Yes, sir," the smaller dwarf managed, holding up a large ring of keys. Searching through them, his hands shook slightly as he inspected each one in turn. Locating the correct shaped strip of metal, he unlocked the door, and the group stepped back to allow their visitor to enter.

Looking around at the circle of faces, Hayt realized their conversation would not be private. Swallowing, he took a second step forward and lowered his voice. "I must speak with you," Hayt addressed the Mate.

"I'm listening," Piers snorted, turning his hands up as he mocked their cramped space before crossing the arms over his broad chest. A formidable man of over six feet, he glowered down at the dwarf as he waited.

Licking his lips, Hayt glanced at the ebony-skinned girl, his brain growing fuzzy as he did so. Breathing heavily, he gasped, "I have come to ask your permission…" he managed before his voice cracked. Swallowing, he tried again. "My uncle has given me permission to ask for Zaendra's hand."

"What?" the girl clipped in obvious surprise as gasps echoed from the others. "Why would you do that, and why would he allow it?" she fumed, having had all night to consider the dwarves and their actions. As much as she had enjoyed the company of the king's nephew, he was one of them and probably not to be trusted.

"Please," he begged, pushing past Amicia to stand before the nymph. Dropping to his knees, he seized her fingers and made his appeal. "I cannot save you all. But if you agree to be my bride, I can at least get you out of this cell, and you will not be sold to the dragon."

"You are certain of this?" Ami snapped, using his shoulder to pull him to face her.

"Yes. My uncle has given his word. I may have Zae and her servant, Oldrilin," he explained. "Please," he repeated more quietly.

"My servant," the girl in question bit, looking down at their smallest member, "Lin does not serve me or anyone!"

"I know this, but it was the only way to secure her release as well. I may take the two of you but no more," the young man begged, sitting back on his haunches as he searched each of their faces in turn.

Standing in the shadow, Reynard watched the proceedings with a lump forming in his throat. When Hayt's eyes reached his, he knew insisting the dwarf leave empty-handed would likely be a death sentence, both for the nymph and his dear little friend. "You will take good care of them?" he whispered.

"I swear it," the king's nephew insisted.

Also looking over the group, Amicia's features grew determined. "Zae, you must do this," she professed.

"I believe I'm the one who has the final say," Piers pointed out.

"Then say it," the blonde insisted. Reaching into her pocket, she produced the hamar gem as she squatted before the mermaid. "Take this with you, as well."

Accepting the offering, Oldrilin's small face sagged. "But Amicia uses the magic of the stone." She had given the gem to the girl long ago and had no desire for its return. Her eyes darting between the others, she searched for some indication of what she should do.

"Not anymore," Ami replied gently. "You must take it. It will do me no good where we are going."

"The dragons will not return you to us," Lin whimpered, tears glistening on her small cheeks in the dim light.

Also taking a knee before their smallest member, Rey fought his tears by blinking rapidly. "Lin, this is for the best. Take the gem and protect it. It is sacred to the elves, and despite our cause against them, we should protect it from falling into other hands." Sniffing loudly, he wiped his arm on his shirt sleeve, noting the heavy silence as the others waited for his final words to his tiny companion. "I will miss you." His voice broke, and she flung herself against his chest, sobbing uncontrollably at his heart-felt farewell.

"We can't do this," Zaendra whined, her own drops of sorry spilling over. "It matters not what the Mate says. I will not leave my friends in such a state."

Still holding the trembling siren, Rey waited for their leader to make the women see reason. As badly as he wanted to keep the group together, he knew doing so would likely be a death-sentence for them. Casting a wavering glance up at the older man, he gave his approval of the dwarf's plan.

Exhaling a loud breath, Piers shook his head slowly. "We don't have a choice." Flicking his eyes over at the door and then back to Ami, he nodded. "This is the only way to ensure you will be protected."

"You fear the dragon will kill us," Meena observed, her hands tracing her husband's arm as she clung to him.

"Aye," he agreed, still staring at Ami. "I agree. You may take her and her servant." Noting the silence that followed, he added with a short laugh, "Be sure to invite us to the wedding."

Staring up at him, Hayt's brow furrowed in confusion, "How –"

"I'm kidding," the Mate cut him off. Leaning over, he grabbed the front of his chest and pulled him to his feet. "Take care of our girls," he added, clamping their benefactor on the shoulder.

"Guard!" Hayt hollered.

"Yes, sir," their jailer called through the bars of the door.

"I have been given permission to bring out the nymph and the siren," he informed him as the two of them gathered their things. "Send a messenger to my uncle to confirm this if you must."

Staring up at him, the dwarf's mouth opened and closed a few times as he considered the request. Making his choice, he replied, "That will not be necessary, sire. I'm sure we know where to find you if you have lied."

Not sure if the statement were meant as a joke or a true jab, Hayt chose to laugh. "That you do. Come along, ladies," he bade as he led the way out through the open portal.

As soon as they exited, Zaendra began to sob loudly. Turning, she flung herself against the gate, bellowing, "I can't bear to leave you!"

"You must," Amicia insisted, holding her through the holes in the bars. "Zae, listen to me. We are not lost; at least not yet. If the king keeps his word, and if this Putwyn is an upstanding dragon, we will stand before the council. Only they can decide our fate."

"But I'm scared," the girl cried, refusing to let go.

"Take her," Ami commanded Hayt, glaring at him with clear green orbs. "You must remove her before anything can be changed."

Dropping his arm over her shaking shoulders, he pulled her away. "Come with me, precious. Please, do not make this harder than it is."

"We will try for their release? Promise me this," she insisted as she followed him with Lin on her other side.

"We will have a few days," he agreed, squeezing her in comfort. "We will ask again before they are removed, I swear it."

Glancing back over her shoulder, Zaendra could see the group pressed against the bars of the door, watching as she walked away. "Then there is still hope," she agreed, offering the mermaid her hand as she followed her intended.

The city seemed less splendid this time around. Arriving at his quarters, she looked about the small room, which was similar to the larger version the group had first been given. "This is your home?" she asked doubtfully, imagining living there with him.

"Yes, I have the dwelling of a single man. We will share it until we have a child, and then we will be given a larger chamber," he explained their customs as he poured water for them. "Wash your tears. You do not want to appear before my uncle in such a state."

Doing as he asked, Zae used the water first, then patted her dark skin with a towel that he provided. Standing in one of his chairs, Oldrilin also prepared herself to face the royal dining hall once more.

"They will know she is not my servant," Zaendra sighed.

"I'm sure they already know. As long as she behaves and follows you around, what can they do but agree?" he quipped with a spastic laugh.

"Perhaps," the girl nodded, taking his hand as they made their way to their morning meal.

The dining hall seemed too large with only the five of them seated at the long table. The room silent, the king and his sister each sat in their normal places. Taking seats in the center facing one another, Zaendra helped the siren into the chair closest to Asyng so that two empty chairs lay between the couple and Baeweth.

"There is no need to be angry," the sovereign chastised at their choice in chairs.

"We are not angry," Hayt replied crisply. "This is a large table, and so these seats make the most sense, with all the extras."

"Ah, but the seats will soon be filled when your children begin to arrive," Baeweth pointed out with a wide grin.

Ignoring the comment, Zae sniffed as she battled her tears, eating a meager meal. Next to her, Lin slurped at her broth until it was gone, then climbed out of the seat and presented herself to the king.

"If you please, your highness," the siren said in her small tinkling voice.

"Yes, what do you want?" Baeweth growled, still picking at his food.

Holding up the stone, the mermaid grinned, "Lady Cilithrand gave the sirens a beautiful gift. I wish to trade it for my friends."

Staring down at her, the king's jaw dropped at the size of the hamar. "You think I would accept the elf's treachery?"

"Uncle!" Hayt snapped in surprise. "She is offering this to you from her heart; it matters not who gave it to her."

"Rubbish," the king replied, pushing back his chair as he prepared to leave the table. "The elf gem is worthless to me, as I am certain it has no value to anyone other than the elves."

Glaring at him, Zaendra's mouth fell open as she prepared to berate him, informing him of how Amicia had been able to use the trinket on more than one occasion to save them. Glancing at her fiancé, she could see the warning in his eyes. Clamping her jaw shut, she held her tongue.

"Uncle," the younger dwarf repeated. "Please reconsider. This is the only thing of value they have to trade."

"Then they will be bartered to the dragon, as promised," his uncle spat, on his feet and headed for the door. "If you wish to have them at your wedding, I suggest you plan for it to happen before Putwyn comes to claim them in six days' time; five, not counting today."

"You would allow them to stand with us?" Zae gasped.

"I am not a monster," her future kin replied, turning to face her squarely. "But I have given my word, and I refuse to break it. Plan your ceremony, and I will allow them a few hours outside their cage to see you are properly wed before they depart."

"Thank you, uncle," Hayt agreed. "Your offer is most gracious, and we will accept. We will plan for the day after tomorrow and see to all the arrangements by then."

"Good," Baeweth smiled, warming to the idea of his nephew putting down some solid roots, even if the girl was an outsider. Leaving the chamber, he already knew the next step would be getting him out of the engineering department and teaching him everything he would need to know to run the kingdom. Whistling as he strolled down the path, he reckoned that this marriage practically assured the young man would one day sit upon their throne.

FIFTEEN

Zaendra's Day

AMICIA STOOD in Hayt's small chamber, her eyes wide as she admired the contrast of the silky white gown as it hung on the nymph's small frame. "This is your day, Zaendra," she sighed, feeling a stab of indecision on the matter.

Meena also there, they had been permitted to help the girl prepare for her wedding. "I'm glad the king has allowed us to share this with you," the older woman stated with a tremble in her voice.

"Yes, most generous of my new uncle," Zae whispered, staring at herself in the full-length mirror that had been provided.

Stepping up beside her, Ami placed her hand upon her shoulder, sharing the reflection. "I'm sorry that I pushed you, love," she said quietly. "I should not have done that."

Raising her arms, Zaendra admired the beautiful silk gown that trailed the floor. One of the dwarf seamstresses had worked non-stop to finish it in the two days since the wedding had been set. Smiling at the image, she ignored the comment, observing instead, "It is fine work. It fits me perfectly, and I had never dreamed of anything so exquisite on this day."

Sharing a glance with the blonde over her head, Meena joined them in front of the glass, claiming the other shoulder as she insisted, "I think what Amicia is trying to say, is that you do not have to do this. We came here together, and it might be best if we left together."

"I know," Zae sighed, pivoting and looking up at her friend. "But I want to do this. Hayt and I have spoken for many hours since our meeting. He is a

113

good man..." She paused, giggling. "Or dwarf. He will make a good husband," she assured with a firm nod. "Oldrilin and I will be well cared for here in Rhong."

Her lip quivering, Amicia pushed her arms around the smaller girl's chest, hugging her from behind. "Now that it's here, I don't know that I can bear it!" Tears running down her cheeks, she swiped at them to prevent their dripping onto the beautiful dress. "Two weddings now we will have shared. One for each of my sisters." And none of them hers.

Turning, Zaendra reached for her neck, dragging her into a proper hug. "Sweet Amicia, with a heart so pure. I will pray for you when you go with the dragon that you will stand before the council and convince them of your worth. When you do, you must return to Rhong, even if only for a visit, that I may know you are safe."

Hugging her, Ami didn't argue. It was her wedding day, after all, and here she cried, threatening to spoil it. "I will, love," she promised. "I know they will hear my words, and I will do my best to convince them of exactly that."

"And we will return," Meena added, placing her hand firmly on Zae's back to comfort her. "Now, wear your smile and be happy in your moment. Alas, it is no ordinary dwarf you wed, and half their kingdom will come to see your vow."

"Yes," Zaendra grinned, pulling away and twirling so that the material floated around her. "His people love me. I can feel it when I meet them; their smiles are warm and reach their eyes. Even Baeweth has accepted me, I am certain."

"Are we ready in here?" Rey asked at the door, interrupting the trio of women, Oldrilin peeking in while holding his leg. She had claimed him the moment he was released from the cell and refused to let go of him until she must.

"I am ready," Zae pronounced, raising her chin and grinning profusely. Accepting a small bouquet of white roses from Amicia, she sniffed at them. "So lovely. My new dwarf kindred have thought of everything."

Taking his arm, Rey walked beside the bride, their steps slow as he guided her to the end of a long walk. There, Piers would take over, and he only had a moment to say what could be the last words that they would share. Inhaling deeply, he whispered, "I have enjoyed our time together, Zaendra."

"Don't," she clipped, her eyes fixed straight ahead and her nose in the air.

"Don't? Don't what?"

"Don't say your goodbyes," she bit through clenched teeth and a forced smile as the kingdom watched their slow gait.

"But I may not have another chance," he replied hoarsely.

"Then they will never be said, and we will both know the love and friendship we have shared. We will remember it fondly, for all times," she finished as they arrived at the end of a long path, where the Mate waited to take her the rest of the way.

"Then so it shall be," Reynard agreed, bending to kiss her gently on the cheek.

"You look quite lovely," Piers complimented, offering his arm.

Accepting the appendage, she smiled up at him. "And you quite handsome, sir." Pivoting, they looked out across the expanse of dwarves that had gathered in the large room she and Hayt had explored the night after they had first arrived in the kingdom.

The high ceiling above glistened with gems and minerals, and the walls lined with walkways were packed with short, round bodies. "There are so many," she breathed, her chest growing tight as those on their level pushed in closer to the path they would take.

"Steady, girl," the Mate soothed, patting the back of her hand. "They are your new kin," he assured.

"Thank you, Mate," she whispered, relaxing a little at his collected air. "You have been so wonderful to know."

Behind the couple, Amicia held Rey's hand as they walked together, followed by Oldrilin, then Meena and Bally in single file. Only one member of their group had been denied attendance, and Animir remained locked in their cell, as Baeweth could not be convinced to allow his presence at his great-nephew's ceremony.

Tears on her cheeks, Amicia watched the beautiful gown glisten in the dancing light of the fires, as torches and lamps lit their path. Catching glimpses of the pure white flowers in her bouquet, she realized that the dwarves had worked hard to give her such a beautiful moment; one they would share as the earth nymph became a part of them, these creatures who dug out and lived within their hidden world.

Giving her a squeeze, Rey fought tears of his own. He had hoped to express the depths of his feelings for their dark-skinned companion, but she had brushed him off, and his words remained unspoken. Drawing a ragged breath, he lost the battle, and his face glistened with droplets that he could not hide, both happy and sad.

Guilt twisting her stomach, Ami glanced up at him. She felt torn at that moment, guilty because she thought of herself as much as she did the girl before her. Yes, Zae had made the only choice she could, but Amicia had wasted so many chances to walk down her own aisle, and now she might never. Swallowing hard, she stifled the cry that threatened to escape.

Just one more chance, she silently prayed, closing her eyes as he guided her. *If I get another chance, I am going to marry Rey. He loves me dearly, and my Lamwen is assuredly gone.* She knew in her gut she should take her vow with the man beside her and would do so if the council allowed them to live.

Arriving at the front of the dwarf cathedral, the group hung back as Piers walked the girl up the steps. At the top of a raised platform, Hayt waited, smiling broadly as his bride approached. Placing her tiny hands in his, Piers gave him a wink as he commanded, "Take care of her, son."

"Always," the dwarf replied, fighting the urge to kiss her lush full lips. There eyes meeting, the kingdom fell away, and for a moment, only the two of them lived and breathed as he drank in their ebony light.

Stepping down, the Mate walked calmly between the members of their group, wiping at his damp cheeks as he rotated to stand beside his wife. Taking her hand, he held her firmly as he lifted his chin to watch the ceremony.

The king himself performed the ritual, and the happy couple knelt before him as he patted their heads and chanted an ancient blessing. Then they were allowed to stand and were presented to a cheering crowd. Clapping and shouting their own greetings, the group of friends smiled and laughed, even when a guard came forward to escort them back to their cell.

"We will not attend the celebration?" Amicia gasped, addressing the single dwarf who would return them to their prison.

"I'm afraid I have been instructed to remove you, quietly if possible," he explained, looking around them at the joyous throng.

"We will go," Meena agreed hurriedly. "We will not poison our friend's beautiful day."

"Aye," the Mate agreed, glancing down at Oldrilin's tear filled eyes. "Say goodbye to her, Rey."

Dropping to his knee, Reynard hugged the tiny creature, then pushed her away. "Take care of Zae," he instructed. "And I will return for you if I am ever able," he promised.

"Unhappy Rey Daye," she sniffed, shaking his large hand with both of hers. "Will miss most assured."

"Most assured," he repeated quietly, standing tall to follow the group as they left the great hall.

Arriving back at their cell, their mood had waned, and they found Animir sitting on the foot of their long bed, staring at his hands. "It is done?" he asked, his gaze still fixed on his fingers as he spoke.

"Aye," Bally sighed, sitting beside him. "I'm sorry they didn't let you come and be a part of it."

"Tis no matter," the elf disagreed. "I am surprised they have not killed me by now. The hatred between our kinds runs deep; I fear we will never overcome it."

Clamping him on the shoulder, the Mate gave him a firm squeeze. "It is the lack of seeing a person when we look at each other that brings such horrid decline. It is easy to hate when we see no face, nor the heart and soul within."

Turning and throwing her arms around Rey's neck, Amicia squeezed him tightly. Her tears unfettered, she sniffed loudly as he held her. No words were shared between them, as she could not bring herself to give him her secret promise; not yet. But soon, their fate would be decided, and she would confess to him her intention to take his name.

SIXTEEN

Broken Chains

"OUR NYMPH MADE A LOVELY BRIDE," Asyng praised, walking beside her brother the morning after the ceremony. "Are you certain her magical blood will not taint us?"

"I have consulted with our elders, and there is nothing to fear, dear sister. I have been assured they do not use their magic in the way of other creatures, such as the dragons and the wizards," Baeweth assured her as they entered the dining hall. "They are closely akin to us in that regard."

"Yes, then I suppose she will do," she sighed as she took her seat. "I am so looking forward to the sounds of tiny feet within our halls. The palace has been a lonely place since Hayt has grown."

"Indeed," the king chortled, raising his glass of grog to toast her. "We have done well, my sister. May our line prosper and the Kingdom of Rhong never fall."

"Hear, hear," she agreed, lifting her own as the happy couple entered the room.

"Ah, here are our newlyweds," Baeweth sang in a boisterous tone. Seated at his end of the dining table, he and Asyng had been discussing their plans for his young heir, but the conversation quickly fell away at their arrival.

Taking the center chair opposite from her husband, as had become their custom, Zaendra looked about her anxiously. "Where's Oldrilin?"

"She no longer dines with us," the woman to her right informed her curtly. "She is with the chambermaids who serve us, and there she will remain."

119

"But Lin belongs to us," Hayt replied, still standing, holding the back of his. "Uncle –"

"Sit, my son," the king commanded. "We have much to discuss now that the union has been consummated."

His face shifting to bright red, the contrast highlighted by his fair hair, Hayt took his seat while avoiding Zaendra's gaze. What had taken place between them in his chamber the night before was private, or at least he thought it had been. "Have your say," he grunted, certain he wasn't going to like what came next.

"We are moving you into the palace," the royal replied, his arm jerking back and forth as he sliced at a hunk of meat. "We have selected a suite, and it has been prepared. Oldrilin and the other maids are collecting your personal things to move them as we speak."

His face shooting up, the young couple's eyes met, and he could see the deep sorrow within her mahogany orbs. "I'm sorry," he breathed, speaking to her in a quiet tone.

"It's not your fault," she replied, flicking her gaze between the two ends of the table. "How could you have known?"

"He didn't," the old king laughed. "It was a surprise for both of you. Your new suite will be fit for a queen, and your husband will begin his training as to the running of a kingdom in the morn. Firen has already been promoted to the role of head engineer."

"Uncle!" Hayt exclaimed. "Training? I am a builder, not a politician!"

"You are my great nephew and heir to the throne of Rhong," Baeweth shouted back. "It's about time you started to act like it. This is the perfect place in your life for a transition. You will take up your role as my advisor, and I will teach you all that I know about diplomacy and caring for a realm."

"Diplomacy," his heir grunted. "Dwarves living beneath a mountain have little use for it."

Ignoring him, Baeweth turned his gaze to the girl, looking her up and down as he added, "If she is able, she shall provide you with many sons, and our halls will again brim with the life of our line."

Her lips forming a perfect "O," Zaendra could not bring herself to speak. *No wonder the king has taken to me.* He has seen the ends within the means, and she would be acceptable in that manner.

"Outrageous," Hayt grunted, his fork in hand as he smacked his fist against the table. "You could have at least asked what our thoughts might have been. What our plans are. We do have our own lives, you know."

"No, you don't. As heir to the throne, your life belongs to the people," his grandmother spoke up. "You have known since your parents died when you were ten that this day would come, and I dare say none too soon."

Staring at the matriarch with wide eyes, Hayt's mind slipped for a moment, trapped in the morning he had learned of their demise. "A plague. A simple stupid illness that swept through the kingdom."

"Yes," Asyng nodded. "It took one-fourth of our people; a heavy loss after the third who died before we left the depths of the southern side, under the mountain. Great hardship we have faced in our rebuilding. Many of our line have fallen, but we hope the addition of the nymph's blood will strengthen our family tree against such future events."

Eyeing the girl, her smile curled Hayt's toes with fear. "What do you mean by that, grandmother?"

"She is an earth nymph," the old woman soothed. "Magical beings with fortitude and the blessing of the kingdom of Eriden. We have forgotten the ways of the ancients through the centuries, but her blood remembers. It will fortify your offspring and return to us something we have lost."

"Ah," Zaendra gasped, understanding more clearly the simple role she would play. *I will be breeding stock and little more.*

Blinking rapidly, fighting his sorrow, Hayt sighed, "I must take my place then." Lifting his chin, he stared at the beauty seated across from him. "You will make an excellent queen, my love."

His acceptance of their future more than she could stand, Zaendra's bottom lip stuck out in a pout. Her heart beating hard against her ribs, she recalled the night he had told her of his position. *But it was to be years before he would take his place as king.* Turning to his uncle, she asked softly, "You must prepare him so soon?"

"I'm afraid so," Baeweth barked, chewing at his meat. "One never knows what might happen to me, and he must be ready to step in and guide our people in my stead if and when that day comes. At near one hundred and forty, I am quite aged, and infirmity might set in at any moment."

Nodding a few times, she sniffed, "I understand. But I will be allowed to see Oldrilin?"

"You will see her, but she is not your equal, and you should remember that," Asyng replied, grinning behind her cup of grog. She had warned her brother that the siren was not a servant, despite Hayt's claim, and now the proof lay before them. "She is your chambermaid. We have few of those who serve here under the mountain, as most are free dwarves, so you should consider yourself lucky that you have brought your own."

"Indeed... lucky," Zaendra agreed, looking back to Hayt with wide doleful eyes. "I'm afraid I have had my fill of breakfast. When may we be shown to our rooms?"

The king clapped his hands thrice with loud pops, and a small dark-haired dwarf appeared. "Yes, my lord?"

"Our new heiress requires guidance to the suite the girls have prepared for them," the king announced.

"Very well, my lord," the butler replied. "This way, my lady." Raising a hand, he indicated the exit.

"I'm coming as well," Hayt coughed, dropping his utensils and leaving his plate only half empty. Scurrying to catch up, he slipped his fingers into hers as they followed their guide. "Are you angry?" he whispered next to her ear.

"No," she clipped, her glare straight ahead. "What is done is done."

His gut roiling, her mate didn't see it that way, but there was little he could do about it; at least for the moment.

Led through a narrow passageway with one guard at the main entrance, they weaved through the special tunnels that had been deemed the palace centuries before, when the dwarf kingdom had opened the caves and begun the construction of Rhong. Making a few turns, they eventually came out in a larger chamber, the space decorated by large pillars of crystals and gems. In the middle of it, a pond with a large rock column on the far end glowed with an eerie blue light as rivulets of water trickled down the smooth surface.

Stopping short, the girl looked around with wide eyes. "What is this?" she gasped.

"This is the common room of our king's palace, sometimes referred to as the garden. The pond is fed from a tarn above, where the water runs down the pillars there in the center, and enchanted stones were brought and used on the bottom to give it the light within," her husband explained with pride.

"It is beautiful," she confessed with a smile that lifted her spirits. "I never expected such an exquisite thing from dwarves." Realizing the harshness of that statement, she cut her eyes over at Hayt. "I'm sorry. That didn't come out the way I meant it. You are such a robust and salt-of-the-earth people. Such a purely decorative place seems so unlike you," she tried to explain.

Staring at her with his clear blue orbs, Hayt inhaled deeply, then blew the air out gently through his nose. "You have much to learn about us, my love," he replied calmly. "But for now, we must see our quarters, and there we can make our plans."

Moving once again, their hallway exited to the right of the garden and consisted of three large rooms and one small one, which would belong to their housekeeper. The largest of the rooms sat alone on the left side of the narrow passage. It held a bed and seating area for the couple. The other two across from it were smaller bedrooms, which undoubtedly would house their family as it grew.

"How quaint," Zae observed, her use of understatement perfectly suited to the lavishness of their new home. "I suppose the commoners among you get by on far less."

Nodding, her husband agreed, "Their homes are much like that which you have previously seen." Accustomed to the king's palace, Hayt had known what they would find. Their walls encrusted with gems and precious metals, their furnishings were the finest in all the kingdom. "I've been in the palace many times, and never once have I thought I would actually reside here," he confessed as their servant made his exit.

Alone, Hayt whirled around, quickly examining the walls and then the chairs and bed. Finding nothing out of the ordinary, he turned to Zaendra, walking straight up to stand before her. Seizing her hands, he held them between his, pressing them to his chest. "If I asked you to run away with me, would you go?" he whispered.

"What?" she gasped, her open jaw expressing her surprise.

"I do not wish this life. If my uncle wants to strip me of my title as head engineer and force me to live as another, then I should be the one to choose it; whatever that life might be. I didn't fully realize it until this moment, but I hold no desire to ever be king."

"Then what shall we do? Where shall we go?"

"First, we must help your friends to escape," he plotted, releasing her and walking a slow circle around her, peering at their gaudy surroundings with distrusting eyes. "That means we will need to act quickly, as the dragon will come for them the day after tomorrow. Tonight, if we can, we will go to them and break the chains that bind them."

Frowning as she pictured her companions, Zae recalled that they were not actually bound. Inhaling, as if to vocalize the point, she caught the words before they tumbled out. "You speak metaphorically," she accused instead.

"Yes, of course," he chuckled. "We will get the guard to open the door, or we will tie him up and steal his keys. We will walk right out through the front door if we are able."

"We should escape through your new vista, instead," Zae agreed to his plan with a wide grin. "We had hoped to go over the top of the mountain, and that would probably be best."

"You were headed to the marshes of the gnomes?" he asked, his eyes wide as he realized how risky that would be. "The dragons might once again locate you if we choose that particular course."

"Well, we cannot hide in the northern woods forever," she countered, licking her lips excitedly. "Oh, Hayt, thank you!"

"Well, you are most welcome, my love; but please do not thank me until the task is complete and your friends stand beside us," he suggested.

"Then let us see what we must do to bring this plan into action," she whispered, as if the walls might hear. "We will need to pack supplies. And the weapons must be retrieved. Yes, we will have much to do this day if we are to flee into the night," she surmised, staring that the marriage bed they had been provided, one they would never share if they succeeded.

Nodding, he agreed by pulling her into a firm hug. "Thank you, Zae. I could not have asked for a better wife, and I will do my best to see us all back upon your journey."

"Then I will pack my bag and see that Oldrilin is also ready to depart," she stipulated. "You will see that we can exit through the new vista?"

"Yes, I will go there now. Stay here within our chamber, and I will return for you for our dinner, as we must dine with uncle and grandmother as if all is well. Then we will take our things and take our leave," he suggested.

"A wise decision, as they will not realize we are gone until tomorrow, unless an alarm is raised," she agreed, already sifting through his things in search of items that he might need, which she would add to her own.

"I will return then, Zae," he said with a smile. Catching her by the arm, he pulled her to face him, lowering his mouth to kiss her once more. Then, stomping through their doorway, his heart raced as he passed through the garden and exited the palace.

Noting the long spear held by the guard next to the outer door, he considered how they would retrieve the group's weapons. Someone knew where they had been taken, but how he could gather the information without arousing suspicion would be difficult. Deciding to ascertain the progress on the vista first and deal with the armaments later, he began the long trek through the maze of tunnels that would take him there.

As he strode along, he thought about the layout of their city. The vista on the northeast corner, it would be close for them to reach from the prison cell, where the group was being held. However, they would also have to pass through the great hall, where their wedding had been held the day before. *It will be unlikely that we will cross unseen,* he mused.

Listening to the rocks crunch beneath his thick leather boots, he scowled as he contemplated the conundrum. *There has to be a way.* Arriving at the gaping hole that had been cut into a clean arch, he grimaced.

"What's wrong with it?" Firen demanded, sauntering up to his former boss.

"Who said anything was wrong?" Hayt demanded, still studying their work.

"Your face, that's what. You look as if it will crash in upon us at any moment," Firen laughed anxiously. "I've only held your place a day, and I'm already in trouble."

Turning to look down at his old friend, Hayt also chuckled, "It is not your work that brings my frown. I am not a politician, and it pains me greatly to have all that I have worked for taken from me the day I wed my wife."

Catching him by the shoulder, Firen gave him a firm squeeze. "I am sorry that I have been promoted in this manner, as well. But it is the king's order; his word is law."

"Bah, I know this, my friend," Hayt agreed, catching the other dwarf in the same manner and returning the fond gesture. Dropping the connection, he marched through the arch into the new tunnel, where he came out a moment later in the cave on the other end. The supports were all in place, and the front would soon be completed. "You have done fine work," he praised.

"We followed your plans," his successor agreed. "Your uncle is wrong to force his life upon you. There are others in your line, more distant kin he could have chosen; some who are eager to sit upon the throne."

"Yes, but I believe he fears their desire to wear his crown," the king's heir sighed. "I am the only one he feels he can trust."

"And how do you feel?"

"I think I would leave if I were able," Hayt blurted, his face growing red as soon as the words had been spoken. Still admiring the roof, he pretended that his remark had been purely innocent.

"If you were serious about such a thing," Firen whispered, pushing his friend towards the cave exit, he waited until they stood alone on the shelf overlooking the forest before he finished, "you would need help to accomplish it."

"Only a fool would help us. As soon as your aid was discovered, you would be the one sitting in a prison cell, or worse," Hayt sighed, realizing he had divulged his intentions to the first person he had spoken to. *Zaendra will be disappointed.*

"Silly dwarf," Firen laughed loudly, then said more quietly. "You will need a diversion. You wish to leave this way?"

"We were thinking we might."

"I advise this be your decoy, my friend."

"And we leave by the front gate, is that it?" Hayt grinned as he cut his eyes over at his new conspirator.

"No, you leave by the southern tunnels."

Spinning to face him, Hayt grabbed the shorter man by both arms and pulled him towards him. Glaring into his shocked features, he demanded, "Through the south tunnels. Have you lost your mind?" Searching his eyes, he could see no sign of changing his suggested path. "You know what's down there!"

"Yes, as does the king. That is why he would never follow you. If you truly wish to get a way, you must go where he will not. Otherwise, your flight would only be temporary. He will send troops to find you and bring you back, and then where would your new bride be?"

Releasing him, Hayt's lungs refused to work for a moment as his heart raced and his mind ran in circles. "You are right. They will come after us, most assuredly."

"You know that they will," Firen agreed, righting his clothes. "But I can help make it appear that you have left via the vista and are climbing the mountain."

"No, if we go by the southern tunnels, then my uncle should know that it is so. He should know how desperately we wanted to get away," Hayt bit, anger seeping into his tone.

"And what of your grandmother? She will be disappointed at your choice."

"She will understand," the boy insisted, slamming his fist into his open palm. "Thank you for the suggestion. We will use the southern tunnels, and with any luck we will avoid facing the daemons who live below. But, if they find us within those dark halls, we would definitely need the weapons that were taken from Zaendra's friends. Can you tell me what was done with them?" Hayt asked, hesitating to push for more.

"I do not know, but I know someone who will. Do not worry," Firen assured with a nod. "I will have them for you and wait for you at the entrance to the pits at midnight, there in the engineer's caves. You will free your wife's friends and pick them up from me there."

"I hate to involve you, honestly, Firen. You have been too dear to me to risk in this venture," Hayt countered, his frown returned.

"You do not have to ask; this I will do of my own accord," Firen insisted. "Now, go make your plans for their release, and I will tend to the rest."

"You are a good friend, Firen. I shall never forget you," Hayt growled as he turned to head back inside, ready to lay the groundwork for the next part of their plan.

SEVENTEEN

A Safe Journey

MEETING in the dining hall that evening for their meal, Zaendra and Hayt had refrained from speaking about their day of preparation until they were safely back in their quarters. Checking the smallest of their rooms when they arrived in their suite, the one fitted for Oldrilin, the girl returned to their chamber with a sigh. "Lin is not here. I thought they were going to allow me to keep her."

"Perhaps she still dines with the other servants and will return shortly," Hayt suggested, quickly pouring over the essentials his wife had packed. "I fear you have brought too much," he observed, laying a few scrolls of parchment beside the parcels she had prepared.

"You say that now, but when that bag is all that you have, you will realize how little it is," she snapped, recalling the hard times the group had faced on their journey from the glen to the north and then again after their cabin had been burned.

"Please don't be angry."

"I'm not angry," she bit, then stammered, "I'm upset she isn't here. We need to be on our way, do we not?"

"Soon," he nodded, shoving everything back into the pack and tying it shut with his pages sticking out the top. "For now, we wait. If you go after her, it might raise suspicions."

"True," she agreed, watching him fight with the size of his parcel. "Don't worry. Meena can shrink some of the items to make them easier to carry once

129

we have freed her, so don't let the size of your bundle upset you. I could have, but I never learned how, as Animir and Ami were taught to do," she sighed."

Surprised at such a notion, he cut his eyes over at her to see that she was straight-faced about the proposed manipulation. Swallowing, he held his surprise in check, as there was a great deal about magic his people had purposely forgotten over the decades. "I'll take your word for it," he nodded, scooping up her hand to give it a squeeze and hoping he was right about the siren, as losing her would be more catastrophic than a few personal items.

"You have figured out everything else? How we will get the others out and to the vista?" she asked, eyeing his rolls of paper.

"Yes, about that," he sighed, dreading informing her of the direction they were actually going to take. Pulling her hand, he turned her to face him. "Do you trust me, love?"

"You know that I do," she grimaced.

"Then please, do not ask or question the choices I have made. Simply follow and do as I say."

Staring at him with wide eyes, fear roiled inside her. "You will not put us in danger, I hope."

Shrugging, he made a miserable attempt at a grin before it fell away. "We are breaking out of Rhong in the middle of the night; you know there will be danger."

"You're right. I don't want to know the details," she gasped, patting him on the chest. Hearing the patter of little feet outside their door, she pulled away and poked her head out. "Lin!"

"You need of me, my lady?" Her large blue eyes upturned, the tiny creature swept the girl's fear away.

"Yes, come and let us speak for a moment," Zae replied, offering her hand.

Back inside their bed chamber, Zaendra fell to her knees before her, swaddling her tiny friend into a firm hug. "I was so afraid when they took you from me," she whispered.

"I have learned my place," the siren explained, also on the verge of tears. "Being a good servant to my friend Zae."

"Yes, you are very good," the nymph agreed, "but now we must make our plans. Secret plans you must follow and do as we say."

Looking up at Hayt with wide blue orbs, Lin agreed, "Oldrilin will, yes."

"Good," Hayt breathed, relieved at least something seemed to be falling into place. Kneeling with his wife, the couple quietly explained their plan to help the others escape.

Hearing their intentions, the siren bounced up and down as she squealed, "Tis a good plan, lady Zae. My Rey Daye be saved!"

"Yes, they will all be saved," Zaendra agreed, taking up a small wrap and unfolding it. "But we must be careful so we are not caught. I want you to wear this, as I think it will help conceal you as we make our way through the tunnels." They would each wear one in hopes of being less visible and to help hide the gear that they carried.

Covered, the small creature could easily be mistaken for a dwarf. "I like the disguises," Hayt praised, donning his own robe and helping Zaendra adjust hers. "Come, and I will show you where you will wait. I will retrieve the others from the cell and pick you up on our way out of the city, along with the weapons that my friend Firen will deliver to us."

"Won't we draw attention carrying these packs? They look rather large, even with the covers," Zae asked doubtfully, her palms growing moist with the thought of what lay ahead.

"Hard to say," Hayt shrugged. "The evening is come, and there will be limited numbers out to see us, much less notice what we carry on our backs. With the robes, we could be anyone, and few will be of a mind to check."

"Then we are ready," the girl agreed, pursing her lips anxiously.

Following him, Zaendra and Oldrilin held hands until they reached the outside door of the palace. There, Hayt and Zaendra walked side by side, the light from his small lantern not really needed at the moment on the well-lit path. Lin trailing behind, her lamp had not been lit, and she hid it beneath her cloak. Glancing back at her small friend, Zae hoped she appeared as if she merely walked in the same direction in her hooded disguise.

"We are doing well," Hayt observed as they passed the center of the massive room. He could not see his bride's face with her hood in place, but he could hear her tense breathing and hoped his words would calm her.

Ahead of them, Zaendra could see the platform where they had stood to take their vows. Reaching for his hand, she nodded, "Yes, we will make it, I am certain." Holding him, the cloth draped over their fingers soothed her, and she found herself a bit more relaxed as they moved unnoticed, or so it would seem.

Arriving on the south end of the great hall a few minutes later, Hayt pointed out a few small caves that went nowhere. "Let's get out of sight." Selecting one that held storage crates, he knelt before the siren. Taking Oldrilin's lamp, he lit it, then commanded, "Hide here, and I shall be back shortly." Her blue orbs full of fear, he could sense the faith she had in his ability to see them through. "Don't worry, Lin. We are halfway there."

Standing and removing his cloak, he dropped his pack and lay the robe over it, careful to place them behind a stack of boxes. Smoothing his clothing, he hoped he would now appear to be out on any normal walk despite the lateness of the hour. Smiling at his wife, he nodded to her, prepared to depart.

"What if someone comes?" Zaendra asked anxiously.

"No one will come," he soothed, rubbing her upper arms firmly. "I hope you don't get too cold. It may be cooler the farther down we go."

"I have a wrap," she informed him tartly. "How do you know we will not be discovered?"

"These caves store the tools for our engineers," he sighed. "All of the work crews will have turned in for the night. No one lives on this end of the kingdom since the king decided this area is too close to the southern tunnels."

"Is that where we will go?" Oldrilin asked, not fully understanding the danger.

"Yes, but you must be quiet, Lin," he beseeched her. Kissing Zae on the forehead, he added, "I shall return," carrying his lamp as he departed.

Folding her hands in front of her chest, Zaendra drew deep breaths to keep herself calm. "He'll be back, Lin. I just know this is going to work."

Alone in their hiding place, the pair sat upon the ground and waited with the small light between them. The flame illuminating much of the chamber, Zae could see crates of all sizes stacked against the walls, presumably holding supplies and probably nothing of use to them.

Her mate had been right about the coolness of the air, and Zaendra pulled her robe tighter around her, then offered her hand to her small friend in comfort. "It won't be long now," she whispered, along with other occasional soothing remarks; but the night wore on, the minutes ticking by as they grew restless.

Eventually noting the pages Hayt had left sticking out from his pack, Zae removed them, unrolling them and pressing them flat against the dirt and rocks of the floor. The edges tattered, they were obviously very old and fought to return to their curled state. Using larger stones to weight the corners, Zaendra lifted the light to have a better look.

"What is this?" Lin asked, filled with curiosity at the drawings.

"I don't really know," the nymph replied airily. "It's a cave, I am certain. Perhaps the way he intends to escape. But these labels..." She hesitated, running her finger over a few before she breathed, "This is a city. Surely this cannot be what lies in the southern tunnels."

"I'm afraid that it is," Firen replied, startling the two women with his silent approach. Seeing them both jump, he laughed as he offered a small wave. "I'm Firen."

Recognizing the end of Amicia's bow, Zae gasped, "Firen who? Are you here to help us?"

"I am," the dwarf confessed. "But I am troubled that our friends are not here yet. How long have you waited?" he asked, dropping his bundle on the ground and having a look at the map for himself.

"I have no idea," she gasped, fighting the panic within her. "What time is it?"

"Tis midnight, the hour I have promised to deliver these and meet Hayt here in the storage caves," he replied, taking a knee and using a pudgy finger to trace their ancient halls.

"It's been hours," Oldrilin whimpered, clinging to the taller girl as they stood.

"They will be here soon," Zaendra smiled as she reassured her small friend. "I'm sure it's all part of the plan." Turning to their benefactor, she continued, "You may leave them with me," indicating the bundle he had appeared to have forgotten. Noting his trance like state, she shifted her attention to his package.

Unwrapping their defenses, she located her spear and clutched it with both hands as she stood straight and proud. Planting the butt end in the soft earth of the cave, the sharp tip glinted about a foot over her head.

"Is that yours?" the dwarf asked, cutting his gaze up and eyeing her doubtfully.

"Yes, it is. The Mate made it for me in Whitefair, and I have used it to kill many times," she grunted.

"I bet you have," he observed, staring at the blade and considering her words. "People?" he asked, standing slowly while curling his tongue.

"Yes, men," she agreed, her eyes bright as she recalled their escape from the oasis. At the time, it had bothered her deeply that she had taken a man's life, but as the recollection of the events had aged, she had come to understand how fighting for their lives had been important, and she would do so again if the need arose, without fear or hesitation.

"Well, I'll leave you then," the dwarf whispered, nodding at the siren. "Good luck to you all on your journey."

"Wait!" Zaendra called, smiling when he paused his step. "Tell us about the map. Where is this place?"

Not turning to face her, Firen's mind raced. "Perhaps it would be best not to dwell on what is to come. You will have your weapons, and your husband will be there to guide you through the worst of it."

"Worst of it," Zae repeated, the air hurting her lungs as she breathed. "You know something, don't you," she accused evenly.

"I know the king will not follow you into the city of Asomanee. He fears the creatures of the darkness; the daemons that reside below. If you can avoid them, you will escape out into the marshes, and you will be free," he explained, not filling in too many details.

"Daemons?" Oldrilin asked, cocking her head as she studied the back of the dwarf, who still did not face them in a secretive manner.

"I dare not say more," he replied curtly. "I bid you a safe journey."

Watching him go, Zaendra sighed, unsure if she should be happy things in their plan had already been altered. If Hayt knew of these creatures, that would explain his request to trust him. Squeezing the handle of her spear and fighting to calm her nerves, she inhaled deeply.

"Will the daemons harm us?" Lin asked timidly, holding the girl's leg as she stared up at her.

"I certainly hope not," Zaendra replied, unable to remove her eyes from the entrance to the cave. "They don't sound friendly at any rate." Fear running her heart, it beat wildly inside her chest. *No wonder the king did not allow them to build their homes here so close to the darkness below.*

Realizing there was nothing to be done, Zae closed her eyes as she sat upon the ground. Leaning back against the rock wall, she listened to the silence of their cave, as the dwarves were too far away to be heard even if they were not yet asleep. Hoping that her friends were safe, she rested, preparing for the battle for their freedom she feared would soon come.

EIGHTEEN

The Abyss

CREEPING along the walls of the cave, Hayt approached the area where his wife's friends were being held. The prison small, only a few cells were contained there, as most prisoners were executed or released in short order.

Pausing when he reached the mouth of the tunnel, he could see the bars of their cell on the far wall. In the middle of the larger central chamber, a small fire burned in a pit, which lit the room. His eyes fixated on it, he could see the flames shoot up and then vanish as it danced.

Shoving his hand in his pocket, he ran his fingers anxiously over the edge of the gem Oldrilin had given him when they had prepared to leave. His uncle didn't take much of a liking to it, but he hoped he would have more luck with the guard. He doubted he could get them freed, but if he could get the door open, it would give them a chance.

Somewhere, out of sight from his point of view, a dwarf coughed. Recognizing the voice as the guard grumbled to himself, Hayt grinned, then walked calmly out into the light. "Good evening, Vael," he grunted, addressing the dwarf who stood near his height.

"Hayt, my lord," Vael replied, standing straight, his arms stiff at his sides.

"Oh, now don't start that *my lord*," Hayt laughed. "I'm still the dwarf I was yesterday."

"No, my lord. Our great king has informed us of your promotion, as it were," the older dwarf countered, his red hair catching the light as it glinted off his long braid that hung down the center of his back. His face covered in a

135

full, scruffy beard, his yellowed teeth showed as he spoke. He obviously revered, or feared, the man before him, which could work to Hayt's advantage if handled properly.

"Promotion," the king's nephew scoffed, turning his back and rubbing his hands together briskly.

"Yes, and congratulations on your new wife," the warden laughed, relaxing only the slightest with the pleasantries. "She was a beautiful bride," he added, his tone less than convincing. "Not a dwarf but fine makings for a queen, none-the-less," he stammered, almost talking in circles.

"Indeed," Hayt agreed, loudly clearing his throat. "I feel so lucky, all these good things happening to me at once," he grimaced, hiding his displeasure at Vael's choice of words about his bride. Opening his palms to the fire, he warmed them, hoping to appear calm. "As I recall, you are quite fond of trinkets," he began, glancing at the ground behind him, watching the other dwarf's boots as he shifted uncomfortably.

"Yes," the guard grunted, "I have a fair collection of unusual fare."

Producing the hamar gem, Hayt grinned to himself, noting the way it gathered the light from the fire, as if it harnessed it. "Good. I have something I think you might be interested in adding to your assembly."

Catching sight of the offering as the king's nephew turned, Vael licked his thick pink lips. "My, that is precious," he observed, his voice still shaky.

"Yes, very," Hayt agreed, glancing at the door of the cell he needed to open. "I'd like to trade it to you for a few minutes with our guests."

"You mean the prisoners!" Vael snapped, instantly removed from his daze, as if he had been slapped. "No, sir! Under king's orders, no one may see or speak to the outsiders. Trinket or no, you may not, my lord!" He still stood at attention, but his displeasure was evidenced by the sway of his body as he resisted.

"Now Vael, obviously you know that one day I am to rule this kingdom. Imagine what good it might do you to have such a favor for me to repay when that day comes?" Hayt soothed, enticing him further with the promise of a future blessing. His heart raced beneath his calm features, as force would be his only resort if the dwarf could not be persuaded.

Vael cut his eyes over at him, calming his body and standing still as he stared at his superior without reply.

"Let us come to an arrangement," Hayt charmed, raising his chin as he sauntered towards him. His hand extended, holding out the prize, he sweetened, "And imagine that day I will grant you any single thing you could wish, once I sit upon the throne."

Staring at him with wide green eyes, Vael flicked his gaze between the stone and his round features. "I could get in so much trouble," he stammered, again adjusting his feet anxiously as he held his post.

"I only need a few minutes," Hayt insisted, giving the gem a twist to further catch the light.

Unable to resist, the dwarf's tongue shot out quickly and flicked around his mouth as he reached for the crystal. His fingers wrapping around it, he panted, "Ten minutes; no more."

"Thank you," Hayt replied, opening his hand to accept the key to the cell. The ring of metal jingled softly as a shaking appendage passed them over. "That's a good friend," Hayt offered, turning to let himself into their cage.

Inserting the key into the hole, he turned it, listening to the click as the lock shifted. Pulling on the bars, the door squealed as it opened. Leaving it wide, Hayt shoved the ring into his pocket and stepped inside, blinking at the darkness of the compartment. "Have I awakened you?" he asked, noting the Mate sat on the far end, while the rest lay stretched across their single bunk that ran the length of the right-hand wall.

"As if we could in such a wretched place," Animir growled, pulling himself up to stand between their visitor and the exit.

"Relax, elf," Hayt slurred. "I have not come to quarrel." Looking past him, he could see the guard remained on the far side, staring into the stall. Dropping his voice, he said more quietly, "We are leaving. Tonight. Zaendra and Oldrilin await us."

His mouth falling open, Piers gasped as he slowly got to his feet, "You're serious."

"Of course. Would I come all this way to prank you?"

Peeking at their guard himself, Animir observed, "You gave him Oldrilin's gift."

"Yes," Hayt nodded as he explained. "She gave it to me tonight while we were preparing to leave. We decided it could still be used to buy your freedom even if the king refused the offer."

"We'll have to get it back," the elf sneered, slapping Baldwin on the foot. "Wake up," he taunted. "We have a visitor."

Sitting up, Bally blinked at Zaendra's new husband. "What are you doing here?"

"There's no time to explain to each of you in turn," the dwarf grunted. "Wake the others and be ready to rush him. He is only one, but we must move quickly if we are to make your escape."

"Did you bring weapons?" Piers asked, giving his wife a shake, then

Amicia. Holding a single finger to his lips, he hissed, "Be quiet and follow. Our new friend is here to see us to an early release."

Glancing at Hayt, Ami knew immediately what danger such a prospect could hold. "You go out and silence the guard. We'll pack the bags and be ready to leave."

"I'll take care of him," Animir grinned, darting from the cell. At the same moment, he lifted a flat palm in a stopping motion, and the gem flashed with a blinding white light as he directed a shot of energy into it. Knocked against the wall, the jailor rolled onto his knees but made it no further before the elf and Baldwin were upon him. Pulling him up, they forced his arms behind him, stripping him of his new toy.

"What shall we do with him, Mate?" Bally asked with an excited squeak in his voice.

"We'll lock him in here when we've prepared to leave," Piers suggested.

"I've got the keys," Hayt countered, producing the ring. A moment later, he had opened another cell. "Put him in here, and we'll not have to worry about him while you pack." As soon as they had shoved him inside, their new friend shut the door with a loud clang.

Turning to face him, Vael grabbed the iron bars and leaned against them. "So, this is how you repay me?" he growled, certain he would pay dearly for their escape.

"I'm sorry," Hayt replied, lifting his chin, "but I cannot allow my uncle to sell these people to the dragons; not for any price."

"We're ready," the Mate cut him off, leading the others to the door.

Accepting the hamar from Animir, Amicia shoved it in her pocket and announced, "I fear this plan will get us killed."

"Aye, it may," the Mate agreed, throwing his bag over his shoulder, "but staying here will only do the same. Let's go."

Following the dwarf, they exited the tunnel a short time later, coming out in the great hall. Seeing movement on the far side, they stepped back into the shadows, hoping they had not been seen.

"Is there another way around?" Meena asked, watching the dwarves on the ledge above the ground floor, certain they had no intention of retiring any time soon by the looks of them.

"I'm afraid not. Almost all tunnels pass through the great hall," Hayt explained with a shake of his head. "Those that do not are private and won't take us anywhere we need to go."

"Great," Bally grumbled. "We'll never get by them."

"We can use the stone, as we did the night we made it into the troll's cave," Amicia offered, fishing it out of her pocket and holding it up.

Observing the faint light within it, Hayt gasped, "How are you doing that?"

"I have a way with the gem," she grinned. "We share a kind of connection, you could say."

"Right," he agreed with a nod. "So how are you going to use it on us?" he pushed, his trepidation intact.

"I will hide us within a shadow," she explained, moving to the mouth of the cave. "Everyone will form a line behind me, each holding the person in front of them. We are going to go slow so that none get disconnected, so hold on and stay calm."

Holding up the gem, the girl waited until their chain had been formed. Then, taking slow, purposeful steps, she entered the great hall. Her feet walking forward, each pressed against the loose gravel slowly to muffle the sound of the tiny stones grinding against one another.

"I –" Bally began as he reached the mouth of the tunnel.

"DO NOT SPEAK!" Piers hissed from behind him, his loud whisper causing Amicia's heart to beat wildly within her chest.

"What are you doing?" she reached out to their leader telepathically.

"He must be silent. I'm sure your shadow does not mask our sounds," he replied in kind.

Breathing through her nose, she panted, *"Ok, but please don't do that again."*

"He'll get us killed," he replied in agreement, *"but I'll be silent from here on."*

Sweat forming on her brow, Amicia wiped at it the best she could with her raised arm. Her mouth dry, she longed for a drink but knew there would be no water until they reached the far end of the path.

Taking a few quicker steps, she noted the difference in the noise the gravel made. *Damn. We can't go any faster.* Forced to keep the pace down, she crept along, the line of the others following her. *Shit.* A dwarf couple approached, moving towards them at a quick gait.

Shifting to the left edge of the path, she looked back at the others, hoping they would do the same. Following her lead, they stood shoulder to shoulder as the lovers walked past them, oblivious to their presence.

"My God, that thing is powerful," Piers observed to her.

"Yes," she agreed. *"Thankfully."*

Resuming their creeping across the vast floor, they slowly closed the gap between themselves and freedom. They weren't sure how the dwarf was going to get them out of Rhong, but they felt certain he wouldn't have broken them out without some sort of a plan.

Over an hour had passed since Amicia first hid them as they exited the open room. Her fingers cramped, she uncurled them, dropping the glowing white stone into her other hand as she worked the digits to restore the flow of blood. "How far now?" she gasped, hoping she would no longer have to provide their cover.

Hearing voices, Piers growled, "Doesn't anyone in this cursed kingdom sleep?"

"Yes, but we are very close to the family quarters. They will be coming and going for some time. I feel we should hide," Hayt explained.

"Hide? And do what, wait for our escape to be discovered before they come for us?" the Mate bit angrily. "Why did you remove us from the prison if it wasn't safe to make our escape?"

Glaring up at him, Hayt replied through clenched teeth, "Perhaps you would like to return to your cell. It's that way," he pointed over his shoulder as he walked ahead to have a look. Seeing nothing, he curled his fingers to encourage the group to follow.

In this manner, they made quicker progress than they had in the main hall but still slower than they would have liked. Having to hide against the walls a few more times, they finally came to an area that appeared to be deserted, and the noises of the families fell away.

"Where are we now?" Amicia asked, still longing for a single swallow of water as her thirst persisted.

"We are on the south end of the kingdom," Hayt explained. "Ahead are the storage caves, where the engineering supplies are kept. Zaendra and Lin await us there. The hour is much later than I had anticipated, but I hope that your weapons have been delivered to them in my absence."

"You had someone helping you?" Bally asked in surprise.

"Yes, a friend I have known all my life," the dwarf explained, leading them through the passages as Amicia provided the light.

"He must be a very good friend to risk himself to help us," Meena observed in a somber tone.

"Yes, very good indeed," Hayt nodded, pointing. "This is it," he announced as they passed through the entrance and Zaendra's dim light illuminated the room.

"Oh my God," the nymph squealed, throwing herself into Piers's arms, earning a surprised glare from her husband. Noting his displeased countenance, she laughed, "Thank you, my love. I was afraid my friends were lost to me forever."

"To the contrary," he grunted, cutting the taller man a dark glare. "But we must move quickly before we are discovered. I fear we may already be missed, as morning is coming rapidly," he informed them as he gathered a few tools from one of the crates.

"Well, thankfully, I again have my staff," Meena breathed, lifting it out of the pile of returned weapons. "I was surprised they bothered to take it from me the night we were marched from our room."

"They must have feared you could use it," Rey surmised, locating his sword and giving it a test swing.

Bally stood motionless for a moment, frozen with guilt. "I'm sorry; I might have mentioned you were gifted to Asyng that last night at dinner," he confessed.

"Forget about it," the Mate commanded, handing him his axe and sword, then locating his own. "We must leave and don't have time to worry about such things."

Armed and ready, the group followed Hayt once again, out of the cave and into the tunnels. Remembering what she had discovered about them, Zaendra slipped her small fingers into his, holding him firmly as he guided them towards the abyss.

NINETEEN

Asomanee

THEIR FOOTSTEPS LOUD on the loose gravel, the group arrived at a section of tunnel that had been cordoned off. Glaring at the wooden planks nailed across the opening, Piers grunted, "We're going in here?"

"Yes," Hayt agreed, applying an iron bar he had retrieved from the crate to the rusted nails. "This is the path to Asomanee, but it was sealed long ago."

"Why?" the Mate clipped, glaring at the shorter blond.

"Don't ask," Zaendra mumbled. "You are much happier not knowing."

Glancing between them, Hayt swallowed, then replied quietly as he continued to unhook the boards. "About two centuries ago, we were driven from the original dwarf city by a dark presence. Few still live who were there for the exodus, but the stories remain," he explained. Having removed the covering up to mid-thigh, he pointed, "We should squeeze through and be on our way."

"Not until you tell us what's down there," Piers snapped, glancing at his wife. Noting the firm set of her jaw, he knew she was frightened and doing her best to hide it.

"There's a presence there. Someone has used a powerful spell to trap it below," she informed him weakly.

"Don't worry, love. We're not going to put ourselves at risk," he tried to reassure her, considering if they had time to go another route.

"We're already at risk," Rey observed, pointing the way they had come. "Unless I'm mistaken, they have discovered our path of escape."

143

"Everyone into the tunnel," Amicia took charge. "Go; now!" She stood behind them, holding up her light and hiding the group as they worked their way through, each crawling under the remaining blockade and dragging their packs behind them. The dwarves were in sight by the time she had fallen to her knees, backing through the gaping hole and pulling her bag under.

On her feet on the other side, their two lanterns lit the dark tunnel only a few yards ahead of them. She expected the dwarves to crawl under close behind, but they did not, giving them at least a chance to escape. With Hayt leading the way, they moved down the path as quickly as they could, while a shouting match echoed through the corridor.

"Follow them!" Baeweth commanded.

"But sire, there are daemons," a voice protested.

"I care not what else may lurk in the shadows! My nephew and his comrades must not escape!" the king screamed.

Silence followed, either as they had moved beyond range of the debate or his minions had refused to go any farther. Realizing they may lose their lead, Piers growled, "Is there any place down here to hide?"

"Yes," Zaendra intervened. She had spent hours studying the map and pointed ahead. "We will come to a tunnel that veers to the left. If we take it, we can hide and wait for them to pass or lay a trap for them if they follow."

"Aye," the Mate agreed. "We will rest a few minutes there and see if we are pursued."

Making the left turn, they filed into a small chamber. Dust hung in the air, and remnants of furniture made of stone lined the walls. Only bits of dirt and piles of debris covered in cobwebs remained. Anything made of organic material had decayed long ago.

"Well, this is creepy," Bally observed, dropping his pack and gripping his axe.

"Creepy or not, I'll take it," Amicia sighed. "And I'd sure love a drink. I don't suppose you thought to pack us some water?"

Staring at her, Zaendra shook her head slowly. "I'm sorry. I didn't realize we were coming this way until we left."

"I have the water stone," Meena advised. "Perhaps one more pot can be supplied." Pulling out their kettle, she placed the smooth blue stone in the bottom and filled it to the brim. "This will give us all a good drink."

Locating her cup in her bag, Amicia scooped it full and slurped at the cool liquid. "Thank you," she breathed when it had been drained. "I was so thirsty when we were crossing the great hall I felt I might faint," she explained as she passed the cup along so the others could have a share.

144

"Have another scoop," Zae advised when they each had gotten a cup full. "We don't want to waste a drop."

Waiting anxiously, the group finished the water and then sat in a tight circle in the center of the room. In the tunnel, no sound reached them, so if the dwarves had dared to follow, they had been very quiet about it.

After the time grew long, Piers observed, "I don't think he convinced them to follow. Whatever is down here must be atrocious to put such fear into dwarves," he surmised, glaring at their would-be rescuer. "Care to explain?"

"It is," Hayt agreed, laying his arm across his wife's shoulders to pull her firmly against his chest. "It would be better if we do not speak of it and simply do our best to avoid it."

"Well, that's not going to work," Reynard disagreed. "How will we know what to avoid?"

"If you see them, you will know," the dwarf countered. "They will be the only living things down here."

"They?" the Mate probed. "So, there is more than one?"

"Yes, thousands from what legend says," Hayt sighed, seeing that he wasn't going to get away with keeping the story to himself. "They are daemon, minions of a dark queen. As I have always been told, they were small creatures, perhaps only a foot or two tall. Not intimidating, but they are gifted with dark powers of fire and ice. To simply be touched by one is a death sentence, and they murdered over a third of us before we escaped the tunnels the night they came."

"When was this?" Animir asked, his face drawn into a thoughtful frown.

"As I said, near two hundred years ago," the dwarf confirmed.

"The great war," the elf grunted. "They are indeed a formidable threat."

"Shouldn't they all be dead now?" Amicia observed. "If they have been living down here for centuries, what could they possibly have to eat?"

"Some creatures do not consume as we do," Animir explained. "Creatures of pure magic do not require sustenance."

"Pure magic?" Baldwin asked, his interest in the beasts growing.

"We will avoid them at all cost," Piers informed the boy sternly. Turning to Zaendra, he asked more thoughtfully, "Did you get a good look at the map? Perhaps we should pull it out and choose our path."

"I did," the girl agreed, retrieving it from her husband's bag and unrolling the parchment. "You'll have to hold the edges, as it has a tendency to curl."

Spreading the guide on the floor, the group peered down upon it. Each drawn to different features and parts, a silence fell over them for several minutes as the reality of their situation sank in.

145

"This place is massive," Amicia observed. "How will we ever cross it undetected?" Thinking of her gem, the very idea of hiding them the entire way made her arm ache.

"We will choose wisely," Piers soothed. "Many of the chambers have but one way in and out, so they must be avoided, lest we be trapped."

Leaning over, Zaendra traced the path. "I aligned the map with what I knew of Rhong. This is the exit that will take us out into the marshes of the gnomes," she added, thumping the cave they needed to reach. "It's almost like a maze, as the Mate suggested, but we can make it through," she added, indicating the connecting corridors by sliding her finger along it.

"Perhaps we sleep," Oldrilin suggested. "Leave when we wake to face the darkness." Her clear blue orbs filled with tears, Rey offered her his hand, which she used to climb into his lap.

"We can't rest too long here," Amicia countered, her pulse slowly rising in her ears. "I do not like this place. The longer we have been here, the more intensely I feel a presence."

"I feel it as well, a powerful creature," Meena agreed, glaring at the elf. "You know more of this, I am certain."

Glancing between them, Animir shook his long locks. "Nothing that would help us," he denied. "But I agree it would be unwise to fall asleep within these halls even with a guard. We should gather our things and do our best to be out of here before we are found."

Still staring at the map, Piers seconded, "I have also memorized the path. Zaendra and I will help keep each other on track as we pick our way through. Everyone put on your robes and cover yourselves the best that you can; we will leave in a few minutes."

Moving to comply, a noise tickled Amicia's senses but not a sound she could easily place. *"Lamwen?"* she reached, searching for the first time in days.

Only silence greeted her, adding to her sorrow. Feeling the resonance again, she glanced at Meena to find the woman's dark brown orbs glaring at her. "You hear it, too," she whispered. "What is it?"

"Yes," the wan replied, pressing her lips together as she swallowed. "I'm not sure of the source, but it is here with us. I cannot tell if it senses us, but it may."

"Let's move," Piers commanded, taking the lead with one of their lanterns. "We won't talk unless we have to, so everyone stay close and keep an eye out... and whatever you do, do it *quietly*," he instructed, emphasizing the final word with a hiss.

Following the Mate, Rey carried his sword, his hood and sleeves pulled down so that his hands and face were only partially exposed. Ahead of him, he could see the light of the small lamp swaying in rhythm with the older man's steps. "This is bad," he mumbled as he turned to look back. Behind him, Zaendra and their new dwarf followed, while the others took up their usual places, Meena, Lin, Ami, Bally and Animir at the rear, also carrying a light for them. "I don't like this," he grumbled to himself, a cold settling over him despite the work of walking.

A moment of clarity coming to her as they slunk along in the shadows, Amicia reached out to Piers. *"Do you think these daemons might fear the stone?"*

"I doubt they are like the goblins," he replied.

"But what if they are?"

"I don't intend to see any, so we won't ever find out," he clipped back at her, scowling to himself as they moved.

"Well, how long will it take to make it to the other side?"

"How should I know?"

"You must have some idea!" she insisted.

"Ami, please be quiet," he snapped. *"I must focus on the path."*

Her lip taking on a heavy pout, the girl left him alone, but not without a bit of resentment. *After all, we might need to know these things. "Just tell me how long... Guess."* she tried one last time.

"An hour," he sighed. *"If we keep up this pace, it will take us an hour."*

Given a quantity to contemplate, the girl resisted the urge to annoy him further. *An hour is good,* she thought to herself. *Not the fastest but not hours or days, either.*

The corridors remarkably similar to Rhong, she considered how long the dwarves might have occupied the city. Thinking of the story of the great oracle, Edeill had said they were given the mountain to share with the elves. *At the beginning of time.* Or after they were created. *A long time ago, either way.*

But the elves plotted how to steal the mountain for themselves. That's what the wolf had said. *Could the elves have something to do with the daemons?* She shivered violently at the thought of it. Her thoughts raced in circles as they wound their way through, keeping her mind occupied and holding out the fear.

The minutes ticking by, they had covered over half the distance when they arrived at a huge room with a ceiling that towered above them. Pausing his step, the Mate allowed the others to catch up. "Dwarves and their damned great halls," he muttered, observing the layers of balconies that lined the walls.

Each of these walkways were fed by tunnels, similar to that he had observed in Rhong. Scooting up beside him, Zaendra sighed, "This is the scariest part."

"Aye, and the deepest within the mountain," Piers agreed. "Once we clear this, we will be very close to the exit and perhaps a bit safer." Turning to Rey, he observed the pouch, ready on his chest. "You better take on your passenger, son. We'll be running so that we cross this room as quickly as we can."

Her eyes searching the darkness, Amicia could still hear, or rather feel, the sounds around her. Her mind drawn to their escape the night before, she sighed, "At least I don't have to hide us all the way."

"I honestly wish that you could," Piers countered, also peering into the shadows. "Everyone ready? We will quicken the pace, running if we are able. There should be little or no debris on this path, and it is a straight shot to the door on the far end; the one we need to take to make the correct section of tunnels beyond."

"Let us hurry," Animir agreed, holding his bow tightly as he waited.

The siren securely against his chest, Rey announced, "We're ready, Mate. Lead the way."

"Stay close, everyone," Piers repeated the command. Turning on his heel, he walked quickly. Glancing behind to see that everyone indeed kept up, he quickened the pace, falling into a light jog. Holding the lamp in his left hand and sword in the right, the light bounced around ahead of them, illuminating the dust covered path made of hard stone rather than the gravel of Rhong.

Nothing moved in the grey areas that fell to the sides, where the light penetrated but was not strong enough to provide full view. His eyes scanning, the Mate's spirits lifted at the thought of their reaching the other side unscathed. They had almost made it , and the doorway they must take loomed ahead when a scream behind him stopped him dead in his tracks.

TWENTY

Creatures of Darkness

FOLLOWING THE OTHERS, Bally lagged behind, hanging beside Animir. At the moment, he wished the two of them had established that telepathic link that Amicia seemed able to share. *It sure would be convenient,* he mused, having a hard time remaining quiet about all that they observed as they passed through the forgotten city.

His mind wandering, he first considered what the miniature daemons might look like. *Hayt said they were fire and ice; I wonder if he meant that literally.* Picturing a small animal, perhaps like a cat or a dog walking on its hind legs, he imagined it bursting into flames. Catching a giggle from the prospect, he barked a small laugh.

Snapping to attention, he noticed he had continued to lag farther behind, and Animir was eight to ten yards ahead of him. "Hey –" he almost shouted, catching himself at the first syllable. *That was close.* His boots clicking louder as he ran to catch up, he panted. *Need to watch yourself here, Bally.*

Feeling a stinging pain, perhaps a bite, on his right leg, a thousand shards of glass pierced his skin. Screaming, Baldwin stopped, shaking his appendage wildly to remove the creature. Remembering his axe, he chopped at it with his blade. The hardened steal sliced the tiny being easily, and it squealed and landed on the floor, seeming to melt into a pile of black goo as its cry echoed through the wide hall. Falling to his knees, he breathed heavily, his chest tight.

Reaching him, the group formed a ring, staring into the darkness for signs of any others.

149

"You fool!" Piers bellowed. "What were you thinking?"

"I didn't see it," the boy stammered, leaning back against his stiff arms as he sat on the stone floor. His wound stretched out before him, the Mate pulled at the material, cutting it with his sword to expose the area up to his knee. "It bit me before I knew it was there," Bally finished meekly.

"Do not touch it," Hayt warned. Glaring at the boy, he added, "He will die. There is no recourse for this."

"Die!" Amicia screamed before she was shushed by the others, kneeling on his left side. "He cannot die."

"I assure you he can and he will," the dwarf insisted emphatically. "Not to sound callous, but we should leave him and go."

"How long?" Piers asked, thinking if they could reach the surface with him. "Minutes... hours. I have no way of knowing," Hayt growled. "I only know the poison within him will spread, and any who touch it will also be at risk."

Staring into their leader's clear brown orbs, Amicia swore, "I can save him. I am certain." Reaching for the hamar gem, she pulled it from her pocket. Folding the fingers of her right hand around it, it glowed brightly between them as she placed her left flat against his chest. Inhaling deeply, she closed her eyes. *This has to work. Please, Bally, don't leave us!*

"We do not have time for this," Meena hissed, indicating the door on the far end.

"I don't see anything," Rey observed, holding the siren firmly against his chest, as if the pack in which she rode were not enough.

"Nor do I," the older woman whispered, "but I hear them. They are gathering out of sight I am sure of it. When they come, we will be swarmed with no chance to fight back."

"Ami, give me the stone," Animir commanded, shoving Piers aside and taking his place.

"What? Why?" she gasped, her eyes fluttering as she panted. Glaring at the markings, Bally's condition appeared unchanged.

"Whatever magic you possess, you cannot change this," Hayt warned, fidgeting where he stood and ready to run.

The conversation chaotic, Animir pushed. "My ancestors sent the daemon. The queen is a dark elf, one of renowned magic. Amicia, please; give me the hamar gem that I may try to imprison her within it."

In the doorway on the far end, a tall, slender creature entered. Standing in the arch, it wore black, like a gown, from head to toe, it's hair the red of burning embers. Holding its arms above its head, its fingers splayed as it screamed. Upon the loud shriek, the area around her feet bubbled with life as the daemons poured in and surrounded their queen.

"We must go, now!" Meena cried.

His hand landing on her arm, Animir held the girl firmly, tearing the gem from her grasp. "You must flee, my queen. Take her, Mate. She is the one who must see the light of another day."

Pulling himself up, Baldwin used the handle of his weapon to stand. Limping towards the exit they had all but cleared, he joined his best friend's plea. "You guys get out of here. Me and Animir will hold them off as long as we can."

"You can't fight," Zaendra challenged. "You are injured."

Catching his bride, Hayt moaned, "We cannot save him, love. They are coming, and we must flee." The pack of daemons had already crossed half the distance between them while they argued.

Seeing no other choice, Piers seized the blonde, tossing her over his shoulder as if she were one of the packs of milled grain she had hidden behind on his ship. "Bring her bag and follow," he shouted, not waiting to see who would keep up and who would be left to the darkness.

Adding the girl's bag to her back, Meena gripped her staff firmly as she followed her husband. Rey close behind, the dwarf and nymph also followed. When they cleared the door, Piers paused to see that the two who would remain behind had turned and faced the oncoming rush.

"Goodbye, my friends," he whispered, holding the lantern up before him as he ran into the next tunnel, Amicia still squirming against him.

Screams and howls echoed through the halls, and Amicia joined in the chant. "Piers, stop! Please! We must help them," she sobbed. "We cannot leave them behind." When he failed to respond, she tried another. *"Animir! Do you hear me?"*

"I hear you," came a weak reply.

"Oh, God," she sobbed.

"Do not cry for me, my queen. This is a fitting end, one I am proud to own."

"No!" she bellowed aloud, fighting to free herself, to no avail.

Pausing his step, the Mate lifted the light so that it shone farther ahead. "We are not alone," he warned.

Gripping her spear, Zaendra's blood boiled. "We will destroy them!"

"Do not let them touch you!" Hayt warned.

"I will not, dear husband," Zae seethed, glancing at Meena next to her.

"Get Lin and Ami to safety," she suggested, "while the three of us take on the fight."

"Agreed," the wan nodded. "We may not be strong enough to defeat them, but we can hold them off while you carry your burdens from this dark place."

"We are almost there," Piers agreed. "Stay close and do not lose your way."

"I know the way," Zaendra challenged, taking the lead. Out of the abyss, a small form scurried towards her. Stabbing at it with a downward thrust, Zae sliced the creature in half. Falling limply to the floor, the daemon dissolved into a pile of dark earth, and the girl giggled with morbid delight as they pushed on, dismembering any that found their way out of hiding to attack them.

At the back of the group, more came at them, but Meena and Hayt were equally skilled with their weapons. Over and over, the challenge came as they fought their way through the rubble, and time and again the tiny bodies parted and fell into small piles of dust.

"There are so many!" Rey cried, swinging his sword at a few that made it past the girl in front.

"We must hurry," Piers urged. "We cannot fight them off much longer."

Ahead of them, the final corridor loomed. Its angle steep, it led directly to a small cave, where the marshlands would greet them once they found their way clear.

"Put me down!" Amicia screamed, resorting to thrashing when she was able.

"Ami, stop!" Reynard fumed. "You only slow our escape!"

"We left them," she cried, no longer able to reach the elf. "We left them!"

"We had to, love," Piers soothed as they reached the incline. In the narrow space, the solid walls would protect them. "Prevent them from running up behind," he ordered, their progress slowed by the condition of the trail. "As long as we do, and if the cave ahead is clear, we will make it."

Crying with every step, Amicia refused to give in. Her heart broken, she feared the future without her dearest friends more than any creatures of the darkness. "Please, take me back," she sobbed again and again.

The minutes ticking by as they stumbled forward, exhaustion pulled at their legs, bringing their momentum down to a crawl. "Keep going," Piers urged. "We can't have much farther."

Moments after he spoke, the earth flattened before them. "We made it to the cave!" Zaendra sang, pivoting to look around at the bare walls. "I don't think they come in here," she observed, based on its condition.

"They do not come to the surface," Hayt agreed. "They are creatures of the darkness and cannot survive in the sunlight."

"I should have used the gem against them," Amicia fumed as the bright light blinded them for a moment.

Placing her feet upon the ground, Piers maintained his hold on her arm, squeezing it when she tried to pull away. "You can't go back, love," he soothed. Catching her with his free appendage, he hugged her against his broad chest as she sobbed.

Meeting the gaze of his wife, he continued, "Is everyone whole? No bites or scratches?" The group had spread out, sitting on the large flat stones that flanked the mouth of the cave to rest and inspect each other for wounds.

"I am fine," Meena gasped, out of breath after their climb. Bending over at the waist, her long hair hung down as she huffed, wafting air onto her exposed neck.

"We are, as well," Hayt supplied, having checked himself and his bride thoroughly.

Pulling Amicia with him, the Mate led them away from the cave. "We should put some distance between us and the entrance in case she decides to run back in."

"She wouldn't do that," Rey countered, recovering as his pulse slowed. "She isn't stupid."

"No, but she's suffered a great loss," the older man explained. "Her mind is clouded, and we must look out for her."

Ahead of them, dense woods greeted them, as no path was easy to discern. The ground covered in grass, moss, and other foliage, it squished with moisture as they marched.

"This is the muddiest place I have ever seen," Reynard observed with a brief laugh, looking around to share it with his best friend. Fighting the overwhelming sorrow, his face scrunched. Unable to breathe, the grief was too much. "Oh God, Bally is gone!" The tears overtook him, and he dropped to his knees, cradling the siren as he wept.

His broken state contagious, they made it no further, their bodies littering the ground as they rolled on the moist earth and mourned.

TWENTY-ONE

Ancient Betrayal

ANIMIR AND BALDWIN stood shoulder to shoulder, blocking the exit their friends had taken. "I don't think we can hold them off for long," the younger observed. "I'm hurting pretty bad."

"We must provide them all the time we can," the elf replied, noting the piles of debris that cluttered the space around them. Using a sweeping motion, the gem glowed brightly as he gathered the material with massive force, shifting it to cover the hole in the wall only seconds before the wave of daemons crashed over them.

Swinging his axe wildly, Bally screamed, catching a few and turning them to dust. Likewise, Animir used his blade, but in the distance, he could see the queen of darkness sauntering towards them. Holding up the stone, he adjusted his grip, waiting for her to draw near. When he could wait no longer, he produced a powerful blast that knocked her forces back, converting a multitude of them simultaneously and rendering them inert.

"You come for us," Animir called when she seemed unaffected by his blow, "but I know who you are!"

"Who I am?" she cackled, the deep lines in her face visible when she stood before them. An ancient creature, her voice rasped, "Who do you think I am, elf?"

"Kedoria, queen of the darkness," he spat confidently. "Galiodien sent you here at the start of the great war; an ancient betrayal of the kingdom of Eriden. He thought he could eliminate the dwarves with you, his evil weapon, but he

155

was wrong. They escaped and somehow have locked you out of their tunnels and caves."

Glaring at him, her eyes glowed as embers. "Your knowing will not save you," she hissed.

"Save me?" he laughed in her face. "I am your master, dark elf!" He held up the hamar gem to demonstrate his power. "You will leave us, or you will die."

"I do not walk among the living," she howled, her hair rustling as the power swirled around her. "You cannot destroy me!"

"No, I cannot, but I can remove you," he challenged, raising both hands with the glowing stone in one and his sword in the other.

"I grow tired, my friend," Bally interrupted, overcome with fatigue. He had been taking swipes at the trickle of daemons who insisted on coming forth while his friend dealt with their mistress. Sinking to his knees, he added, "I believe this is the end."

"Baldwin!" Animir snapped, his eyes twitching between the old woman and the boy he had grown to love. "I wish there were something I could do," he breathed, wondering briefly if the witch before him could remove the poison.

As if she had read his thoughts, a twisted grin formed on her wrinkled lips. "You will watch him die, elf. I do not possess the power nor the inclination to change his fate."

"And so it shall be," Animir sighed. "You have been a great friend, Baldwin Carter. I am pleased that I have known you."

Raising her aged fingers, Kedoria rocked her nemesis with a wave of energy, knocking him a step back. Holding the stone firmly, he resisted, producing a shield of light that held her away from them.

"Try again, wench," he taunted, his eyes narrowed as he studied her.

"You are stronger than you appear," she observed. "How is it you travel with such a ragged lot?"

"This ragged lot," he laughed back at her, then growled, "we are friends on a great quest. We deliver the destroyer to Adiarwen, that the prophecy shall be fulfilled."

"The girl," Kedoria laughed. "She does not yet know who she is. If she did, she would have faced me."

"Yes, but she will soon learn. There is still time for sweet Amicia to turn the tide," the elf professed.

"Ami?" Bally stammered. His vision blurred as he glared up at the warrior next to him. "Ami is the destroyer?" The words brought a brief smile as he realized the importance of their journey, one he had been a part of. In that moment, he knew his friend must escape and help finish what they had begun so long ago when they crashed upon the shores of Eriden.

His heart racing, his fingers had gone numb and he could no longer swing his axe. Thinking of Piers and the care he had put into forging it, he realized the group would still have need of it, even if he were not the one to wield it.

Forcing his legs to stand, he slipped the handle into a loop on the elf's pack, so the axe hung off the back of his gear. Collapsing to his knees once more, a calm settled over him. "Amicia must be protected."

"Yes, her rank outweighs us all. She is a great dragon, Bally. Queen of Eriden, but she is not yet aware of her destiny," his friend explained. "She is the reason I have come to stand against my people."

"And she is the reason you cannot remain here with me. Animir," Baldwin said faintly. "You must go. Get out of here and leave me to the darkness."

"I can't," Animir insisted, using all his strength to hold the queen of daemons at bay.

"Yes, you can," the boy faltered, his voice weak as his chest ached more with each breath. "We have shared many adventures, but yours has not yet ended. Do what you must to return to the others, and do not let my death be in vain."

"Bally –"

"Don't. Go now. Find Amicia and see that she makes it… that she one day does sit upon her throne."

Laughing wildly, the dark elf slurred, "You will both die here, mortal."

"Goodbye my friend," Animir whispered, creating a distraction to blind the queen with a blast from the gem. In an instant, he performed a transposition, passing through the barrier he had formed and materializing on the other side. Not pausing, he ran through the tunnels the others had traversed only minutes before.

His hand holding the stone up for light, he could see piles of fresh daemon dust, which brought a brief smile to his lips. *They made it. I know they did.* As a few of the vile creatures leapt at him, he added their remains to those that littered the hallway, each one lifting his spirits in a morose fashion.

Arriving at the base of the final tunnel, Animir heard Kedoria scream from behind. Looking up the steep incline, he knew his pace would be slowed. Seeing the soft earth at the entrance, an idea sprang into his mind.

Kneeling, he drew a circle upon the ground. Adding runes for north, south, east, and west, he finished it with other symbols between those, so that the charm was complete. Standing in the center, he gripped the gem as it hung by his side, waiting for the dark elf to stand before him.

"You shall not escape me!" she shrieked when she had closed the distance between them.

"No," he agreed, "but my friends have made it to the surface, and you will not follow. You have lost, crone."

Drawing near, she examined the ring drawn in the dirt, his feet firmly planted in the center of it. Pacing, she seethed, "What trickery is this?"

"None," he replied calmly, his poise a thorn he used to prickle her, keeping her on edge. "Have you not seen it before?"

"A protective charm," she agreed. "Very old magic. You are from a line of magical elves," she observed. "Where is your family gem?"

"I traded it away," he confessed. "I was banished from using my power for many years. It was only after I joined the company of mortals that I regained my strength."

Raising her eyes, she glared at him, her gaze narrowed into thin slits, "And you think this makes you a match for me?"

"I am a match for you because I was made to be," he alleged. "We are each born to our fate. It is learning to accept it that makes life so difficult."

"You insolent child –"

Animir cut her off before she could hurl the wave of energy at him; the stone before him, he called forth his own curse. In a flash of light, the dark elf disappeared, and the light within the gem was snuffed. Standing in the darkness of the cave, he could see nothing, but the hamar felt heavy in his hand.

"I did it," he breathed, confident he had succeeded. The path to his left, he reached for the wall and shuffled his feet to find the incline of the final tunnel. He had never stood in a blackness so dense, and he could feel it pressing in upon him.

Taking small, deliberate steps, he began the climb to the surface. The air thick, he hoped that he did not come upon the bodies of his friends before he reached the light of the sun, as he still had no proof that they had indeed survived.

Arriving at the cave that covered the exit, Animir paused, sinking to his knees as he breathed deeply. The air fresher, light filtered into the wider space. Lifting the stone, he studied his handiwork, finding that it was now opaque, like an onyx, with the dark elf trapped within.

"I really did it," he grinned. Getting to his feet, he stumbled forward, hoping to find his friends before the sun set. The world would be a sadder place for them that night, but he had survived, and what's more, he had captured the creature of the darkness. "Bally was right; his death was not in vain," he consoled himself as he stepped into the light.

Outside the cavern, Animir looked around at the marshes. The ground moist, it oozed with small shallow pools of water standing in a few spots. The rest of the earth was covered with a lush green film, either of moss or grass. A few hundred feet before him, the trees sprang up, and dense woods hid what lay beyond.

Taking a few steps, his strength hardly enough to walk, he marched, deliberately placing one foot in front of the other. Seeing his friends sprawled across the turf just short of the forest, he resolved to make it to them and did so after a few minutes.

The group still lying on the ground and caught up in their anguish, they did not notice Animir until he was upon them. Collapsing next to them, he only then realized how severely his battle with Kedoria had drained him, and he was completely spent; but he would live.

"Animir!" Ami cried as he lay beside her in the flesh.

"Yes, sweet Amicia; I have made it through the darkness," he confirmed weakly.

"Is Bally with you?" Rey demanded, sitting up with hope in his voice.

"I'm afraid he was not able to walk after only a few minutes," the elf replied, his heavy heart reflected in his somber tone.

Falling over with a heavy thud to lie flat on his back and stare at the sky, he licked at his dry lips and blinked at the blue above as if in disbelief. Still holding the hamar, he lifted it above him and turned his hand, presenting it to the girl. "I'm afraid the gem will never be the same."

Accepting the stone, Amicia stared down at it, her cheeks streaked with fresh tears. "Oh, Bally. What has this cost you, my friend?"

"You have bound the vile creature," Meena observed, pulling herself together and wiping at her damp flesh. "Good. Amicia never needed the stone. Her power comes from within, and one day she will learn to reach it without the aid of such a device."

"Perhaps," Animir agreed. Lifting his chin, he stared into the Mate's pure brown eyes as he stood over him, the red rims attesting to his sorrow. Rolling over, he got to his knees and bowed his head before their leader. "Our dearest friend is gone, but his dying wish was that we complete our quest."

"We will," Piers agreed with a firm nod. "For now, we must devise our shelter, as the sun is already low in the sky. I see that you have brought Bally's axe," he observed, thinking it a peculiar thing to do.

"He hung it on my pack, I assume so that we would still have use of it, but all else that he carried is lost to us." His voice cracked, but he held the pain at bay. "He fought bravely to the very end. Choose where you would like to set our camp, and I will see to the wood for the fire." He caressed Bally's weapon as he spoke, a silent vow that he would carry it always.

Selecting a group of trees that held a clearing of sorts, the group quickly realized staying in the marsh would be unlike any place they had been so far. The wetness of the ground meant they would be cold and damp before morning even with the fire.

Realizing the direness of their situation, Reynard pushed his grief aside. They all were hurting, but they would need clear heads if they were to survive in this strange new land. Taking charge, he announced, "Meena, we will have need of one of your spells. Animir may gather the wood, Piers and Hayt can fetch some wild game, and the girls can see to the gear and fire for the stew while the two of us prepare our shelter." Dumping the contents of his pack, he tossed the empty bag over his shoulder and stood ready for everyone to comply with his suggestions.

"What do you have in mind?" the older woman demanded as she followed him towards the cave they had barely escaped.

"Your power to shrink things will come in quite handy," he mused. Arriving at the large stones that lined the base of the mountain where the mouth of the cave loomed, he tapped one of them with the toe of his boot. "I figure if we take a few of these, we can sit upon them while we eat, and then lay across them for the night."

"That's impressive," she agreed, setting to work on selecting the best for that purpose. Giving one of the large flat specimens a tap with her staff, she shrank it perfectly to the size of a small loaf of bread.

"Not really," he debated, shaking his head as he scooped the stone into the pack. "I just wouldn't relish lying upon the damp ground, not to mention all the bugs and snakes that might like to join me."

Laughing at the image in spite of himself, he thought again of his best friend. *Damn. It will take me a long time to get over him, if I ever do.* Such friends are hard to come by, and Baldwin had been his best ever since he signed upon the Sea Serpent; *ages ago.* Watching Animir gather their supply of wood in the distance, he mused, *Never have I felt such joy and sorrow at the same time.* But at least one had been returned to them, and he would not discount the happiness he felt at regaining their elf.

Digging into the task at hand, Rey refused to linger on the thought for the time being. He knew that losing was a part of living, and he had more pressing things to worry about and other friends to look after. His bag full, they carried the stones to the area they had selected, and he arranged them in a circle around the designated pit for the fire.

"I believe these will work beautifully," Meena observed as she reversed the process, adjusting the size of each so that they would suit one member of their group comfortably. Arranged like the petals of a daisy, the flames burned in the center and the rocks flared out from it. "Now, if I could turn them into feather mattresses, that would be a feat."

Laughing at the idea of it, Rey and Animir exchanged a glance, taking comfort in the presence of the rest. "Having the stones will be a blessing," the elf agreed with a nod, equally impressed with Reynard's ingenuity.

When their tasks had been accomplished, the group languished on their ring of stones.

"This was a brilliant idea," the Mate praised, patting his giant rock affectionately.

"I have my moments," Rey agreed with a small grin. "Are we taking watch tonight, the two of us?"

"Three," Hayt snapped. "The elf should rest, but the rest of us can split the night to thirds." Cutting his eyes over, he glared at the pointy-eared creature through narrowed lids.

"Thank you, but I do not require special treatment," Animir growled, poking at their fire with a long stick and sending sparks into the sky.

"Rubbish," Piers grunted. "You have fought bravely today, trapping the dark elf. You deserve a good night of rest, for certain." Turning to address the other two males still in their group, he added, "I'll take the first watch, and I'll wake Rey for the second; he can trade with you for the last, Hayt."

Glaring at them, Animir didn't bother to argue. Their group had become set in their ways of looking out for one another, and the dwarf had been accepted among them. Inhaling deeply, he nodded, unwilling to disrupt their raw emotions by insisting any different.

TWENTY-TWO

The Gnomes of Falconmarsh

THICK FOG HUNG over them when the group awoke the following morning. Lying beneath it, flat on her back, the hard stone held her form rigid beneath the white cloud. "Anyone else awake?" Amicia asked softly, not wishing to be a nuisance.

"Aye," Piers replied. "Fine weather we're having," he observed with a laugh.

Turning her head, as he lay on the stone to her left, Ami could see the faintest of outlines. "Indeed," she giggled, then sighed. "My rock kept me dry, but it's hard on the bones," she complained playfully as she shifted her gaze to the other side.

Rey on the stone to her right, he had been watching her through the haze for some time. "You would have preferred the turf?" he queried.

"Not at all," she replied, sitting up and stretching to remove the stiffness from her limbs.

In the center of their camp, Animir piled fresh wood and stirred their fire. "I assume we will have left over stew for breakfast."

A loud pop sounded outside their ring and everyone froze to listen intently.

"I don't think we are alone," Meena whispered. Rising slowly, she stood, then squatted between her and Zaendra's stones. Her fingers curling around her staff, she clutched it, waiting for the attack to come. When it did not, she called loudly, "Who watches us?"

"Pfft," Rey laughed, getting to his feet, "do you really expect them to respond?" The fog thick, he couldn't see the girl next to him clearly, much less what lay beyond their clearing. "I doubt they can see any more than we can."

Also rising, Piers joined the banter, "Easy, now. We don't want to start anything with the locals." Recalling their small friend from the northern woods, he seconded his wife's request, "We are here to visit the gnomes. Would there be any willing to speak with us, as this is their lands?"

More twigs cracked, but the feet that broke them retreated rather than move into their camp.

"I think you scared them away," Amicia sighed, thinking of her merdoe. Pulling it from between her breasts, she squeezed it, calling to the unseen creatures. *"We mean you no harm. Please, come and speak with us."*

"And who is us?" a small voice replied.

Ami smiled at her success. *"I'm Amicia Spicer, mortal of the rim. We have come on a quest and seek the company of gnomes. Have we reached Falconmarsh?"*

"You have reached Falconmarsh," the voice announced aloud, stepping into the ring. Holding up his hands, he warmed them at their fire, giving Animir a firm nod as he did so. "Elf."

"Gnome," came his stiff reply. Turning to study the girl, Animir quipped, "Making friends without us?"

"Not in so many words," she squirmed, pushing her blanket off so she could stand. "I reached out and he replied."

Eyeing the group, the small creature appeared to be assessing their intentions, as well as the dynamic of their party. "You are in charge?" he asked of the girl.

"Not... exactly," she sputtered, folding her cover and placing it at the head of her makeshift bed. Pulling her brush from her pack, she ran it through her golden locks to make herself presentable. "Piers, I believe it's your turn."

"My turn," he laughed, calmly watching the encounter. "You seem to be doing all right with it."

"But I'm not in charge here," she fussed in return.

The gnome small, even more so than the mermaid, he cut his beady dark eyes around the circle, taking each of them in. Arriving at Oldrilin, he demanded, "How did you come by these parts? We seldom have visitors from other realms, much less serpents of the sea."

"Serpents?" Rey asked in a loud whisper as he stared at his small friend, unsure if he should be offended at the remark.

"We came through Asomanee, by way of Rhong," Meena explained, indicating Hayt with an open palm.

"And what use have you for gnomes?" he asked, turning to glare at the girl who had not behaved as a mortal of the rim. His eyes fixed upon her, he watched her primp, as if she were trying to hide from him. *"Amicia of the rim,"* he pushed, invading her thoughts and demanding an explanation.

"I prefer not to speak telepathically while others are present," she explained aloud as she secured her braid. Turning to face him, she gave him a small bow. "It is rude."

"Rude," he laughed in return. "You are no mortal of the rim," he slurred. "Explain yourself and be quick about it. I have been sent to assess your presence here, and I am leaning towards asking for a hasty removal."

"Removal," Reynard interceded, "but we just got here! And we fought off daemons to do that." He had been holding his anger, but it pushed at the brim of explosion.

"Please, sir," Amicia tried again. "I have come to this land in search of my past," she explained, kneeling before him to look him in the eye. Noting the pudge in his cheeks, she smiled, "I hope that we can be friends. We have made so many since our arrival here."

"As I see," he agreed with a small nod.

"Yes," she grinned. "If you are here to assess us, then we have a request; we would like to speak to your leader."

Cutting his eyes over at the elf, the gnome grunted, "We do not trust those who travel in the company of elves." Turning his back, he made for the trees.

"Your highness, please," Animir called after him. "I have left the pledge of my kin long behind. These are my friends, and I stand apart from all that my line has imposed upon you."

Pausing, but not turning to face him, the creature inhaled deeply. Sensing his power, the elf stood up straight, spreading his arms as if to welcome the magical search. His eyes wide, he waited for the verdict.

"It has been many moons since you stood within Jerranyth," the gnome claimed.

"Yes," Animir nodded, licking his lips. "Even when I lived among them, I was not whole within the kingdom of Lady Cilithrand. Please, grant us an audience."

Looking around at their pitiful camp, the gnome sighed. "I suppose you will need shelter... food and the like."

"We are capable of tending to ourselves," the Mate bit tartly, finally taking charge. "However, we would like permission to be here."

"Permission," their inspector laughed, pivoting to glare at the girl. "You have our permission. You may use wood from the trees to build a proper shelter. In a few weeks, we will meet with you to discuss your plans for the future."

Seeing the gnome move forward, the way he had come, Piers pushed, "We have not come to impose, nor do we wish to make our residence permanent. The sooner we can speak to your sovereign, the better."

"I am the sovereign," the gnome replied, disappearing into the fog without another word.

"Well that was helpful; not," Rey spat angrily.

"Don't be an ass," Amicia corrected. "They have allowed us to remain, and we should do as they ask. Make a shelter and wait, that is what we do." Turning to Piers, she looked for him to confirm her orders.

Staring at her, the older man felt disinclined to do so, as he strongly agreed with Rey. "We can't wait around here for long," he split the middle.

"And we cannot force them to comply," Meena joined the debate. "Gnomes are standoffish creatures with little use for outsiders."

"Few in Eriden seem to have use of outsiders," Rey bit, his mood still foul.

"What has gotten into you?" Amicia breathed, looking him up and down. "We just lost our friend, we are in a strange land, and we need to give the locals a few days to warm up to us. How hard is that?"

Glaring at her, his chest heaved. "You are right about that; we have lost our friend. The rest, I'm not so sure about. This gnome insulted two of our group members outright, and who knows what he thinks of the rest of us." Lifting an eyebrow at her, "I don't want to stay here, for what it's worth, princess," he mocked.

The fog had been dissipating as they squabbled, and Hayt took the opportunity to speak up. "May I say something?"

"What?" Rey, Ami, and Piers chorused.

"The dwarves and gnomes were once close allies. At least as close as any ever have been to my kind," their newest member explained. "Let's do as they ask, and when they are ready to speak to us, let me do the talking."

Staring at him, her mouth hanging open, Zaendra gasped, "I thought you wanted no part in diplomacy."

Shrugging, her husband replied, "That was different. This isn't so we can line our pockets. We have a quest to fulfill, and I believe I can persuade our small friends to help if you give me the chance."

Studying him, Piers stroked the hairs on his chin. "Your people have been cut off from them for over two centuries. What makes you think they will honor your alliance now?"

"I don't know that they will," Hayt shrugged, "but I know my odds have to be better than those of the elf."

"True," Animir confirmed. "I say we put together a shelter and then let the dwarf try."

"Aye," Rey grunted, ruefully. "I might as well agree, as I can see none of you are willing to take my side." Cutting his eyes over at Ami, he glared at her, disappointed that she had not.

"I'm sorry, love," she said softly. "We are only a few, and fighting them or forcing our way is unlikely to help, that's all."

"Then we are agreed," Piers announced, ending the dispute. "We need to locate a place for the shelter and decide upon its construction. I think we should keep it small and simple, as in the end we really don't intend to be here very long."

A week later, the group had constructed a crude camp at the edge of the marshes where they had come out of the mountain; four shelters that faced a central fire. Each consisted of a roof made of grass and moss, with the opening being about four feet in height, which covered a patch of ground about six by six feet square as it cascaded to meet the earth in a single slant.

Meena and Piers took the one on the south side, while Hayt and Zae held the "room" on the north side of the fire. Animir and Rey shared the east and Amicia and Oldrilin the west. Placing four large stones in front of their structures, the fire heated them, radiating warmth into their dwellings throughout the night.

Inside, they used the bark of trees to line the ground, providing some protection from the damp conditions but allowing for a bit more comfort than their stone beds. Admiring their work when the chore had been completed, Amicia felt a great deal of satisfaction in their ability to adapt.

"I believe we have done well for ourselves," she observed as they gathered for their evening meal. Each pair sitting on the stones in front of their shelter, she smiled down at Lin. "Maybe the gnome lord will see us soon and we won't have to stay here long."

"Oh, Amicia," the siren laughed, as if her words were a joke. "Gnomes are eccentric creatures."

"Let me guess," Rey interrupted, "friends to no one."

Coughing a spastic laugh, Piers agreed, "We've heard that before. Pretty much about every realm in Eriden."

"Well, we each value our privacy," Meena defended.

"Yes, we do," their visitor announced himself as he came out of the shadows, entering their camp from the forest side. "We wanted a few days to study you; we hope you don't mind."

"And I suppose we have passed inspection," Piers growled, turning his spoon in his hand as he returned the glare.

"You have," the gnome agreed with a grin. "My name is Thirac, head of the elders."

"Elders," Animir observed with a grin. Nodding at Hayt, he indicated that the dwarf should take over their introductions, as planned.

Standing, the dwarf silently agreed. "Thirac, I am Hayt, heir to the throne of Rhong."

"Previous heir," Thirac corrected bluntly.

"Yes, of course," Hayt stammered, rubbing his full belly with his palms as he adjusted his stance. Suspicious, he growled, "You know of our escape from Rhong?"

"It took me a few days to decipher it, but I believe I have worked it out," the gnome replied evenly.

"You have an orb," Meena speculated.

"As do you," the gnome replied, bowing to her. "Why is it a surprise? Because the dwarves have shunned their ancestral rights?"

"If it is that small gold globe you are speaking of, we have shunned nothing," the dwarf spat. "My uncle holds ours for safe keeping."

"Ah, but he declines to use it," Thirac chuckled. "He fears it, I think, from what I have seen."

"Yes, after our ancestors were forced from Asomanee, the use of all magic was rejected in our new caves," Hayt agreed, feeling at a disadvantage. He shifted anxiously, feeling the weight of their scrutiny. "We believed it was the use of such trinkets that allowed the darkness to fall upon us. We used the last of our magic to barricade them out, and it has been forbidden to practice since."

"It was not your fault," Animir input quietly. The others turned to face him, his tone requiring further explanation. Cutting his doleful gaze over at his new friend, he sighed. "The elf king sent Kedoria into your caves to destroy you."

"You confess this openly?" Hayt growled.

"What fault is it of mine? It happened over a century before I was born,"

Animir defended. "I merely wish to point out that those dwarves of magical decent gave up their gifts without cause."

"Correct," Thirac chimed. "And now you see why we have little trust for those who share our kingdom."

"We do see," Amicia sighed. "But hopefully your magic orb has shown you our intent is not to harm."

Turning his attention to her, the gnome studied her, his eyes looking her up and down. The pause long enough to grow uncomfortable, the Mate cleared his throat but remained silent.

Cutting the glare over to him, Thirac nodded. "We will leave you to your dinner. We will hold a feast for you in Falconmarsh in three days. Come at sunset, and we will formally welcome you to the marsh at the ceremony."

"How will we find it?" Rey asked in surprise as their visitor turned to go.

"The princess knows the way," the gnome called over his shoulder before he disappeared into the woods.

Curling her tongue, Amicia sighed, "I do wish people would stop calling me that. It's like I have it branded on my forehead or something."

A round of glances passed through the group, then Piers announced, "Well, now that we have three more days to kill, I have a proposition."

"What sort of proposition?" Meena asked with a grin, recalling the day the two of them met.

"Haha," the Mate coughed a laugh, growling at her playfully before he quipped, "Not that kind. I've been thinking about Bally. It almost feels as if he is still with us, and I was wondering if we should hold some sort of ceremony for him."

"You mean a funeral?" Amicia gasped. "His body is lost in the great hall of Asomanee."

"'Tis true," Piers agreed with a firm nod, "but that does not mean we cannot erect a memorial or give him a proper farewell. I think he deserves to be remembered."

"He will never be forgotten," Reynard bit pointedly.

"No, of course not," the first mate countered. "I'm not implying that he would or could be. I am simply suggesting that we give him... a grave. A place that we can visit when we wish to think of him."

"I do not see the point of this," Animir agreed with Rey. "What good could carving a stone bring?"

"It is our tradition," Amicia sighed, thinking of the cemetery where her adoptive parents had been lain. "Like Abolia," she observed. "They buried their dead with stone markers as well. Do others not follow this custom?"

Blinking her wide green eyes, it occurred to her that they had not seen such a place anywhere else in Eriden.

"No, we do not," Meena replied sadly. "Bodies are summarily burned throughout Eriden, not planted beneath the ground."

"Oh," Piers grunted, the image gruesome and nowhere near what he had in mind when he mentioned a memorial. "Well, it was just a thought." Folding his hands, his gut twisted in anguish that he had unintentionally reopened their wounds.

"I think it's a good idea," Amicia agreed. "He was a mortal of the rim, after all, not of Eriden. He deserves to have a proper funeral." Smiling weakly at the Mate, she added, "Don't you think so, Rey?"

Swallowing hard, the man across from her cast an uneasy glance around the ring of faces. "I suppose that we could," he speculated, not ready to admit his friend would never return.

"A good idea," Oldrilin sang, her happy voice in sharp contrast to the emotional state of the others. "Bally be remembered by stone."

"Aye," Piers nodded. "I'll set to work carving it in the morning, and you may choose where we will set it," he suggested, indicating Rey with an open palm.

"You already have the headstone?" Rey clipped in surprise, bordering on anger.

"Well, yes, you could say that," the Mate sighed, running his fingers through his hair. "I found it a few days ago, while we were working on the camp. That's what gave me the idea."

"It's a good idea," Amicia reassured, cutting Rey a silent plea to end the debate. "Tomorrow we will make the arrangements, and on the second day, we will hold the ceremony."

"And on the third, we meet with the gnomes. Perfect," Rey growled, getting to his feet and leaving the group as he wandered off into the darkness.

TWENTY-THREE

Written in Stone

WALKING THROUGH THE WOODS, Amicia and Rey searched for the place Baldwin's memorial would be placed. It would stand for all time, after all, and therefore the location must be precise. Reaching a small divide, they glanced at each other, as if to question their direction.

"I'll go this way," said the girl.

"Aye," Reynard agreed, sticking to their previous path. They had explored a great deal of the area in the few days they had been there, and he felt she would be in no danger going alone. Entering a clearing, a circle of trees opened up before him as it had the time the group met the southern pack.

"This is different," Rey observed to himself, stepping further into the exposed space. Turning in a slow circle, he admired the height of the massive trunks. "This is very old; almost sacred," he added more confidently. "Ami, come! I wish to show you what I've found!"

Not far, the girl smiled at his enthusiasm. He had taken Baldwin's death the hardest of all of them, she felt certain, and he had yet to speak of his friend in the past tense; as if he had not accepted that he was gone. *Perhaps this day will help him say goodbye,* she mused as she closed the distance between them.

Entering the ring, Ami gasped, "Oh, Rey. This place is enchanted."

"Literally?" he frowned.

"I think so," she breathed, joining him in the center and turning exactly as he had, staring up at the branches overhead. "It's perfect."

171

"Then this is where our friend's memorial will stand."

"Yes, let's go tell the others. We should mark the trail that we may find it easily, as well," she suggested.

Holding up Bally's axe, he grinned, "Already planned to."

Knocking small bits of bark from the trees as they moved, the pair arrived at the clearing before the cave easily, then sauntered over to their new and improved camp. There, behind the slanted structure closest to the path to Asomanee, Piers knelt on the ground. A chisel and hammer in his hand, he gouged at the rock, removing bits to form the words he felt in his heart.

Staring at them, tears formed in Rey's eyes. "We've found the location," he croaked.

"Good. I'll be done here shortly, and we can gather," the Mate spat, having already cried his lot.

Glancing at the dark entrance to the cave, Rey sighed, "Will the daemons remain there without their queen?"

"I don't know," Amicia replied with a shake of her blond locks. "I'm sure none of us wishes to return and find out." Swallowing, she thought of Baldwin's remains lying on the floor of the great hall. *Even for him, we shall not go back,* she sighed inwardly.

Turning to her shanty, she knelt and crawled inside. She shared hers with Oldrilin, so she had more room than any of the others, she supposed, but making the transition had been difficult. She was spoiled by the cabin, she felt certain.

Running her fingers over her blanket, she recalled that it had been Baldwin who helped her pack it the night they fled Jerranyth. He had always been there, in his little brother sort of way. Even now, she could almost hear his chatter as he would have made random observations about the marshes, where they now resided.

Brushing out her hair, the sound of hammering against the stone mixed with her memories and brought on her sorrow. *Even Piers has wept,* she mused. Tying the locks back with a ribbon that pressed tight against her head but allowed the back to hang free, she knew there would be plenty of tears to go around soon enough.

Standing, she hung her blanket over the front of her quarters so she could change. She had sustained a tear in the shirt during their escape from Rhong, but Meena had stitched it for her. The set had been laundered to dry overnight, and she squeezed at the fresh firmness of the material, smiling at the thoughtfulness of the older woman. *We will see each other through.*

Getting dressed in a place where she could not stand frustrated her, especially in her raw emotional state; but under the circumstances, there was little she could do. The clothing she would wear once belonged to Bally, and her memories churned as she fought to put them on; the hold, the Mate's quarters, and the night the ship sank. *Oh, Bally.*

Dressed and presentable, she removed the blanket, folding it and laying it across her bed. Her movements slow and deliberate, she forced herself to the next step as each was completed.

"You look lovely," Rey praised as she did so.

"Thanks," she replied, not looking at him. She had been thinking of him a great deal over the last few days, and she recalled the promise she had made to herself in the prison of Rhong. *It feels odd now, with Baldwin gone;* more urgent somehow, even more than it had when only the dragon had been lost. *He won't ask, though,* she surmised. She had made it clear enough, and he would respect her wishes. *When the time comes, I will have to convince him to do so.*

Turning, she managed a weak smile. "Is the stone ready? You seem to have stopped your clanging," she said to Piers.

"Aye," he nodded, brushing his hand over the letters. "Meena will shrink it, and I will haul it to the location you have selected."

"I'm pleased to help," his wife chuckled, bringing forth her staff and completing the task. Glancing around at their expanding camp, they had shrunk and brought nearly all that they had owned within the cabin the night they fled. If and when they had a permanent place to settle, they would be off to a good start, thanks to her magic.

Wrapping the memorial in his blanket, the Mate realized it was unlikely it could be damaged between there and the circle of trees. Grinning at the stares of the trio, he laughed, "Call me sentimental. Where are the others?"

"We are here," Animir informed him, as the remaining four of their group had been hovering close by, waiting for their march into the woods.

"Aye, let's go then," Piers directed, nodding at Rey. "Please, lead the way."

"I marked the path," the younger man informed him, strolling along the front of the tree line. Arriving at the first marker, he pointed, "We will be able to visit the memorial whenever we like."

"Well done," Hayt praised, thinking of the stone statues that adorn the front of Rhong. "My people are carvers as well and build sculptures of our fallen kings. Somewhere, on this side of the mountain, stands a grand collection of my ancestors."

Smiling at the thought of it, Amicia asked, "Would you hunt for it?"

"Perhaps," he agreed as they filed onto the narrow path. "If we remain here long enough, I may do so."

The trees of the swamp grew close together, with thick foliage in between; one of the reasons the group had opted for the clearing outside of them to build their small shelters. A feeling of wonder settled over them when they arrived at the clearing and the canopy opened above them.

"Tis beautiful," Zaendra observed, her eyes fixed on the blue morning sky. "The perfect resting place for our young friend."

Rey winced, keenly aware that Bally's body would never rest there, or anywhere for that matter. Pursing his lips, he fought the urge to point out that fact, as the girl had meant nothing by the comment.

Kneeling, Piers opened the cover and positioned the grey stone, then moved so Meena could return it to its correct size. Taking a knee again, the Mate used the cloth to polish his final words to his underling.

TWENTY-FOUR

Baldwin Carter

Brother ~ Son ~ Friend
You will be missed

STARING AT THE INSCRIPTION, none held a dry eye. Even Hayt, who had known him the shortest amount of time, wiped a tear. "He was a good lad. Curious fellow, with his incessant yammering," he recalled. "The meal he sat across from me next to grandmother was torture." He laughed heartily in spite of the glum occasion.

"Aye, the boy could ramble," the Mate agreed. "I remember the first day he came on board the ship. Three of the crew complained," he laughed as well. "A born talker if ever there was one."

"Why brother and son?" Amicia asked. "We knew so little about him. None of the stories he told were true."

"They were all true," Rey countered somberly, his hands folded in front of him so he could hold them still. "They were true because he told them and gave them a spark of life." He sighed, shaking his head, "He was my brother."

"He was my son," Piers added. "We knew what was important, love. Nothing else mattered."

Standing in front of them, the siren opened up and moaned loudly, her song filled with her pain as she mourned. Her tiny body shaking, she carried

175

the others with her, over the edge with her dirge, each wailing and weeping openly.

Wrapping Meena with his arm, Piers offered her comfort, even in the time of his own undoing. As the deluge ebbed, he offered, "Would you like to say something?"

"I can't," she huffed, dabbing at her eyes with a small cloth. "Why should the young be taken so unfairly?"

"We all make this journey some time," Animir observed. "Even those considered to be immortal will one day walk this path."

Amicia sniffed, "Do you think he is in heaven? I mean, we all believe in the afterlife, do we not? In one form or another..."

"I believe that we do," Piers agreed, his voice steady as he dug at his eyes with his thumb. "Of course, it is different from people to people."

"The elves believe it is the love of family and friends that assures our passage into the afterlife," Animir confirmed. "Years of life well lived."

"The winning of battles," Hayt corrected, standing taller.

"In that case, you must not have many kin there," the elf retorted, "as your people have hidden beneath the mountain for eons."

"We fight when the time is right," the dwarf shrugged, glancing at Zae as he added more quietly, "mostly among ourselves."

The confession garnered a fit of giggles from the others, and for a moment, it was as if Bally had never left them. It was just the sort of observation he would be prone to make, and it calmed them somehow, as if he had spoken through their new friend.

"He will live on through each of us," Zaendra agreed. "Even in the dark place, his body will return to the earth, as it should." Reaching for her husband's hand, she held it firmly.

The sky above bright blue, Amicia looked up, recalling the last service she had attended; the one for Arely Spicer. It had been a beautiful day then as well. "He will not be forgotten," she agreed, "and his life was not lived in vain."

Slowly, the group disbanded. Zaendra and Hayt left first, pushing further into the woods in an effort to share a few minutes alone together. Meena and Piers left in another direction, probably for the same reason.

"Would you like a ride back to camp?" Animir offered, noting Lin's shriveled state.

"I believe I can make it," she replied, staring up at him, her blue pools still filled with sadness.

"I will walk with you then," he agreed, "in case you change your mind."

Watching them go, Ami and Rey remained within the circle. They had cried hard with the others, but their tears had not yet been spent. As soon as their eyes met, a fresh wave fell upon them, and he offered her his arms.

Accepting, Amicia sank against his chest, rocked by the depth of his suffering. She had hoped he would face the pain, but she had not been prepared for the magnitude of it. "He's really gone," she sobbed, her face pressed against his white shirt.

"Aye," he sniveled, stroking her hair. "If there had been anything we could have done, we would have," he assured.

"Do you blame yourself?" she asked, surprised by his words, *Or me?* She added mentally.

"There is no blame," he assured, sensing her unspoken question. "Sometimes there is nothing to be done and our end is simply upon us. No reason, no regrets."

"He's in heaven," she stated firmly. "We had a little church, there in Nalen. My parents –" she started, then faltered. Changing her choice of words, she began again. "Gus and Arely took me there often. Not every Sunday, but near enough."

"Aye, we had one as well on the island of my parents' farm." Thinking of the small structure, the doors opened and the image of a wedding sprang into his thoughts. Shaking the dream away, he regretted picturing the happy occasion on the day of his best friend's memorial.

"We will visit there one day," Amicia promised, her sorrow renewed. "We will see your family farm, your little church, and I will be happy to share them with you," she finished, clinging to him as if she would never let him go.

Rocking her back and forth, Rey sighed, feeling his layers of protection being lifted away. If they stayed much longer, his core would be exposed, and he might divulge more than he had intended. "I think we should go," he managed.

"Please, a little longer," she begged, pulling away and looking up at him with her large green eyes.

Unable to resist her, he nodded. "A few more minutes," he quietly agreed, unsure if he could take the battering his heart suffered every moment that they remained.

TWENTY-FIVE

The Right Time

TEARS STREAKING HER FACE, Amicia sighed, "Thank you for staying. I don't really know how to say goodbye. I've lost so many these last few years.".

"I know," Rey groaned, wiping at his own drops of sadness with his right hand. He shoved his left into his pocket, his shoulder drooped as he worked to collect himself. "He was like my annoying little brother, which was funny," he observed with a short spastic laugh. "When I was growing up, that was my job. He turned the tables on me." Sniffing loudly, he confessed, "I wake each morning expecting him to return."

The girl had suspected as much. The breeze catching her loose hair, Amicia peered at him through the strands as they floated across her face. "We will both miss him."

"Aye." Meeting her gaze, he saw the darkness brewing in her clear green orbs. "What's wrong?" he asked sharply, catching something in their depths he couldn't place.

Her lip quivering, she stammered, "I'm so afraid, Rey. I've not mentioned it for some time, but Lamwen has never returned to me."

"The dragon?" he sputtered, his mind turning. "This is an odd time to be worried about him, don't you think?"

"Yes, the dragon," she spat angrily. "He is also someone I have recently lost. I loved him, which I am certain you don't understand. He was as dear a friend as Baldwin Carter, maybe even more so. He protected us, and I shared

179

so many hours and days, months and years with him." Fresh tears on her face, her cheeks flushed.

"It wasn't that long," Rey clipped, a hint of outrage in his voice. How could she bring him up *now*?

"It was for me," she sighed, turning her back on him. "I hardly expect you to appreciate how deeply fond of him I had become."

Pursing his lips, Reynard calmed his tone so as not to offend her further as he probed, "What does it mean to you when you say that you loved him?"

"Exactly that. If he had been a man, I could have seen us as so much more," she confessed, her voice wavering.

His heart pounding against his ribs, Rey clenched his teeth. "And?"

"And, I've been thinking about my future," she sighed, not having planned to have this conversation with him this day but well aware of what she wanted to say. Turning to face him squarely, she demanded, "May I ask you something?"

"You know that you can ask me anything, my love," he breathed, her expression calming him in an instant. Reaching for her, he grasped her arms and squeezed them firmly. "What is it that you need?"

Licking her lips, fear ran through her trembling form. The afternoon breeze suddenly cool against her bare skin, she randomly thought of her sweater still lying on her mat with her quilt. "Is it me or is it chilly this morning?" she stalled.

Smiling at her spirit, he nodded. "A bit. Should we return to the shelter for your sweater?" he asked, tracing her thoughts easily.

"Oh, Rey. You know me so well," she sighed, her fingers catching the buttons on his shirt as she skimmed over the front of it playfully. Clearing her throat, she steadied her nerve. "I've been thinking about my future… and my past. I have squandered chances before, and I do not wish to do so any longer. I know that you have deep feelings for me, but you have been such a gentleman. Near on three years we have known each other, and yet only a few kisses have we ever shared."

"Aye," he agreed, his chest tight at her seeming diversion.

"I feel I have squashed something I should have allowed to bloom."

Staring at her, his hazel orbs swimming, he clarified, "You think it is time I should court you."

Lifting her chin, it dimpled as she croaked, "No, Rey, I do not wish for you to court me. I wish to be married."

"Married!" he squealed, dropping her arms and taking a step back as he gaped at her.

"Yes. I feel like I've been holding things up, and if I had not been such a fool, you would have asked me by now," she confessed, closing the distance he had put between them. In a softer voice, she cooed, "If you ask me, I'll say yes."

Blinking at her, his mind raced, tracing the time he had known her. "And you wish to be my bride, just like that. No courtship, no public dalliances, no formality."

"No formality," she agreed with a small smile. "I didn't come to this decision lightly. I have thought of little else since we arrived in the marshes, perhaps even before we left Rhong. The idea first occurred to me while we were still prisoners there, and I swore to myself if we made it to our freedom, I would take my vow with you; that is if you will have me."

Her lips perfectly turned, Rey's heart melted. "Of course I will have you," he breathed. "How could you think I ever would not?" Seeing the joy wash over her, he hesitated, holding her still at arm's length. "But I must know the reason, Amicia. Is it for love that you will take my name or fear that has persuaded you?"

Her brow creased, the light left her eyes. "Do not ask me such questions, Reynard Daye. I have suffered much upon this journey, more so than you can fathom. Although I am still young, I feel in my heart the age that has come through each trial we have faced. Do you wish to wed or not?"

"You know that I do," he gasped, sweeping her into his arms. "Piers promised me that one day you would be mine, and I have looked forward to it ever since."

"Piers promised," she giggled, warmed by the strength of his embrace.

"Yes, the first day after I awoke in Riran. You had gone to visit the mermaids, and we spoke of you and your love for him. I was so jealous, Amicia. Even now I fear you have only chosen me because he married Meena and your dragon friend would not make a suitable mate."

Blinking back tears, she consoled, "I'm sorry it would appear so. I cannot deny my love for either of them, but when choosing with whom I will spend the rest of my days, there are more things to consider than just my heart."

Relaxing his grip, his gut wrenched. "You do not marry me for love."

"Stop," she laughed, more determined than ever to gain his agreement. "Do not twist my words. I do love you, but I have always known that there was more to choosing a husband than that. Love over time can grow stale, and I must also have a friend and companion as well as the flames of passion."

Stepping back, she gazed up at him, taking in every line of his masculine features. Her fingers trembling, she brushed at his long ringlets that had escaped their binding, which framed his bearded face. "Such a handsome man. Your eyes speak of love when they look upon me."

"Aye."

"Your hands feel of devotion when they have dared to touch me."

"Aye," he nodded.

"Marry me then. Let us face all that lies ahead as one."

"I thought you wanted to know who you were before you gave your pledge," he insisted as a final argument.

"I have learned enough," she said, shaking her head gently. "Enough to know if we don't take the chances we have, they may be lost forever. I wish to take this chance. Say yes, Rey."

"Ami…"

"Say yes, Rey."

"Amicia."

"Say… yes… Rey."

"Aye," he whispered, glaring at her, then hugging her once more with a squeeze that kept her from breathing until he let her go. "I will speak to the Mate and ask him to perform the ceremony. I assume it will be a small gathering; nothing so spectacular as that of Zae and Hayt, or even Piers and Meena for that matter."

"Nothing like them," she agreed with a nod. "Our small group and nothing more." Sliding her fingers into his, she squeezed him. "A private ceremony will be all that we need."

"Then we shall have it," he agreed, finally lowering his lips to press them firmly against hers before releasing her and walking away to search for their leader.

His thoughts churning, the young man oscillated back and forth as he tromped through the marshes, his doubts eating at him from the inside. *She loves you,* one side insisted. *She has no other option,* the other tallied.

"Enough!" he growled aloud, hoping to silence the two halves of himself. Spying the Mate splitting wood with Bally's axe, he walked directly up to him and asked, "Need any help?"

"Aye, you are right on time," Piers laughed, happy for the distraction from his brooding thoughts. The loss of their youngest member had been hard for him, and he had been giving it his best effort to hide the depths of his pain, but the morning's service had left him feeling drained. Dropping the tool, he hoisted the elven bottle he had filled with water to enjoy while he toiled.

Taking up the handle, Rey studied it for a moment, his thoughts drawn to his young friend who was no more. Inhaling deeply, he gave a loud sigh, then placed a log on the stump and split it cleanly with a full swing.

"I have a favor to ask," he began after he had laid waste to a few of the portions of wood.

"Oh?" the Mate grimaced, sitting on the ground and sipping from the vessel of cool liquid.

"Amicia and I wish to be married," Rey informed him in a rush.

"You want to do what?" the Mate asked incredulously, glaring up at him. "Have you lost your mind?"

"No. I am in complete control of my faculties," Rey grunted, glaring at the older man with the axe hanging at his side.

"But Amicia has been adamant that you should not court her. Even during the best of times when we lived in the cabin, she stood against it. Why would you ask her to marry you, especially now?"

"I didn't ask," Rey hesitated, uncomfortable at the first mate's reaction. "We have shared a talk, and she suggested it."

"She suggested it."

"Aye, and you know this is what I've always dreamed of," the younger man admitted in a subdued tone. "Please understand; Ami has offered her hand to me, and I have accepted. Will you marry us or not?"

"Why must I be the one to marry you?"

"Because the captain went down with the ship, remember? That means you take his place and by rights should perform the ceremony."

"Oh, you won't talk me into it that easily," Piers growled, getting to his feet so he could impose his height upon his friend. "I strongly warn against this. You know she is still discovering herself. What if she finds out some horrible thing that you simply can't live with?" Thinking of his promise to Meena not to share what she had surmised about the girl, he hoped it wouldn't come to breaking his word.

"There is no such thing," Rey replied, running his hand over the top of his head and smoothing his long waves of dark hair. "I love her, Mate. There is nothing I could not accept about her."

"I'm not so sure about that," the Mate replied, turning his back as he rubbed at his mouth and beard anxiously. *Fuck*, he swore under his breath. Raising his shoulders as he drew a deep breath, he calmed himself. "This isn't something you can take lightly. Maybe I should speak to her. If you make this vow, it cannot be undone. This is an 'until death' kind of deal, and I would hate to see either of you do something you would regret."

"You said yourself that one day she would be mine! What has happened that you are so set against it?" Rey demanded, the anger seeping into his voice. "Come on, Piers. We're friends, or at least I thought we were!"

"We are friends," the Mate replied, turning to face him squarely. Placing his hand on his shoulder, he gave it a squeeze. "That was near three years ago, son. Much has happened since then. But if you are certain… if both of you are certain, I should say," he paused, swallowing before he finished, "then I would be honored to hear your vows."

"Thank you," Rey breathed, his smile wide when he realized they would be wed. "We will decide on the time, but rest assured it will be soon."

"I leave you to the chopping then," Piers grunted, taking his bottle as he trotted away.

Watching him go, Rey twirled the axe, spinning it in his palms. *She will be mine,* he swore to himself with a wide grin. Cutting his eyes up at the sky, he hoped Bally really had been watching and that he would be there to see the day Amicia became his bride.

TWENTY-SIX

Secrets About Secrets

"I MUST SPEAK WITH YOU," Piers informed his wife without preamble when he arrived at their camp.

"Oh?" she replied, smiling up at him from her mending. "Our clothing has suffered greatly this time around. Fortunately we brought what remained of our sewing supplies and I can –"

"Please, leave it," he commanded, placing his wine bottle on the ground and glancing between Zaendra and Oldrilin. Pulling at her arm, he silently urged her to follow.

Close behind, she trailed him into the woods straight east from their camp. "What is it?" she demanded when they were alone. Arriving at a small opening in the trees, they had put a fair distance between them and the others.

"I'm afraid we have a problem," he replied, wringing his hands anxiously.

"Always," she laughed. "Our lives have been one disaster after another since we met. What is the cause of this latest bit of chaos?"

"Ami and Rey wish to be wed," he supplied, facing her squarely.

"Oh my. That does present a problem."

"Exactly," he clipped, raking his hand through his dark locks and freeing the knot. "I tried to talk him out of it, but he insisted. I didn't divulge anything, and I haven't spoken to her," he finished weakly.

"You thought you would leave that up to me," she sighed.

"What's going on?" Animir interrupted as he and Hayt joined the couple. "Are we sharing secrets away from camp?"

185

"This doesn't concern you," Piers barked, hoping to keep the situation between him and his wife. "Please, leave us be."

"If it concerns the group, it concerns us all," Hayt countered. He had taken a liking to the elf once he got to know him, and had no problem supporting him on this cause.

"They are concerned about Amicia," Zaendra bit tartly as she and Oldrilin also sauntered into the clearing, which had grown crowded with the six of them standing within it.

"Oh, that's just great," the Mate growled, unhappy their private conversation had been overheard.

"Please, dear husband. Let us discuss this situation openly," Meena advised.

"Openly?" he chortled. "Perhaps I should call the happy couple over, then. I'm sure we can squeeze them in," he bit, wafting a hand around for emphasis.

"Happy couple?" Animir observed in surprise. "Have they announced their intentions?"

"Aye," Piers grunted, bobbing his head, "which is a bad idea from what I know of the situation."

"Because Amicia is a dragon," Zaendra observed.

Staring at her with wide eyes, the Mate's tone softened. "Who told you?"

Quiet laughter erupted around him, and their leader looked upon each of them in turn. "You all knew."

"Of course we knew," Hayt smirked, slapping the taller man on the back. "She is a magical being."

"What our dwarf is trying to say is, Amicia's inner being shines brightly within her. The more she uses her powers, the greater it will show," Animir explained. "The gnomes, rest assured, will address her as our leader tomorrow night despite our intentions. All that we have met know who, or what, she is."

"Except us," Piers breathed, shaking his head and feeling foolish. "Rey doesn't know and neither did Bally. We can't see it, but all of you can."

"That is correct," Oldrilin agreed, bowing her head at the mortal of the rim. "Much we have to share, much we need not say."

The Mate's features twisted as he interpreted her comment and asked, "Are you saying we should or shouldn't inform Rey? I mean, I don't think we should allow them to wed, personally."

"We cannot prevent their wishes without due cause," Zaendra observed. "If they wish to be joined, it is not our place to judge or stand against it."

"But she's a dragon!" the Mate fumed.

"Do you wish to reveal this to her? She is not yet aware," Animir pointed out. "You would have to tell both of them why you stand against their nuptial, as it is their choice to make."

Silence fell over the group as they abruptly reached the point of their conversation.

"Do we have the right to stand in their way?" Meena finally asked quietly. "As far as they are concerned, she is a mortal of the rim. If one of you knows a way to break her curse, speak of it now."

"I know of no such magic," Zaendra stated defiantly, her dimpled chin raised. "And I do not think it is our place to force a wedge between them."

"There is a wedge between them," Piers grunted. "They aren't the same!"

Cutting her eyes over at him, Meena's expression collapsed. "As are we, my love."

"That's different," he dismissed with a wave of his hand. "I knew what you were, and I loved you anyway. Rey doesn't know she's..." the words fell away as he pictured the young man he had known long before they came to the Kingdom of Eriden. "He won't care. He is head over heels for her, and I am certain it wouldn't matter. Is there any hope of returning her to her dragon form?"

Glancing between the others, he waited, each of them silent as they considered the implications. When no one volunteered a resolution, he sighed, "Well, I say we let them marry then. I for one do not wish to break the news to either of them."

"You do not think she should be told?" Hayt asked pointedly.

"No. If we cannot help her gain her true form, what would be the point? She is likely to spend the rest of her life trapped in the body of a human. She might as well be able to live like one." Glancing around at the others, Piers could see the doubt on their faces. "Come on. What do you say then? Who will go and tell her?"

The seconds ticking by, none were quick to volunteer. When each had stepped back out of their circle and informally withdrawing from the discussion, Piers concluded, "Then we are agreed. Meena, if you wish to try and dissuade her, then you may do so, but the consensus is that the wedding will take place whenever they have set the time."

"I am not certain of this course of action," Animir informed him, "but as I do not wish to be the one to break this news to her, I will agree."

"As will I," Hayt snapped, glancing at his bride. "Zae?"

"I will not speak of it," she replied, her lips pursing into a pout.

"Ami must discover her own heart," Oldrilin agreed while shaking her head side to side. "If it was my place to tell her, I would have long ago."

"Then the secret is sealed, lest anyone outside our group reveals it," Piers affirmed. "Let us then return to our chores and speak no further of it."

Picking their way back through the marshes to their camp, the three women returned to their sewing. Taking up her needle, Meena glared at the cloth, her heart filled with mixed emotion. Part of her wanted to reveal all to her young friends, but she understood why it would be cruel to do so. If Amicia were to remain in human form all the days of her life, knowing she was a dragon might force her to spend that life alone. The very idea filling her heart with sorrow, she informed the others, "I'm afraid I must speak to Ami."

"Well, then you are in luck," the girl giggled, joining them from the north side of the clearing. Dropping to her knees, she crawled into her shelter to retrieve her pack and the item still hidden within it. "I have exciting news," she beamed, obviously happy at their plans.

Seeing the eagerness on her face when she stood, Meena smiled, her doubts removed in an instant. She would never do or say anything to crush her young friend's joy. "We have heard your happy news," she informed her with a nod. "Congratulations. I was coming to find you that we might discuss your wedding wishes," she added with a laugh she hoped covered her previous misgivings.

Glancing around, Amicia also giggled, "I'm afraid the marshes will have to do. I have the dress we made for me last winter," she informed them, pulling it from her pack. It had been rolled into a tight bundle and shoved to the bottom. "However, it isn't very fresh after all we've been through."

"It will be fine," Meena smiled. "I know a trick for such things." Taking the garment, she carried it over to a tree limb, where she hung it so that the bottom cleared the ground by close to a foot.

Next, she poured a small bowl of water and placed it beneath the gown. Surrounding the vessel with smooth stones, she used her staff to tap them gently, causing them to glow brightly. The water warmed quickly, and steam rose into the air, penetrating the delicate fibers. Pressing her hands together, the cloth sandwiched between, the wan worked her way up, pulling downwards and smoothing the fibers as she went until it shimmered like new.

"It's beautiful," Amicia gasped, pleased with the result. "You have a trick for everything, don't you!"

"I have lived many years, yes," Meena laughed. "You will make a beautiful bride."

"Know any spells for flowers?" Zaendra grinned. Glancing around them, the marshes were only decorated in shades of green.

"I don't really need flowers," Ami sighed, still fingering her dress. "All I need is my circle of friends to stand with me as I embark on a new life."

The words stealing her breath, Meena knew she would not speak against their intentions. "And you shall have it," she agreed.

Hiding the gown so Rey would not see it, Amicia set about preparing their dinner. Animir and Hayt produced the meat while Zae and Lin gathered the vegetables. Sitting in their circle that night, the group spoke in soft voices, each enjoying the company and doing their best not to spoil the occasion for the happy couple.

Once they had eaten, Rey announced, "We will hold the ceremony tomorrow morning if that's all right. That way we will be joined before we stand before the gnomes."

"Why not now?" Piers replied in a surly manner, still disgruntled with the cowardice of the others, as well as his own.

"Now?" Amicia gasped, her clear green eyes darting around at the gathering.

"Perhaps tomorrow would be best," Meena clipped, glaring at her mate. "We did hold Baldwin's memorial only this morning."

"It would end the day on a happy note," Rey observed, the lump in his throat bobbing as he swallowed nervously.

Silently glancing again at the others, Amicia could see the doubt on their faces. Still, sooner was better than later as far as she was concerned. On her feet she announced, "It will only take a few minutes for me to change. Let us gather in the clearing so that Bally can join us."

"Bally," the Mate snapped, pushing himself up to stand. "You know he isn't really buried there."

"No, but it's our place of remembrance," Ami replied happily, digging in her bag for her brush. "You all go and await us there," she ordered, pointing at the men with the mirror. "I promise we won't be long."

Seeing that she was serious, Rey reached inside his shelter to retrieve his blanket as the other three men reluctantly gathered at the trail to Bally's marker. "You go on, and I'll join you in a minute," he informed them, heading further up the line of trees.

"What are you doing?" Piers yelled after him.

"I've got something I need to do," he shouted back with a wave before he disappeared on another trail. Pushing his way through, he located a secret place he had discovered but not shared with any of the others. There he set up a surprise for his bride, then left to return to the place of their ceremony.

Approaching the ring of trees surrounding the engraved stone, the girls had not yet arrived. His three friends appeared anxious, causing him to laugh. "I thought I was the one supposed to be nervous."

"Hmmp," Piers grunted. "Just preparing to officiate, here," he lied.

Rey looked around with a peaceful gaze, as the circle had felt sacred since the first time he had laid eyes upon it. Rubbing his palms against his pants, he sighed, "I guess this won't be much of a wedding."

Above him, the full moon shown brightly down upon them. "It contains all that it should," Animir informed him.

"Aye," the Mate agreed, his features forced into a smile. He had agreed to do the honors, but he currently wished he had some of the troll beer to help him with the proceedings.

They didn't have to wait long, as Ami was in a great rush to finalize their agreement. Wearing the dress, her hair had been combed and hung loosely about her shoulders. Coming into the clearing, she paused as the other women moved to stand beside the others in a full circle.

In the center stood Rey, facing Piers, who would hear their vows. Staring at her with wide eyes, the beauty of his intended took his breath away, and he knew he would not trade their simple ceremony. When she arrived beside him, he whispered, "I have waited so long for you, my love."

Blinking back tears, Ami nodded, "And your patience shall be rewarded."

"Well," Piers announced, clearing his throat. "At this point, I have to admit I have never performed a wedding, and it was never a regular occurrence on any ship on which I sailed."

Turning to face him, the couple waited patiently for him to go on. Staring at them, the Mate realized he would have to make something up if he couldn't remember the words, so he began to improvise.

"Reynard Daye, you have professed your devotion to this woman?"

"Aye," he breathed, breaking into a wide grin.

"And you swear upon your soul you will live each day to come for her, for as long as you both shall live?"

"On my soul?" Rey faltered. "I don't think that's how it goes, Mate."

"Shh," Ami rebuked, working to keep a straight face.

Glancing at her, he agreed, "Ok, on my soul, I swear to live each day for her."

"And you, Amicia Spicer," Piers turned to her.

"Yes," she nodded firmly.

"You renounce your name and take his, that you will forever walk by his side, so long as you both shall live."

"I do," she agreed, her features erupting into a wide grin.

"Then as the captain of… our group and the leader of our clan," he said as he shrugged, "I pronounce you husband and wife."

Gasping at the abruptness, Amicia's smile faltered. Glancing around at their ring of friends, she could see the strained expressions. Her gaze arriving at Rey, all her doubts fell away at the pure adoration in his hazel orbs. "I do," she breathed again, reaching for him and pulling his mouth to hers for the first kiss of the rest of their lives.

When their lips parted, Reynard silently claimed her hand and pulled her in the opposite direction of their camp. Glancing over his shoulder, he could see the others returning to their leaning shelters, and they would have the night to themselves. Pushing through the trees, he boasted, "I have located a suitable place for our wedding night."

Her heart racing, Amicia followed, having not thought that far ahead. "Will we be alone?"

"Yes, quite," he laughed, parting some taller shoots of foliage with thick stems and broad leaves. A moment later, they arrived at a small pond surrounded by dense woods. The moon had moved to the west but lit the small clearing brightly. Spread on the ground next to the water, lay a single blanket; all the protection they would have against the night.

"Oh, my! It's lovely," Ami breathed, her heart rate unimproved as her pulse thumped in her ears.

Staring at her, he wondered if she had ever held another. He didn't care; she had vowed to be his for the rest of their lives, and that was enough for him. However, he didn't have much experience with women; realizing that could be a problem, he longed for a moment to have been as worldly as Piers. His anxiety growing, he laughed, "I'm glad you like it. It will be our secret place."

Turning to face him, she smiled up into his tense features. "Do not be afraid, my love," she reassured. "We will share this night and many others." Taking charge, she kissed him once more, but this time more slowly as she searched for the fire within him.

TWENTY-SEVEN

Return of the Captain

THE FOLLOWING MORNING, Amicia and Rey left their private love nest, his quilt rolled and tucked beneath his arm. Walking next to her, a smile danced upon his lips, and his heart skipped a beat each time he stole a glance at her beautiful profile.

Her dress mussed and her hair a frizzy mess, Amicia felt less enthusiastic about their first night as husband and wife. "I wish I had thought to bring a few essentials," she sighed as they neared their camp, her hand pushing against her out-of-control waves.

"Let me help you tame it," he offered, dropping the blanket. Catching the locks, he forced them into a clump. Pulling the tie from his own hair, he used it to bind hers into a reasonable semblance of a bun.

Staring at his freed ringlets, Amicia groaned, "Thank you, but now you are unkempt."

"I do not mind it," he shrugged, noting her foul mood. "Are you not happy, love?"

Not meeting his gaze, she indicated the camp, "Everyone is awake and appear to be eating without us. We should go," she huffed.

Inhaling deeply, Rey calmed his nerves. Their vow had been spoken and consummated. They would be joined for as long as they both lived, so forcing a fight on their first morning as one would be unwise. "As you wish," he replied softly, taking her hand and guiding her towards their friends.

Entering the circle around the fire, one of the large rocks had been left empty for them. Glancing over her shoulder, Ami could see her things were no longer in the shelter where she had left them.

"Uh, you've been moved," Piers pointed out, stroking his beard anxiously at her displeased frown. "Since the two of you are now a couple," he added, wafting his hand at her new dwelling.

"Thank you," Amicia replied tartly. "To be honest, I wasn't sure you approved of our union. Now, if you don't mind, I'd like to change." Kneeling on her new bed, she fumbled through her pile of belongings, locating her pants and shirt.

"Let me get you some privacy," Rey offered, hanging his quilt over the front of their shelter so she could dress unseen.

"Thanks," she snapped, squinting into the darkness until her eyes had adjusted. Pulling the coverings onto her legs, she slipped out of the gown and traded it for the comfort of her shirt. Then untying her hair, she brushed at it angrily, fuming under her breath.

She could not say exactly what had spawned her rage; she only knew the moment she awoke in their little clearing by the pond, she had felt it. Even a cooling dip to bathe before they dressed had failed to remove it. A gnawing, dripping anger, it poured over her, and nothing that had happened since she first opened her eyes seemed to soothe it. To the contrary, every step she took and move she made appeared to stoke the livid flames.

Outside, Rey took his seat upon their rock and waited for her to join him. Tapping his palms against one another anxiously, he glanced around at the others. Silence followed his bride's sharp words, as each of them feared they had not been fully successful at hiding their doubts.

Emerging from her shelter, Ami took her seat next to Rey with a loud grunt. The girl's emotions hard to read, she appeared equally displeased by the light of the morning after, or perhaps at their efforts to be helpful; it was hard to say as to the cause of her demeanor.

"We want you to be happy," Meena truthfully observed as she handed her a bowl when the girl was settled. "We did not mean to upset you by the move."

"Yes," Animir seconded. "Oldrilin and I will share the other shelter so that you may sleep as husband and wife," he added, also hoping to appease her.

The flush on the couple's cheeks instant, Piers laughed at their innocence. "Ah, newlyweds," he observed. Feeling like their father more than usual, he soothed, "You'll get used to it."

His gaze fixed on the fire, Rey's heart raced. "Thanks for not mentioning it," he grumbled, taking slow bites from his bowl of morning mash.

Eating eagerly, Amicia hoped to remain out of the uncomfortable conversation the men seemed to be sharing. Glancing at Zae, she could see the covert smile on her lips and realized the cause was hopeless; she was a married woman, and the time for embarrassment over such things had passed.

Taking her spoonsful more slowly, she glanced around, noting that the others seemed to have moved on. "What will we do today while we await our visit with the gnomes?" she asked, wishing to clear her dark mood with something pleasant.

"I'm going to work on our mending a bit more," Meena supplied cheerfully.

"Yes," Zae agreed. "We will need to do what we can this day. If the gnomes agree to help us reach Adiarwen, we won't have another chance."

"Adiarwen," Rey repeated softly, as if he had forgotten about their quest. "I never really thought we would make it that far," he confessed.

"I hope that we will," Piers countered. "We must stand before the dragons and plead our case if we ever hope to make a permanent home here, or to be returned to the one we left behind."

Amicia's eyes shot up to meet his the moment that he spoke. *Home.* She hadn't thought of that. Swallowing, she glanced at her husband, seated beside her. "I think we should remain here, in Falconmarsh," she suggested.

"What? Why?" Rey stammered. "I thought that was the plan – to meet the dragons and ask to be returned to the rim, or to some other place where we could live on our own; neither here nor there, but something in between."

Blinking at him, the girl sighed, "I'm afraid they won't allow it. If we stand before them and they deny our request, they might strike us down."

"Then so be it," Animir growled. "Bally gave his life to see that we stood before the council. I believe we should honor his wishes."

Before the argument could escalate further, a shadow passed over their camp, causing the group to look up in unison. Above them, a large dragon made a slow pass. On their feet, they moved out into the clearing, where they could maintain their line of sight as the beast moved away.

"What the hell?" Piers spat as the group formed a loose circle, all staring into the sky as the creature turned again.

"Does no one think we should hide?" Zaendra asked, her voice heavy with concern.

"No," the Mate growled, shading his eyes as he stared into the morning sun. "I'm done with hiding."

Ami watched the dragon turn, her heart racing at the unmistakable colors.

195

It's him. She knew it in her gut. *"Where have you been?"* she asked, reaching out to him but getting no reply. *"Answer me, damn you!"*

Flying lower with each pass, the dragon glided across the heavens, its massive wings stretched wide. On the fourth pass, Rey observed, "I see a definite scar on the left, and the colors are right. Ami, I believe your friend has returned," he managed calmly, holding the dread from his voice. If she had been communicating with the dragon, she had made no mention of it to him, but it would explain her altered attitude so soon after they had wed.

Landing in the center of them, Lamwen touched down gently, and no sound was produced beyond the air as it passed over his massive wings. Facing the girl, he waited, watching her blond strands catch in the wind as she glared at him.

"Lamwen," Amicia whispered. Her anger ebbing at the reality of him, she stumbled a single step towards him before catching herself. Cutting her eyes over at her husband, she gasped, "Oh God." Her heart racing, she could not have anticipated the rush of emotions that overtook her, both exhilarated joy and pure terror surged through her veins.

"I must speak with you," Lamwen informed her, his gaze fixed upon her stricken features.

Anger replacing all other emotion, Ami ground her teeth as she bit, "Where the hell have you been? I called to you –"

"I was unable to reply, my queen," the dragon snorted, swinging around as he studied the rest of the group.

Swallowing, Piers blinked back tears. The beauty of the beast before him a wonder to behold, he only wished that Baldwin had been there to share it. "Speak then and be gone, dragon," he commanded, afraid of what his sudden return could mean after all they had endured.

"Not yet," Lamwen growled, completing the turn and facing the girl once more. "I must converse with Amicia in private. Then I will be ready to share my tale with the rest of you if you will hear it."

"You're damn right we'll hear it," Reynard near shouted, hurt by the pain his love had endured at the dragon's callous actions. "Ami has been worried sick about you, but you couldn't be bothered?"

His protectiveness clear in his tone, Amicia's heart ached for him and the awkwardness of the captain's return. "It's ok, Rey. I will hear him." Addressing Lamwen, she commanded, "Have your say."

"Not here," Lamwen replied, lumbering towards her so that his hot breath surrounded her smaller frame. "Climb upon my shoulders. I will carry you to a place where we may speak in private."

"Why can't you simply take a walk?" Meena interceded, joining the conversation. "You share telepathy, as well, so one of those options should suffice." The older woman had no desire to see the girl removed from their midst, even by her supposed friend.

Staring into Amicia's green orbs, the dragon made no reply. Instead, he waited for her to comply. When she closed the distance between them, he groaned with satisfaction, leaning forward to provide her with easier access.

Hoisting herself up and placing her leg over his back, she sat upon his shoulders so that her thighs rested against his massive wings at the point they joined his torso. His neck before her, the scales were rough beneath her hands as she caressed them, searching for the best hold.

"I am ready," she announced when she was certain of her grip.

Leaping into the air, Lamwen spiraled straight up, the wind rushing into their faces. Hundreds of feet above the marsh, he leveled out and headed due east.

The air cool as it gushed against her, Amicia clung to him tightly. To her surprise, it was not fear that greeted her on their ascent, and a delight she could not have explained exploded within her, crushing her anger beneath it. The air moist when they reached the water, she laughed out loud as he dove to skim just above the waves, sprinkling her with spray.

"Lamwen, it's beautiful!" So many days she had stood upon a cliff, overlooking the ocean and dreamt of that very moment. *"I have so longed for this."*

Hearing the happiness in her voice, the dragon's heart raced. *"You were meant to fly."*

"I believe that I was," she agreed, recalling her childhood home and pushing herself up to catch more of the air as it crashed against her face and chest, much as she had since she was a child. Ahead, she could see a collection of rocks jutting out from the surface of the waves. *"What's that?"*

"Dragon Rock," he replied, slowing as they landed on the jagged stones.

His wings flapping beneath her, Amicia marveled at how easily he had carried her. "Do you bring girl's here often?" she laughed aloud, her delight apparent.

"No. You are the first mortal I have carried," he supplied as she slid from his back to stand beside him. "Take care; some of the footing is not firm."

"I will," she agreed, moving gingerly as she paced the length and then width of the small island. Made entirely of stone, nothing grew on the small section of earth protruding from the sea. "It's amazing," she declared, turning to face him with a full grin. "Thank you for sharing it with me."

"Ah, you have missed me and the excitement I bring to your days," he observed.

"Very much," she sighed more quietly, feeling a little deflated. "Why did you not reply to me? Obviously you were alive, but you allowed me to believe you were lost to me forever."

"I had my trials to face, and I could not help you with yours," he groveled, feeling ashamed at his course of action. "I regret any pain it has caused you. You made a beautiful bride, for a mortal."

"You were spying on me," she accused, her eyes narrowed as the last bit of her bliss evaporated. Her features crinkled, she fought to hide the pain. "You let me marry him," she sobbed.

"That was your choice to make whether I agreed with it or not. Would you have decided differently if I had spoken my warning?"

The air caught in her lungs, Amicia glared at him. How could she say the words? She loved Rey deeply, but she knew in an instant his availability had been convenient, and her actions would cost them all in the end. "Speak your words and take me back," she growled, angry at the position she found herself in.

"I have something I must share. I have hinted at the truth from the first time that we spoke, beside a brook as you entered the lands of the north. Do you recall that day?"

Searching her memories, she did not have to look hard to find the night she had first gone to him. "You became my secret friend," she whispered. "I remember every moment of it."

"I intended to kill you that night, Amicia. I still have not discerned what about you prevented my doing so," he informed her evenly.

Drawing a ragged breath, tears formed in her eyes. "I wish that you had. Or better yet, that you had succeeded the night you sank our ship. Then my suffering would never have happened."

"You wish to die?" he asked in surprise. "You have fought so rigidly for your life and those of your friends."

"Yes, we have fought, but it has been for nothing, it would seem. Everything is wrong," Amicia cried, clenching her fists so that her nails dug into her palms. "My parents, or who I thought were my parents. From the moment they found me, my life has been an incredible lie. They used me as much as they sheltered me, then left me before I was ready to stand on my own without them."

"They cared for you, Amicia," the dragon countered. "Without them, you might not have survived to find your way home."

198

"Home?" she clipped. "I wouldn't call this home despite all that has happened. I've been trapped in this place for *years*, Lamwen! I can't leave, and I can't stay," she wailed. *What am I to do?*

Watching her tremble as she ranted and unable to hear her private thoughts, the beast did not reply.

"Did you hear what I said?" she shouted, then broke down into a loud bellow. "My friend is gone! Baldwin is never coming back, and I feel like it's my fault. I wanted this. I wanted to find the place where I belong, but I had no idea what coming here would cost me."

"You are part of Eriden, princess. Do you think there could have been another way?"

"No. As much as I hate to admit it, I can't," she hesitated, searching for the right words. "I can't help it. I brought Bally here with my longing. I hid on his ship, and it cost him his life."

"It is not your fault," the dragon growled.

"It is!" she insisted. "Everything in my life is skewed, and I have cursed my friends with my company. I belong here, but I don't. I brought my friends here, but I didn't mean to. I married Rey and I shouldn't ha–" she stopped short. "I mean, I love him, but that's not why I did it." Her lips blue from the chill in the air, tears dripped from her jaw. "I was afraid I would lose all my chances, and now I can't take it back. I have ruined everything, and I don't even know why."

"Because you are a dragon," Lamwen slapped her with the words he had come to say, glaring at her without blinking.

Her lips drawn into a pucker, the veins in Amicia's neck bulged. "Stop it. I thought you were my friend."

"Oh, my sweet princess," he replied with a loud gasp of air. Lowering his head, his warm air surrounded her as he breathed. "I wish I could hold you and remove the pain from your broken heart, but I dare not in your current mortal form."

Her hand shaking, she reached for him, resting it against his jaw. "Do you really mean that? If I were born a dragon, we could have been lovers," she dared to suggest, torn with the knowing she could not have them both and probably would not have either soon enough. Her face scrunched, she added, "But I'm not really a dragon, Lamwen."

"You are a dragon, Kaliwyn," he insisted, pushing against her palm.

"How?" she sobbed. Tears streaming over her flushed cheeks, she recalled his telling her when they met that it was her real name. Closing her eyes, she waited, certain her heart would burst with the weight of his words. "I'm ready for the truth."

"The truth," he agreed, puffing warm air over her again before he began. "You were forced into the form of a mortal child the night Gwirwen claimed the throne. Your father was stripped of his crown and title as the supreme dragon; forced to live in a stone prison atop Adiarwen. He remains there to this day, where he mourns the loss of his only living child... you, my princess."

Blinking rapidly, then staring into his burning orbs, Ami searched her mind. Somewhere, in the depths of her memories, she could feel the flame of her past smoldering like an ember within her chest. "Ziradon is my father."

"Yes," he hissed. "You were born to be the queen of our kind, ruler of *all* of Eriden."

Swallowing, she studied him, dropping her arm, then rubbing the fingers against her pant leg. "That hardly seems possible."

"You have seen the power of the dragons," he insisted, stepping towards her and sitting upon the rough stones. His warm breath surrounding her, it held the cool air of the ocean at bay, and she leaned into it, drinking it in as she knelt to press herself against him.

"I have seen," she whispered, her heart aching. "Lamwen, you have become so dear to me. I feared you were gone, and only then did I realize how deeply I had come to love you."

"Love me?" he faltered, his heart beating out of control. "Before you say too much, princess, I should warn you. Female dragons are rare, and –"

On her feet, she backed away. "Don't." He glared at her, so she pushed, "Don't pretend like you don't feel it. I know that you do," she spat, her voice cracking.

"As I was saying," he replied, clearing his throat, "my feelings and even yours are irrelevant. Even if you are able to sever your union with the mortal when you regain your dragon form, you and I would never be allowed to mate. Females are rare, and as the queen, you will be expected to choose a member of the council, that the bloodline would remain pure."

Closing her eyes, more streams coated her cheeks. Wiping at them angrily, the girl felt broken, as if all the light had gone from the world, leaving her only darkness and sorrow. "You will be by my side, Lamwen. If I live all my days in this body, or if I somehow regain that which you claim is mine, I will never lose you again." Her green eyes opening slowly, she glared at him through the narrow slits. "Do you understand?" she whispered.

Feeling the depth of her emotions, he nodded, pushing himself up to tower above her. "I will be your faithful servant for all the days that remain, my queen."

"That's not what I meant," she clipped, crossing her arms angrily.

"It is all I can offer," he sighed, ready to take her back to the others. "Come. We must return to Falconmarsh and form our plans. Now that you are aware of your true self, you must be ready for the battle when it comes."

"Only if you promise me that we will one day be as one. Otherwise, I would rather remain a human and spend my life with Rey. He has done nothing to deserve this loss," she observed. "I have taken my vow with him, and it would take much to persuade me to break it."

"I can make no such promise, princess," he insisted, growing weary of her obstinance. "Besides, all of Eriden is at stake. We will do what we must to save it."

Her heart skipping a beat, Amicia's mind turned to the story of the creator, the destroyer, and the legends many of those of Eriden believed to be true. "The prophecy," she whispered.

Glaring at her, he barked, "Do not be distracted by fables. We have one moon to set things right, maybe two, and then all will be lost. The elves have turned against us, and if they are to be defeated, we must move quickly."

"The elves," she stammered, her face scrunched in confusion. "What can they possibly do?"

"I'll explain when we have rejoined the others. For now, I have said what I brought you to hear. Climb upon my shoulders once more and allow me to carry you back," he commanded.

"Fine," she grunted, knowing he would not divulge his tale until she had obeyed. "But first, you must prove this to me."

"Prove it how?" the dragon snarled, angry at her impetuous denial.

"I want to see my father. Take me to the cliffs that I may look upon him."

"Have you any idea how dangerous that would be?" Lamwen laughed at the suggestion. "I am wanted, hunted by the king's guard, and you are a fugitive as well. We would be seen, and you would be burned to a smoldering heap upon my back."

"I'm not going with you unless you take me to see Ziradon!" she spat, crossing her arms over her chest.

Staring at her small frame, a calm washed over Lamwen. "Very well, my queen." Bowing before her, he waited for her to mount him and take her seat at the back of his neck.

"And no tricks!" she shouted as she adjusted her position. "I'm ready."

"I would never deceive you," he replied. "I promise I will fly you over that you may see him, but I cannot guarantee that we will be able to land."

"Fly us over then, but I want to speak with him if we are able."

"I'm not sure if that is wise, princess. Your father may not recognize you in your current form."

"I don't care," she growled. "I will have words with him if I am able."

"As you wish," Lamwen sighed, leaping from the cold wet stones and heading north, towards the giant cliffs of the dragons.

TWENTY-EIGHT

Unspoken

STARING INTO THE SKY, Rey watched the dragon fly into the morning sun. It bothered him deeply that Lamwen had returned, especially as his bride had confessed the depths of her love for him only the day before. Recalling her admission to be private, at least the others would not know of her unspoken desires.

"She'll be ok. Lamwen would never allow her to be harmed," Animir soothed, clamping his friend on the shoulder.

"Aye," Reynard breathed, hardly above a whisper. "Still, I am concerned. What could he possibly need to share?"

Shaking his head, the rest of their group remained frozen in place as his mind turned.

"He is a dragon," Lin observed. "Dragons have secrets, Rey Daye."

"Secrets," he repeated, frowning. "Yes, I have wondered why in the hell he has followed her all this time. Like they've been spying on us but he can speak to her. It's not right."

Sharing a glance with his wife, Piers could almost see the reasoning unfolding within the younger man's mind. "Don't let it trouble you," he offered.

"But it bothers me," Rey scowled. "It bothers me a lot. Doesn't it bother any of you?" he growled. Losing sight of the speck in the distance, he turned, taking each of them in turn.

"It's ok," Meena soothed.

"Why is it ok?" he countered, studying her with a small pout. He could tell the return of the dragon had disturbed them as well, but they seemed to be pretending it away. "What's going on?"

The anxious looks they shared with one another did nothing to quiet his churning thoughts. "Anyone?" he bit more loudly, offering his open palms as persuasion to divulge what they knew.

The others studied the ground at their feet, no longer able to look upon him or each other. Wringing her tiny hands, Oldrilin sniffed. Kneeling before her, Rey slipped a finger beneath her chin, lifting her tear-filled orbs to meet his.

"Lin," he breathed. "You are my special friend, are you not?"

"Yes, Rey Daye," she sang, a droplet of sorrow spilling over to stain her cheek.

"Tell me then. What is it that you know?"

Looking up at the others, she silently pled for help. Her bottom lip sticking out in a full pout, it trembled as she dug at her eye with a small fist.

"Why is she crying?" he bellowed, standing and turning to face Piers.

"Why are you asking me?" the Mate shouted back.

"Because you're in charge. That means it's your job to know what's going on, so I'll ask again, why the hell is she crying?" His hands clenched into fists, he raised them slowly. If he didn't get answers, his intent was clear.

Closing his eyes, Piers exhaled loudly. "I see little point in hiding the truth any longer. There is something special about Amicia, Rey. There is a reason she has been drawn to this place. A reason she can use magic and merdoes."

"Ok, so what's the reason?" Rey squirmed.

"Well, it's something special about her. I could see it almost as soon as we landed. She behaved differently, and everyone we have met has seen it, only at the time I didn't know why," the Mate elaborated, only frustrating the man before him further.

Seeing the mess her husband was making of the tale, Meena intervened. "Amicia is a dragon."

Reynard stared at her in a state of disbelief, sputtering, "That's absurd. How would she... " He fumed, opening his hands and kneading them as if molding with clay. "She's a girl," he finished.

"She was transformed, when and by whom we can only speculate," Animir spoke up. "My guess is she is the lost princess, daughter of Ziradon."

"Lost princess," Rey quipped. "You don't say. I mean, we all mock her with the term. Why wouldn't it be true?"

Turning his back, he left the group and marched north along the edge of the trees. Arriving at the one that marked the path, he turned, fighting his way to the clearing where Baldwin's memorial had been set. Not stopping until he stood within the clearing, he sank to his knees before it.

The others had followed and filed into the area after him. "I'd like to be alone," he informed them, his chin pressed against his chest.

"We must speak, and then you may be as alone as you like," Meena countered.

"We must speak," the boy growled, getting to his feet. Rage in his eyes, he fumed, "You knew of this, but you did not tell me." Standing toe to toe with Piers, he shouted, "Admit it!"

"I told you what I could, son. But you did not want to hear my warning," the Mate explained, as this was the dark secret he had been alluding to when they talked about his performing the ceremony.

Grinding his teeth, Rey's chest heaved. "You all knew, but none of you would speak of it. And how could she herself do this? Taking my name with such a secret!"

"Amicia does not know, or at least she didn't," Hayt spoke up. "I'm sure that is why the dragon has taken her away; to enlighten her in private." Glancing at the others, he breathed deeply, almost relieved that Lamwen would handle the chore none of her friends had wanted.

"How could she not know?" Rey gasped. "I mean, she's magic. She has powers," he observed, wriggling his fingers to illustrate. "She brought you back from the dead for fuck's sake," he tossed at the Mate.

"Aye, she is a powerful beast," his leader nodded. "But she may never be freed from her mortal form. This is why we chose not to spoil your union. She will need you, Rey. Especially if she is trapped in her body forever. None could love her as you do."

Curling his tongue, Rey considered the notion. "I said that, didn't I. There could be no secret so dark I would not love her."

"You did," the older man agreed. "Was it not true?"

"It was the truth," Rey nodded, tears spilling once more. Glancing down at Bally's stone, he wished more than ever that his best friend was there. "This is what he died for. Amicia is a dragon."

"He knew the magnitude of her secret," Animir testified. "This is why he told me to flee, that I might help her fulfill her destiny."

"Her destiny." Rey's mind raced. "She is the destroyer; a lover of men and dragons."

"I believe so," the elf agreed.

Realizing the magnitude in his words, Rey half smiled. "I love her so deeply. I swore upon my soul to be there for her for the rest of my life."

"Hopefully it won't come to that," the Mate teased.

"It very well may," Animir countered. "The dragon has returned for a reason."

"It's time," Rey nodded. "Yes, she told me that he had not spoken to her since the night we fled the cabin. But she loved him very deeply," he added, then amended, "Loves him very deeply."

"She loves you as well," Piers challenged. "She would not have made such a vow if she had not."

"Do you forgive Oldrilin?" the mermaid asked, looking up at him sadly.

"You know that I do," he gasped, having forgotten about her suffering in the midst of his own. Kneeling before her, he wiped at her damp cheeks. "Cry no more. We must be strong, as our Ami needs us to be."

"How long do you think he will keep her?" Zaendra asked, observing the sun would approached midday. "If it is not soon, we will miss our meeting with the gnomes."

"She knows the way," Rey nodded. "I'm sure he will bring her back."

"I could reach out to her," Piers confessed. "We still share a connection, although we do not use it often."

"If the hour grows late, then we should," Rey agreed. "For now, let them be. If she has half as much trouble understanding or accepting this news as I did, she will need time to process it."

"Then we will give it to her," the Mate suggested, "but we should return to the camp and prepare our belongings. With so much up in the air between the dragons and the gnomes, we may have to leave in a hurry."

"And the elves," Animir added.

"What about them?" Meena asked in surprise.

"They've been building an arsenal for years," he shrugged. "If there is trouble, you can bet they won't be taking anyone's side but their own. It has been no secret the elves wish to rule all of Eriden; this could be their very chance to make that happen."

Swallowing, Rey nodded. There was a great deal at stake, and more than just a broken vow. "All right, let's follow the Mate's orders and do our best to be ready to depart as soon as our girl and the dragon return."

"Are we going to tell her?" Hayt asked. "Or should we look surprised when she announces her big news."

"I hadn't thought of that," Piers sighed. "Perhaps we should hold our tongues and allow her to share when she is ready. Right, Rey?"

"Right," the younger man agreed, turning to stomp down the trail back to camp. "We'll let her decide when and how she comes out with the truth." Deep down, he hurt at what had transpired, but there was no one he could blame for the pain. "And if I get to keep her in the end, all this will only serve to make our connection all the more special," he mused, mostly to himself as he led the way out.

TWENTY-NINE

Rise of the Dragoness

SITTING on Lamwen's shoulders felt less exhilarating than her first flight, the one to Dragon Rock. Her fingers holding tightly to his rough scales, the cold air rushed over her, blasting her damp cheeks. She wanted to converse with him, but after his revelations, she decided to use the time to think.

Collecting her memories of her childhood, she wondered if her father would want to know how she had been raised. It saddened her that he had been imprisoned the entire time she had been away, and she held that fact as a testament to the cruelty of Gwirwen.

Thinking of the dragon who had done such horrid things to her family, she hated him. A loving and giving person at heart, saying that she hated anyone was hard to fathom; but she did. *How could he be so unkind?* Removing her from her home and placing her in a foreign land to be raised by strangers was bad enough; to make her father suffer with that knowledge – unbearable.

Fresh tears spilling over onto her face, the girl wiped at them angrily. After doing so, she pondered if she cried because she was a mortal or if dragons also had tears within them. The thought gave her chills beyond the coolness of the air.

"I'm a dragon," she whispered. Her next thought of Rey, more drops of sadness gathered in her eyes. *How can I tell him this? I gave him my hand; I took his name. We should spend our lives together, but how can we?*

Her emotions raw, she watched the land in the distance as it approached. A large cliff jutted out over the sea, bare rocks with caves that opened above the frothy waves below. *My home,* she sighed to herself, *the one I remember. It was exactly like this, a cottage on a cliff hanging over the ocean.* Her heart beat faster as they approached, and she could see a few brightly colored forms either sitting in the mouth of their caves or flying around above the stones.

When they were close, Lamwen climbed, his angle steep as his wings pumped to raise them high into the air. Her grip not as firm as it had first been, Amicia leaned back and looked down, taking in Adiarwen from above. Spying what could only be her father's prison, she gave up wiping at her tears and let them flow freely.

Gwirwen will pay for this, she fumed. Her breathing ragged, she felt the rage within her; but this was not the time for it. She needed to get on the ground and visit Ziradon if she were able.

"May we land?" she asked of her guide.

"I will make a turn and approach from the north. You will be able to speak to him, but again, I don't know for how long. If anyone discovers us here, we will both be killed."

"I understand," she replied, her heart racing with a mix of excitement and terror.

As promised, Lamwen made a wide circle. Coming in from the north, they landed a few hundred yards from the arched stones, where the foliage began. As she climbed down, Ami again removed the moisture from her cheeks. Seeing the redness of her eyes and flush in her skin, the beast wavered.

"Kaliwyn, I am sorry for all you have endured and for what is to come."

"It's not your fault," she replied, forcing a smile she hoped appeared genuine. "Our reunion will be glorious, in any case. After this, we must also determine if and when I will be able to regain my dragon form."

"Go and speak with your father. I will remain here in the shadows of the trees, but I can be there in an instant if you need me. If anyone sees you, run back to me, and do not stop," he commanded.

Thinking of the hamar gem and what Meena said about it, she grinned. "I'd like to try something." Reaching into her shirt, she pulled her merdoe out, removing it from her neck. Clasping it tightly, she closed her eyes. Taking steps backwards, she moved away from the dragon but still faced him.

"Kaliwyn!"

"Yes, I'm here," she giggled, turning and strutting across the open space. *"You can't see me, can you?"*

"N-no," he stammered, watching... nothing. *"How have you accomplished this?"*

"A trick the wan taught me. I am hiding within a shadow. I have never

done it with the merdoe, but Meena says that I don't really need the gem; the power is mine, and I simply must learn to focus it," she boasted.

"Be careful, my queen," Lamwen warned, shaken by her abilities and her cavalier attitude towards them. *"You may be a powerful dragoness, but there is always someone stronger."*

"Ah, Lamwen," she laughed, breaking into an easy jog as she approached her father's cell. Massive in form, she looked up in awe at the size of the rocks and the grotesque way that had been pulled up into the unnatural formation.

Arriving at the base of one of the pillars, she placed her free hand against the rough surface. Feeling the stone, it was course, with veins or rows of deeper grooves. *I want to remember every detail,* she sighed. *The day I regained my name; and my father.* Her emotion's up and down, as a ship caught in a wild storm, she rode atop the waves at the moment, her joy warming her to the tips of her toes.

Working her way around, she came to a gap between the pillar and the next. Standing in the open space, she could see a massive creature lying on its side in the center of the open chamber formed by the arches. Keeping her hand closed firmly, she wondered for a moment if Ziradon would be stronger and able to see through her hidden state.

"I smell you," a deep voice growled, "mortal of the rim. Why have you come, and how did you get here?"

Instant bliss washing through her, Amicia released the merdoe. "Oh, father!" she squealed, running towards him and falling against his neck, as if she had done it a thousand times before. Fresh tears stained her face even as she laughed with glee.

"Father," the supreme dragon gasped, turning his giant nostril and inhaling deeply. "Kaliwyn, could it be?" Blinking rapidly, his eyes filled, and her question of dragon tears was answered as a single drop spilled over, wetting her when it dripped upon her.

"Yes, my lord, it is I!" she gasped, laughing at his reaction. "Lamwen has delivered me that we may speak. I have so many questions, and I..." She faltered, unsure how to explain.

"You have come to me," he observed, his voice rasping, as he seldom used it. "My sweet princess."

"Yes, father," she agreed, clinging to him once more. His smell different than that of Lamwen, she sighed, "I know you. I remember the scent of you."

"Had you forgotten, my child?"

"Yes, I had. For all my life, I have been a mortal of the rim. I only learned this very day about all that I was before that. I've been on a journey for so

211

long, learning in bits and pieces, and growing stronger all the while." Taking a few steps back, she gazed up at him. "I wish I could share it all this day, but I can't stay long. I promised that I would go back and not get caught, but we will return."

"We?"

"My friends have been with me since I came to Eriden," she explained quickly. "Quite a mixed lot we are; elf and dwarf, nymph and siren, and, of course, mortals of the rim. We will find a way to restore my form, and you will be freed, my beloved king."

Clenching her fists, Ami recalled her hatred for the dragon who had claimed her father's crown. "And Gwirwen will be punished for his treachery. But I must go for now," she sniffed, taking a few more steps back, then turning to hide her tears.

"Kaliwyn," the aged dragon hissed. It pained him to hear such words fall from her lips, as they were not the kind utterances of the child he had known and raised.

Afraid of his possible dislike of her plan, Ami fled, preventing hearing anymore. Closing her hand around her trinket, she pulled the shadow over herself, then stepped through the rocks before she broke into a hard and fast run. Not stopping until she stood before Lamwen once more, she waited, observing him in his hiding place.

His eyes fixed on her father's prison, he waited for her return. His body tense, she could tell he was anxious for her safety. *He loves me,* she speculated breathlessly, *and if he does not, he certainly pretends well.*

The idea of his concern pleased her. She had not yet decided what she would do about Reynard and their vows, or with the fact that Lamwen was beneath her; but she would. And if she chose the dragon, she would never allow what was proper to stand between them, whether the dragon council liked it or not.

Relaxing her digits, the girl reappeared as she announced, "I have returned."

"You were able to speak with him?" Lamwen asked coolly, leaning forward so she could take her place on his back.

"Yes. We did not share much, but he was pleased to see me, I am certain."

"Of course he was pleased," Lamwen gurgled, waiting for her word she was comfortable and he could take off. "I dare say you were the most important thing in his life before you were taken."

"Rubbish," she countered, giving him a pat. "I'm ready. And you can't tell me a king doesn't have things more important to worry about than a girl."

"When that girl is his only child, there is nothing more important than that," he replied, then leapt into the air before she could say more.

Flying to the west rather than straight south, Lamwen carried her over the northern forest. Looking down at the trees and ground below, Amicia sighed to herself. *What a beautiful place.*

Reaching out to the dragon, she asked, *"How long will you remain with us?"*

"I thought I was welcome any time."

"You are," she smiled at his surliness. *"I wasn't sure if you would take me up on that, though. You never came down the mountain before to meet my friends; not once."*

"Things were different then." Then he had believed he still held the rank of captain of the guard and favor in Gwirwen's eyes. Today, he had nothing but the girl, her friends, and a few outcast dragons to rely upon; a grim prospect he had done his best not to think heavily upon.

Turning south, Lamwen climbed, but not too steeply, as they approached the central mountains. Beneath the crust, the dwarves were busy building and tinkering with their mining. Staring down at the main gate, Amicia could see the statues that decorated the bridge. "What a funny people," she mumbled.

Patting Lamwen's neck, she returned to their conversation, her heart warmed at the simplicity of the lives of most of the races in Eriden. *"You are welcome to join us, my friend. I feel I have much to learn from you now that I know who and what I am."*

"Yes, you do have much to learn, but I'm afraid there will be little time for lessons."

"Why?" she demanded, sitting up straighter as he leveled out. Ahead, she could see the marshes and knew they would be there in a matter of minutes.

"I will explain when we have joined your friends. I have much to share, but I fear your Piers isn't going to like any of it."

"My Piers," she giggled, leaning forward to breathe in his scent. Thinking of her father, she recalled how he had smelled. *I never would have noticed such a thing before.* Could simply knowing she was a dragon be changing her perception of things? Her heart skipped a beat as she realized that her life had been forever changed on that day, in so many ways.

As the camp drew near, a shaft of dread pierced Amicia's heart. *"Lamwen!"* she gasped.

"Yes, princess?"

"Today, when you have your say with the others," she faltered, unsure of her request, *"will it be necessary to tell them of my secret?"*

"What secret?"

"You know," she groaned, *"that I am a dragon. Must they be told?"*

"Shouldn't you want your friends to know?" he growled.

"I do want to tell them," she quickly agreed, *"but I want to do it in my own time and in my own way. Can you grant me this one request?"*

"You want me to keep this as another secret between us," he mused.

"For the time being. It would mean so much to me if they were to find out under the best possible circumstances, and I'm afraid having just lost Bally, and now you coming back, this is not the time."

"If this is what you believe, I will honor your wishes," he agreed.

"Thank you, Lamwen," she shared as she patted his neck. *"You are a dear friend to me, and I really am glad to have you back."*

THIRTY

Dragon's Light

APPROACHING the clearing where he had retrieved the girl, Lamwen flew in a large loop to inspect the area. Seeing nothing of consequence, he landed between the camp and the cave.

Caressing his neck, Amicia smiled. "Thank you, my friend."

"You are quite welcome, my queen," he replied warmly, bending so that she could climb off.

My queen, she turned in her mind. His words brought a quickness to her breathing. *He means it.* So often those of Eriden had referred to her as royalty. *I must live to their expectations and do all that I can to set things right,* she silently vowed.

Her feet firm upon the earth, she looked up at him. "Will you come with me? We are expected to visit the gnomes at dusk, so our time will be limited," she explained.

"I will await your signal to join you," he promised, lying flat. "If I am asleep, you will have to wake me."

"Asleep!" she gasped.

"I jest, Kaliwyn. It should not be more than a few minutes for you and your friends to settle, and I will join you," he explained.

"Yes, that's more like it," she grimaced, considering if he were bound to follow her orders now that her status had been revealed. Leaving the thought, she turned, tromping across the rocks to the back side of the western slant.

215

Not able to see much over the top, she made her way around, where she paused. "What the hell are you doing?"

The group scattered, they were obviously packing, and what she should have asked is why.

"Ami," Rey breathed, standing to greet her. Around him sat piles of miniature gear. Even their pot and elvish wine bottles had been diminished.

"You are packing?" she managed as he reached her, pulling her into his arms.

"Yes. We thought it would be a good idea in case things didn't pan out with the gnomes," he supplied. "I see Lamwen is waiting. Does that mean he will now explain where he has been, or has he already shared?"

Closing her eyes, Amicia listened to the thump of her heart within her ears. "I'm so happy to see you," she said, not answering his question. Her grip firm, she wondered if it were the last time she would ever hold him in such a manner.

When she finally opened her clear green orbs, she stared at their bunk; the one they had never slept in together. "I'm sorry, Rey," she sighed. Their blankets folded and sitting on their bedding, everything else appeared to have been shrunken and or packed.

"Don't be sorry, love," he replied, releasing his grip but finding her hand to replace the hug. Wiping at a stray tear, he grinned.

Seeing the love in his hazel orbs, Amicia's gut wrenched. Her secret eating at her, she glanced around at the others, who had all paused to watch them… and she knew. "Oh God."

"What?" her husband asked gently.

"You already know, don't you," she observed flatly. "It's not a secret."

"Your dragon's light is bright, Amicia Spicer," Meena explained, straightening from her arranging of tiny bolts of cloth. "I told you the moment we met I could see it within you, and it has only grown in the time I have known you."

"I see," the girl half smiled, raising her chin. "Well, then I guess there is no need for formality." Turning to the dragon, she waved, then suggested, "We should sit on the stones. He will come in as close as he can and share what he knows."

"Has he already told you?" Reynard repeated, clearing their rock so he could sit beside her.

"No," she clipped, taking the seat. "He took me to Dragon Rock, a small island off the eastern shore, where he explained my identity. Then we flew north, and I visited my father."

"Your father," Zae gasped, sitting to the girl's left. "Ziradon lives?"

"Yes," Amicia agreed, taken aback by the extent of her knowledge. "You even know who I am?"

"Of course, princess," Animir agreed, smiling at her from across their pit. "All you have met in Eriden have known you are a dragon, and most have guessed of what line."

"Then perhaps you can tell me how to regain my form," she clipped, not amused that they had apparently neglected to share their knowledge with her.

"That we do not know," Oldrilin whined, holding her palms up towards the sky. "Some magic is very powerful, and it took many to steal your form."

"I see," Ami acknowledged, accepting the explanation. "So, why didn't you tell me you knew I was a dragon?" she accused, turning to her mate.

"I only learned while you were away," Rey countered. "They kept the secret from both of us, out of love I suppose."

"Love!" she bit back, glancing around the circle as the remaining seats were filled. "Love to lie and hide the truth."

"It was for your own good," Piers snapped. "If you are unable to return to your dragon form, we felt you were better off not knowing." Looking up at the creature who had landed, but still towered over them as he sat, he continued, "Now, are we ready to begin?"

His lids half closed, Lamwen studied the mortal who appeared to still be in charge. "If you say you are ready, then I will begin," he growled, unsure he liked the idea of his queen taking orders from him.

"We are ready, Lamwen," the girl informed him more gently. "Please, start with the night of your disappearance."

"Ah, the night I was called before the council," the dragon began. "Pardodan came to summon me as I watched over you, and I stood before our leaders just after dusk. A great fire burned, as is our tradition. They questioned me, and I became aware by instinct that you were in danger."

Recalling the night in question, Amicia nodded. "Yes, we were eating when I received your message. We left the meal and began packing, as my friends have today," she recalled, indicating their gear with an open palm.

"I thought I might have been able to reach you, but I was attacked. The last time we spoke, I had been fleeing and arrived on the northern border here to the marsh. In the lush fields, I sprawled as the others caught me, beating, biting, and tearing at my flesh," he documented, his head hanging as he described the events.

Up close, Rey could see the fresh scars on his face and neck and interjected, "They hoped to kill you."

"Yes," the dragon hissed. "I managed to take to the air, but I had been badly injured. If it had been by the light of day, I would not have survived. From the marsh, I flew out to sea, and my attackers gave up after only a short distance, thinking I had fallen and would not survive."

"Did you go to Dragon Rock?" Amicia asked, her eyes wide.

"No. They know of that place, and I feared they would find me there. Instead, I flew straight out, refusing to give in to my exhaustion. When I could take it no more, I turned to the south and looped around, coming in to Jerranyth under the last of my power," he explained.

"You sought the elves?" Animir asked in surprise. "Were you not afraid Lady Cilithrand would turn you over to the supreme dragon?"

"Afraid yes, but what choice did I have?" Lamwen spat. "I landed outside her window, as I have done many times. When I called to her, she came and had me sent straight away to one of the gardens. Furthermore, she commanded that I be hidden, and if any came in search of me, they did not discover my presence."

"Well, that's not right," Reynard grunted. "Why would she help you?"

"For the same reason she gave Kaliwyn the hamar gem," Lamwen laughed, the sound sinister.

"Cilithrand did not give Amicia the gem," Animir corrected.

"She gave it to me," Oldrilin beamed, not grasping the meaning behind it. "A special gift between the elves and the sirens."

"It was no gift," the giant creature rebuked gently, his voice softened noticeably when he spoke to the tiny mermaid. "She intended that it find its way into Kaliwyn's hands, that she may discover her strength and stand against Gwirwen."

"Then Animir was right about the queen's treachery," Piers pointed out.

"It would appear so," the elf nodded, happy he had taken their side and chosen to stand against her. "As I said, we had been working to fill the armory since he came to power, near twenty years now; preparing for the day she would make her move against him."

"And that is exactly what she has done," the dragon agreed. "By the time I awoke, your party was within the holds of Rhong. I reached out to Kaliwyn but did not speak to her. I could offer no aid, and after watching to see that she must find her own way out or be turned over to the dragons –"

"Putwyn," Ami interrupted.

"What about him?" the dragon countered.

"He was the one who struck a deal with the dwarf king. Baeweth was to trade us for payment," she added. "Do you know him?"

"Putwyn," the dragon growled. "He served me, or I thought he did. He stood with Gwirwen's men on the night I was attacked, betraying me to their cause."

"Perhaps he was playing both sides," Meena mused, her features drawn into a puzzled frown.

"Pardon?" Lamwen asked her to clarify.

"The dragons had us. If he had left them to collect us, or kill us, the dwarves would have been none the wiser," she explained.

"Tis true," Hayt vouched for her reasoning. "When my uncle summoned me, his orders were clear; connect the tunnel to the cave so we could be the first to get to you. He intended to sell them to this Putwyn after seven days," he addressed the dragon at the end.

"Then it would seem he was at your aid indeed," Lamwen growled, sitting up for a moment and studying the skies. "His actions led to your escape. If Gwirwen has discovered this, we will not encounter him again."

"How are we going to find out, anyway?" Zaendra spoke up. "I mean, if you have followers, do you speak to them telepathically, as you and Amicia do?"

"I'm afraid telepathy is not a common gift," the dragon sighed, dropping his head closer once more. "I will have to go to Adiarwen and hunt the caves for any who might follow my call."

"Adiarwen," Amicia repeated. "Won't that be dangerous?"

"Yes, but I have no choice," Lamwen explained. "I have only shared telepathy with a few others in my lifetime, and therefore we must communicate the normal way; by word of mouth."

Staring at the girl, the group fell silent as all eyes shifted to her. "What?" she countered, uneasy at the undue attention.

"How many have you been able to reach, my child?" Meena asked cautiously.

"What, telepathically?"

"Yes," the older woman nodded.

Counting on her fingers, Amicia hummed, "Well, six or eight, I guess," she faltered. "Does that matter?"

"You are a powerful dragon, Kaliwyn. If any doubt remained, your talents attest to such," Lamwen growled.

"Perhaps," the girl frowned, then her features brightened. "If I knew who you wanted to contact, perhaps I could reach out to them for you!"

Laughter rippled through the circle at the simplicity and yet brilliance of her plan. Nodding his large head, the dragon agreed, "That is not what I meant, but it might work just the same."

"Then what did you mean?"

"I was thinking about your regaining your true form," he explained. "It would be unlikely that you could transform at will, but you might only need one or two others to help you accomplish the task."

"Too bad you can't turn all of us into dragons," Reynard muttered under his breath.

Turning to stare at him, Amicia cried softly, "You wish to be a dragon?"

Staring at her, his mouth hanging open, he collected his nerve. "I do not wish to be left behind," he confessed.

"Oh, love," she whispered, leaning against him and resting her head against his shoulder. "You shall never be left behind, I swear it."

"Well, this is all well and good," Piers interrupted, "but the sun has neared the end of its path for the day, and we have an appointment with the lord of the gnomes. Are you coming with us?" he asked, looking up at their guest.

"I can if you wish," the dragon replied evenly, "but before you go, there is one last thing you must know. Once I had decided I could not aid my queen, I left the comfort of the elven gardens. Flying to the east and west, I discovered that she has indeed invaded Riran and Esterbrook. Who knows; perhaps even the lands of the wizards have fallen."

"But how could Cilithrand be so bold?" Piers demanded. "She must know the dragons will stand against her."

"The dragons are divided," Lamwen explained calmly. "Ziradon is still loved by many. Gwirwen did his best to extinguish the flame, but there are a few who still support him… and his heir."

Her heart racing, Ami did not take her eyes off the massive head as he spoke. "What can we do to help? Surely there must be something."

"We cannot stop the elves; not for the time being. First, we must right what has happened within our own realm, my queen. We will rally with our own forces and count our supporters. There have already been skirmishes, so I am unsure who remains," he confessed. "Today was the first I have seen of Adiarwen since the night I fled. Not yet one moon, but it feels much longer. Once we know our numbers, we can plan our attack. And of course, some-where along the way, we should try to return you to your dragon form," he concluded, studying the mortal who held her hand. "I do not know who might wield such power; it took several to imprison you in the first place, so as I have said, I doubt you can accomplish this feat on your own."

"I think we should go, you and I, and allow my friends to hide here in the marshes if the gnomes will allow it. You have all grown too dear to risk further in a dragon civil war," she claimed with tears in her eyes.

The backlash immediate, all seven of her comrades spoke at once, each detailing why they should be included in her forces. Gaining the floor by holding up his hands, Piers waited until the other voices had died away before he contested, "I guess you can see that is not going to happen. As much as we mean to you, you are equally loved by us. We started this quest together, Amicia Spicer, or Kaliwyn, or whatever you choose to call yourself; and we will finish it the same... as one."

"Hear, hear!" Hayt shouted, standing on his pudgy legs. "I was the last to join your adventure, but I will not be left behind when there is a fight to be had."

"Nor I," Animir agreed, also standing. "You will not strip us of our right to serve, my lady."

"My lady," Ami muttered, recalling how many times she had asked him not to call her that. "All right, you can come. We'll figure out how we are going after we visit with the gnomes. For now, we should tidy up and be on our way."

Standing, Piers watched the massive beast as he moved away to give them room. As soon as he was out of earshot, he turned to Rey. "I have a chore for you and Oldrilin."

"What kind of chore?" the younger man asked in surprise. "I thought we were off to visit the gnomes."

"We are, but you have more pressing matters. I need you to take the siren in her pouch. The eastern shore is not far, and there she will return to the water. She must swim south and verify the condition of Riran." Kneeling before their smallest member, he asked more quietly, "Can you do this?"

Staring at him with wide blue eyes, Lin's lip trembled. "I fear the water these days. I have not transformed since we fled the dragon's fire."

Understanding his reasoning, Reynard also knelt. "Please, Oldrilin. I'm sure this is important, or the Mate wouldn't have asked."

"You don't trust Lamwen," Amicia gasped, joining their smaller meeting.

"It's not so much a matter of trust," Piers sighed. "He has not earned my unquestioned loyalty. If things are as he says, he will however earn a bit of it. Besides, we need a message to be delivered if the sirens are to take our side."

"Then I will go," Lin nodded. "I will do this for the group and return swift as I am able. What message shall I convey?"

"Good," their leader grinned, giving her a nod. "You will tell Olirassa what has happened and that Amicia is prepared to make a stand. We will welcome the mermaids if they still wish to pledge allegiance to Ziradon and his followers."

"What if she doesn't?" Ami asked, afraid where that might lead.

"She will," he assured with a crooked grin. "Remember, she could see who you were the moment you landed on her beach. If she wasn't going to support you, she would have killed us all and not given it a second thought."

"That's true," Ami gasped. "So, I am the reason we were taken in."

"Love Amicia, all the sirens do," Lin sang.

Turning to Rey, the Mate completed his instructions, "Take her after we leave for the meeting. Maybe we will get lucky and the dragon won't notice you are gone, or won't make a scene over it if he does."

"Aye," Rey agreed, already searching for her pouch to strap across his chest.

"Do your best, Oldrilin," Piers encouraged with a grin. "When you have spoken to the queen and confirmed their standing, come back to Rey, and we will wait for your return before we act."

"Ok," she nodded. "This I will do."

Breaking up, the group fell about changing, washing, and doing their best to appear presentable to the gnome elders. Her hair brushed and braided, Amicia stood beside their slant when Rey joined her.

"Care for a short walk?" he asked, holding out his arm while indicating the path they had already begun to wear towards Bally's memorial.

"Certainly," she smiled, relieved he did not appear cross with her. "I'm sorry for all that has happened," she qualified when they had put some distance between them and the others.

"Do not be sorry," he replied, devotion burning in his hazel orbs when he paused and faced her. "I would have it no other way."

"But I have hurt you," she insisted, grazing his beard with the backs of her fingers. "I have made us both as fools before the others and the world... A dragon and a mortal of the rim."

"No. You gave me exactly what I longed for, and the fault is therefore mine." Hugging her, Rey sighed deeply, content in the brief moment he had lived with her as his bride. "I swore upon my soul to cling to you all the days of my life, but I would have even without the swearing. I will fight by your side, Amicia, for as much and as long as I am able."

Grinning at the Mate's vows for each of them, she observed, "It was a unique wedding. I'm sure there has never been one quite like it."

"Or ever will be again, my dragoness."

Her heart aching, Amicia pushed herself against him. Where she had felt shame only hours before, only serenity remained. "No matter what happens, I will always love you, husband."

"And I you, wife." Catching a few strands of her hair, he caressed them. Inhaling the scent of her, the bond between them was stronger than it had ever been.

"Aw, how touching," Piers sneered, interrupting their moment. "Let's go, you two. We have demons to fight, and this time, they are the flying kind."

Scowling at him, Amicia spat, "I take offense to that."

"No offense, princess," the Mate chuckled, glancing at Rey before he added, "Let's get over to Falconmarsh and see if the gnomes will be willing to help."

Smiling up at Rey, Amicia nodded, "We'll be right there." Curling her arms around his neck, she pulled her beloved down for a kiss, then whispered, "Your dragon heart is strong, my love. I promise you if there is a way we can be together when this is over, we will be."

"Aye, my queen," he countered. "I'll see you when Oldrilin and I have returned from the coast."

"Be careful," she whispered, his forehead pressed against hers.

"And you, my love," he countered, dropping his lips for a final taste before they parted ways.

Books in the Dragon of Eriden Series
Whisper of Suffering
Journey of Darkness
Betrayal of Honor
Kingdom of Ruin
The Complete Set (All 4 Books in 1)

Maps of Eriden & The Rim of Mortals

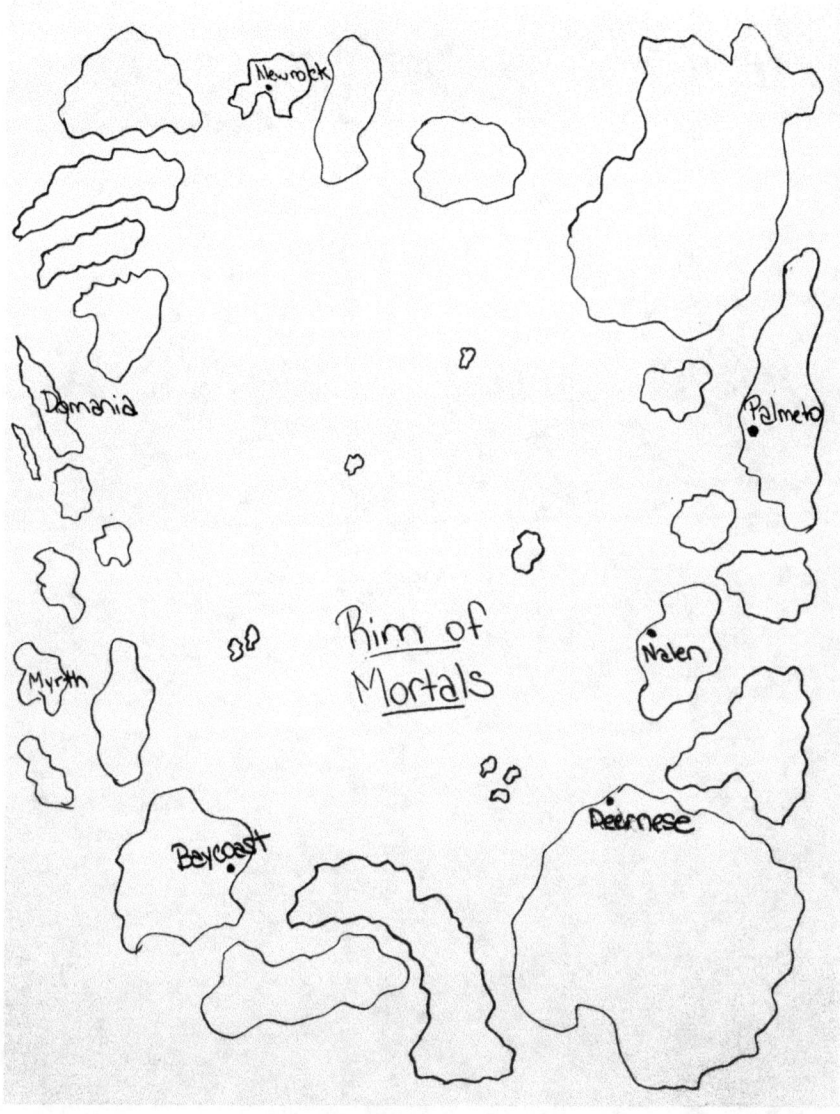

Characters by Race

Humans

Amicia Spicer is a young woman from Nalen discovering her true identity as the story unfolds. Her mother has revealed a secret about her origins upon her deathbed, and Ami is looking for the place she belongs in the world.

Reynard Daye is a young crewman aboard the Sea Serpent. He survives the destruction of the ship and joins the unlucky group of mortals as they crash upon the shores of Eriden.

Piers Massheby is the first mate aboard the Sea Serpent. He is a strong leader and guides the group through their perilous journey in search of a way home.

Baldwin Carter is the cabin boy on board the ship. He is mostly along for the ride, being young and inexperienced at handling the hardships that the group faces along the way.

Minor Human Characters:
    Rupert Miller – Amicia Spicer's friend from Nalen, he expects that she will become his betrothed when her parents no longer need her.
    Gus Spicer – Amicia's father.
    Arely Spicer – Amicia's mother.

Shamus Smith – blacksmith in the desert city of Whitefair.
Geoffrey Tabard – trader from Whitefair.
Humphray Heron – trader from Whitefair.

Sirens

Olirassa is queen of the mermaids. She is the sovereign and protector of the city of Riran.

Oldrilin is Reynard Daye's caretaker in Riran. She becomes caught up in their escape and is swept away onto their adventure through Eriden. Her devotion to Rey is sincere, and she proves to be a valuable member of their group. She seems to have little magical ability but is able to transform into a large black fish.

Elves

Cilithrand is the queen of the elves. She resides in a magnificent palace in Jerranyth, located on the southern end of the elf lands, which consists of the lower end of the central mountains of Eriden.

Animir is an elf of higher class that has been outcast from his station. He no longer feels a part of his elf kin, and helps the group to escape Jerranyth, thereby joining them on their quest to find a way home. He had been banned from using his innate magical abilities, but with the freedom of the group, he explores his talents and regains his ability as a strong wielder of magic. A resourceful member of the group, they value his friendship and utility.

Minor Elf Characters:
    Sadrir – serves the group while they are in Jerranyth.
    Anerion – lead huntsman to Lady Cilithrand.
    Galiodien – Cilithrand's father and former king of the elves.
    Cothiel – female companion to Piers in Jerranyth.

Nymphs

Preivia is queen of the nymphs. She is the sovereign and protector of the city of Esterbrook and the surrounding areas known as the glen and the meadows.

Zaendra is an earth nymph. She is pleased to meet the group when they come into the glen and attaches herself to their company. Spending time with them while they reside in their cabin, she packs her things to leave with them at their departure, as she has always wanted to explore more of Eriden and sees this as her chance. She has some magical abilities and proves to be a valuable member of the group.

Wolves

Uscan is the alpha of the southern pack of grey wolves. His loyalties are often murky, but he holds an affinity for Amicia Spicer. He acts in her best interest both as a friend and advisor. As for the southern pack, they protect the Shadowlands, a cursed area of woods that acts as a natural barrier between the glen and the mountains of the elf lands.

Edeill is the alpha of the northern pack. His loyalties are also in question. His pack of great white wolves are the protectors of the northern woods, and they patrol a much larger area than their southern kin.

Minor Wolf Characters:
    Mirean – scout sent to Esterbrook for the southern pack.
    Aelalle – beta of the northern pack.

Wizards

Meena Gavaan is a wan, a female wizard, but unlike most, she was born with the ability to use magic, which is forbidden within their people. She has led a difficult life and faces tough choices throughout the story. She meets the group upon their arrival in the desert community of Whitefair and agrees to help them for a price. She leaves with them when they flee the oasis and travels with them on their journey, earning her place within the group with her special magical skill set and talent for using her powers in practical ways.

Minor Wizard Characters:
    Jaco Gavaan – Meena's deceased husband.
    Gradien Silversmith – magistrate of the wizard city of Whitefair, he is a powerful wizard, but also a bit of a scoundrel.
    Corvack – head of the security force in Whitefair.

Trolls

Yaodus is the king of the trolls. He is a powerful wielder of magic, which is rare but not unheard of among the trolls. He is distrustful of everyone outside of their community and takes his role of protector of his kind with the utmost of dedication. He is an unlikely ally of the group after Amicia convinces him of her worth, and his help is often the difference between life and death for the mortals and their friends.

Traok is Yaodus's eldest son. He is met several times, as he acts as the liaison between the group and the troll community on several occasions.

Dwarves

Baeweth is the king of the city of Rhong. As their sovereign, he is the protector of the growing city beneath the mountain. However, his family and people have endured a great deal in the last few hundred years. They have denounced the use of magic and are rebuilding after a daemon drove them from their previous home of Asomanee.

Hayt is the king's great nephew and heir to the throne. He holds no desire to ever be king and devises a way to win the trust of the group, then helps them escape rather than see them handed over to the dragons. He is a skilled engineer, and his abilities and knowledge prove useful to the group on their quest.

Minor Dwarf Characters:
　　Asyng – the king's sister and Hayt's grandmother, she is Baeweth's advisor.
　　Firen – Hayt's good friend and fellow engineer.
　　Vael – Another acquaintance of Hayt's, he is the guard on duty when the group prepares to escape.

Daemons

Kedoria is the queen of the daemons. Her loyalties to the elves are shaken when she is captured by Animir and recruited by Amicia. She commands the daemon forces, but they are only able to live in total darkness, which severely limits her utility within the group. She has a few named minions, but they are only briefly mentioned in the events of the story.

Gnomes

Thirac is the sovereign or king of the gnomes, also called the head of the elders. He is untrustworthy and holds little concern for the Kingdom of Eriden. Their people watch events unfold and record them in their tomes, which are stored in their great libraries hidden inside of the old trees of the marsh lands.

Sevoassi is the gnome the group encounters in the northern woods. He is a trickster who helps them escape the northern pack and gives Amicia a special red orb of unknown origin or purpose.

Minor Gnome Characters:
   Ziyath (grumpy) – member of the order of the ossci, the highest and most powerful of the gnomes.
   Mizath (happy) – member of the order of the ossci, the highest and most powerful of the gnomes.
   Yimath – member of the order of the ossci, the highest and most powerful of the gnomes.

Dragons

Ziradon is Kaliwyn's father and rightful Supreme Dragon of Eriden. He is overthrown at the beginning of the story by Gwirwen, who imprisons him that he may suffer for the rest of his days. A powerful wielder of magic, he is seven hundred years of age. During his life, he has lost two wives and all of his sons. Princess Kaliwyn, his dragoness and heir to the throne, is all he has in the world.

Gwirwen is the current King of Eriden, but only because he was successful in taking over the throne. He is not as strong as Ziradon, and certainly not as wise. His poor choices lead to certain destruction, as the prophecy of the destroyer appears to be fulfilled by his doing.

Kaliwyn is the daughter of Ziradon and rightful heir to the throne of the Supreme Dragon of Eriden. Forced into the form of a mortal as a young dragoness, she is taken away to Nalen, where she is found and raised by human parents. She is not aware of her true self and must discover her dragon heart before it's too late.

Lamwen is the captain of the king's guard. He is assigned to protect the coast of the continent and leads the guard in that role. When the group makes it ashore, it is the guard's job to eliminate them. When their attempts prove unsuccessful, he is reassigned to spy on the group, where he learns of Amicia's identity. Becoming her friend and guardian, he is eventually welcomed by the travelers and becomes vital in their success.

Minor Dragon Characters:

Ziewen – female dragon, loyal to and eventually mated with Gwirwen.

Pardodan – loyal to Gwirwen, he longs to improve his rank in the king's guard.

Vaudien – loyal to Gwirwen, he takes Lamwen's place as captain of the king's guard when he is removed.

Kilawon – Kaliwyn's mother and Ziradon's late mate, who was murdered by Gwirwen.

Jarrowan – Lamwen's friend and supporter, he spends time with the group and even experiences human form for a few days.

Putwyn – a less than decisive member of Lamwen's followers who betrays him, then wishes to rejoin them. Most noted for helping the group escape the dragons by arranging for Baeweth to help them.

Onothwyn – a lesser member of the king's guard who helps to hunt the group.

About the Author

Anyone who knows me could tell you, I am a friendly kind of person, never met a stranger and take up conversations anywhere at any time. I work hard, and my mind never seems to shut down, as I wake up often in the middle of the night with ideas pouring out and demanding to be dealt with. Of course that means much of my books were written in the middle of the night.

I grew up and still live in the great state of Texas where everything is bigger, where we have warm weather and a central location. I love my state, my town, and my family, which includes my four sons, my significant other, and many friends as well.

I have thoroughly enjoyed writing this story and hope that you will love reading it just as much. And of course, there will be many more adventures to come.

You can follow Samantha Jacobey at:
Website: www.SamJacobey.com
Facebook: https://www.facebook.com/SamJacobey
Twitter: https://twitter.com/SamJacobey

Also by SAMANTHA JACOBEY

A New Life Series

http://myBook.to/ANewLifeSeries

An epic adventure, TORI FARRELL's life IS one wild story... escaped from a biker gang and running from drug lords... used by the FBI and hoping to protect her present from her past... IT'S DARK - IT'S BRUTAL, and it's WORTH EVERY MINUTE OF IT!! (Mature Adult, 18+)

Summer Spirit Novella Series

http://myBook.to/SummerSpiritSeries

No one EVER had a summer romance like this… Charlie visits another plane, parallel to our own, where Summer Angels and Dark Angels battle over the fate of man. A unique twist on an old idea that will keep you guessing; will Charlie and Clarisse ever find their HEA? (New adult)

Irrevocable Series

http://mybook.to/IrrevocableBoxedSet

From affluent beginnings, BAILEY DEWITT's life has become a broken mess... after her parents died unexpectedly, she didn't think it could get any worse. But when the arrogance of man catches up and puts the entire world into a dooms-day spiral, there will be only ONE PLACE she can run to - the ONE PLACE she wanted desperately to escape. (New Adult)

Teach Me to Prey

http://hyperurl.co/e9qs9f

In this standalone thriller, JASON TRUITT and his friends have gotten their way for years. Deceit, sex, and foul play aren't normally covered in the curriculum, but they're doing whatever it takes to get under BECKY STEWART's skin. When one of the boys turns up dead, it's a race against time to save the others; a STUNNING STORY that will get your heart racing and leave you breathless by the end… (New Adult)

The Wicked Awakened

http://hyperurl.co/2qsgl6

A Halloween novel; a five-hundred-year-old witch wants to turn SARAH MATTHEWS' body into her new home… A twisted tale involving a coven hell bent on seeing that she succeeds. Who will come out on top in this epic battle of wills? (Mature Adult, 18+)

The Binding

http://myBook.to/TheBinding

One cursed diary will change two strangers forever...Can Meri and Rider use her mother's old book to figure out why someone is after them? Or will the guilty party succeed, ripping the tome away before killing them and then slithering back into the darkness…

Also From Our Lavish Family

The Norn Novellas
A. Nicky Hjort
https://www.lavishpublishing.com/authors/nicky-hjort-1/

The Norn Novellas are all chapters in the epic saga of the youngest and most fickle of the four Norn Sisters. The same feisty immortal creature who must escape her inherent inner darkness to learn the meaning of life.

Each story takes a classic fairytale and spins it on its head, as we learn that maybe Norse Mythology was so much more than legend. And to think, you thought you knew those old tales so well.

Meet Za and find out what really happened...

When Tundra Turns to Ardnyt - Book 1: In the center of a magical world there grows a beautiful and terrible chasm of climbing plants. On one side of the Ivy Wall we find the hell-of-Tyndra, on the other, the heaven-of-Ardnyt. But legend has it that in the middle...lives a preternatural beast that imprisons and tortures the children from both sides.

When the war against time begins, Azza will have to cross over the Ivy Wall, something that has never been done before by a living being. But if she does make it through, she just might discover who she really is and how she became trapped in this alternate reality.

A fairytale at heart, this is the first chapter in the epic saga of the youngest and most fickle of the four Norn Sisters. The same feisty immortal creature who must escape her inherent inner darkness to learn the meaning of love.

A veritable palindrome from start to finish, the narrative of Where Tyndra Turns to Ardnyt journeys through duality to discover what shocking truths emerge when up becomes down, life becomes death, suffering becomes release, and the most unexpected endings become the most surprising beginnings.

Welcome to a place where forwards and backwards are exactly the same direction. Here Where Tyndra Turns to Ardnyt.

Where Ebon Sounds Like Ivory – book 2: Norse legend has it that the arms of the Yggdrasil tree—a sacred instrument of Odin—are ever-reaching, and its survival is necessary for life itself to continue.

During Winter's Solstice, when the search for her mortal mother begins, Za will have to cross over the Ebon Branch of the Dead—a feat that has supposedly never been survived intact. But if she does make it across and back home, she just might discover why she and the other three Norn Sisters of Fate came to be.

A fairytale at heart, this is the second chapter in the epic saga of the youngest and most fickle of the four Norn Sisters. The same feisty immortal creature who must discover her true origins to understand her inherent inner darkness. Only this way can she learn the meaning of unconditional sacrifice in the name of impenetrable love…when, as her destiny would have it, all the branches of such a powerful tree tremble treacherously in her tiny little hands.

A veritable unraveling of Snow White, the narrative of Where Ebon Sounds Like Ivory journeys through the most horrible of realms where shocking truths emerge. Here where death mimics life, obsession masquerades as devotion, and the most unexpected endings become the most surprising beginnings of a classic tale. One…you thought you knew so well.

Welcome to a place where the darkest of melodies births a miraculous tune of surrenderance. Here Where Ebon Sounds Like Ivory and Christmas, as we know it, begins.

Behind Blue Eyes Series
Sara J. Bernhardt
https://books2read.com/BlueEyesBeginner

A father's desire to save his child presents him with an unthinkable choice that leaves him darker than human, forced to roam through time alone as he searches for the place he belongs.

Adam Gold – Book 1: Fleeing the French invasion of Geneva Switzerland in the 1700s, Adam Gold books passage to America with his family. On the ship, Adam's daughter falls fatally ill. A mysterious man comes to Adam with a way to save his child by turning Adam into something darker than human.

The Medallion – Book 2: Adam Gold, an immortal with sweet eyes of blue, rushes through the centuries on a quest for reason and a thirst for revenge. To cope with his pain and regret, he sleeps away the years and awakes in a new era with a powerful, ancient vampire who sets her sights on him.

Golden Shackles – Book 3: When the ancient queen, Sekhmet snatches up Adam, he is faced with a terrifying decision. To help aid her in her vile plans or dare to stand against her.

Plus 3 more segments!